Praise for Manda Collins's delectable Regency novels

A Good Rake is Hard to Find

"A fresh and promising start to the series."

—*Publishers Weekly*

"An exciting mystery and a powerful love story!"

—*Fresh Fiction*

"This book has fighting, fast driving, mystery, a super bad guy, and some sweet love." —*Romance at Random*

"Warmth, wit, wicked sensuality and an intriguing whodunit take this story over the top." —*Romance Junkies*

Why Lords Lose Their Hearts

"This sweet and sensuous novel has an undercurrent of mystery that will keep readers riveted."

—*Publishers Weekly*

"Collins' tale blends intrigue and desire in a story that is an unusual and intriguing combination of chilling and sweet." —*RT Book Reviews*

"A suspense-filled tale, *Why Lords Lose Their Hearts*, the third book in author Manda Collins' *Wicked Widows* trilogy, is a witty, sensual historical romance that will captivate readers from the very beginning. Filled with warmth, clever dialogue, engaging characters, sizzling chemistry, mystery, danger, surprising plot twists, tender romance and true love, this story is a delight."

—*Romance Junkies*

"Fresh dialogue, suspense, revenge, a most unlikely villain, and of course romance, make *Why Lord's Lose Their Hearts* a definite must-read!"

— *Reader to Reader Reviews*

Why Earls Fall in Love

"With its shades of *I Know What You Did Last Summer* and strong gothic overtones, Collin's latest is a chill seeker's delight. Along with the surprising climax, readers will thoroughly enjoy the well-crafted characters, the charming setting, and the romance that adds spice to the drama." — *RT Book Reviews*

"Sparkling romance amid mystery." — *Publishers Weekly*

"Combining love, wit, warmth, suspense, intrigue, emotion, sensuality, interesting characters, romance, and plenty of danger, Ms. Collins' has created another enthralling story." — *Romance Junkies*

"Award-winning author Manda Collins brings sensual historical romance to a new level with wit, heat, and beautifully written detail, finely drawn characters, and a flair for fun." — *Examiner.com*

Why Dukes Say I Do

"Witty and smart, Collins' prose flows smoothly as she merges a charming, compassionate love story with gothic suspense . . . Add strong pacing and depth of emotion, and there's no doubt this is a winner."

— *RT Book Reviews* (Top Pick, 4½ stars)

Also By Manda Collins

Ready
Set
Rogue

MANDA COLLINS

St. Martin's Paperbacks

This is a work of fiction. All of the characters, organizations, and events portrayed in this novel are either products of the author's imagination or are used fictitiously.

READY SET ROGUE

Copyright © 2017 by Manda Collins.

All rights reserved.

For information address St. Martin's Press, 175 Fifth Avenue, New York, NY 10010.

ISBN: 978-1-250-10986-6

Our books may be purchased in bulk for promotional, educational, or business use. Please contact your local bookseller or the Macmillan Corporate and Premium Sales Department at 1-800-221-7945, ext. 5442, or by e-mail at MacmillanSpecialMarkets@macmillan.com.

Printed in the United States of America

St. Martin's Paperbacks edition / January 2017

St. Martin's Paperbacks are published by St. Martin's Press, 175 Fifth Avenue, New York, NY 10010.

10 9 8 7 6 5 4 3 2 1

Chapter 1

The Marquess of Kerr was having a very bad day.

As if breaking an axle on his ancient family traveling carriage on the most deserted portion of the drive from London to the south coast hadn't been inconvenience enough, there was also the fact that his favorite horse was miles back, tied behind the coach carrying his baggage and valet. To compound his situation, after instructing the coachman and outriders to wait for help, he'd set out on foot for the coaching inn some three miles up the road only for the skies to open up and release a deluge not felt on Earth since the Great Flood, he was convinced.

If it hadn't been for a chance meeting with his cousin the day before, he'd not have been traveling to the downs at all. But the news that his late aunt Celeste had done what she'd always threatened—left her estate to a bevy of blue stockings—had meant beating a hasty path to her manor house near the village of Little Seaford before any of her hangers-on arrived. At least that had been the plan when he set out. At this rate all four harpies would have descended upon Beauchamp House before he had a chance to so much as hide the silver.

Thus it was that when he reached the Fox and Pheasant

he was not only wet, muddy, and exhausted, he was hungry. Which, as his old nanny could attest, made for a very grouchy Torquil, indeed.

Despite the rain, the inn yard was bustling with activity, as the bright yellow mail coach, which had just arrived, released its passengers into the already crowded doorway of the hostelry.

Cursing beneath his breath, Quill elbowed his way through the crowd until the quality of his garments seemed to register with them and, despite their own fatigue, the passengers began to defer to him. All save one.

Had he been in a better mood, he might have noticed the auburn-haired lady's curvy figure or her warm brown eyes behind her spectacles. But he was too annoyed by her blatant disregard for him as she shoved in front of him carrying a small, but obviously heavy, trunk. And as if that weren't enough, she had the bad manners to drop the aforementioned trunk directly onto his booted foot as he attempted to slip around her.

"Hell and the devil!" he cursed as the weighty box landed. Despite the thickness of his boots, they were no match for whatever it was she traveled with.

"Oh dear," the woman said, crouching at once to clutch the handles of the offending thing. "I am so sorry. I should have waited for the coachman, but I was so afraid to leave them, you see. They're quite valuable."

But when she heaved on the trunk, it was obvious that she'd need a bit of help lifting it. Wordlessly, Quill pushed away her hand that gripped the handle and took both sides in his own grasp and lifted it.

"What are you carrying in this, madam?" he asked as he jostled it up close to his chest. "It feels as if you've weighted it with gold bars."

It was only then that he took a moment to really look at

her. And was intrigued despite his annoyance. She really was quite pretty despite the spectacles and the obviously dated gown.

Before she could respond to his question, however, the innkeeper rushed over. "My lord, I am so sorry you were accosted by this"—he waved his hand in the direction of the lady, as if unable to come up with a suitable description for her, finally settling upon—"person. I'll have our finest room made up for you at once. Be gone with you, madam. His lordship has no wish to be bothered by the likes of you."

Wordlessly he gestured to a footman, who stepped forward to take the trunk from Quill, wincing as he did so.

"There's no need for rudeness, Stepney," Quill chastised the innkeeper. "It was an accident, nothing more. Please have your man carry the lady's trunk wherever she has need to take it."

"Oh that is too kind of you, my lord," the young woman said with a bright smile. "I would have left them in the coach, but one hears such tales about the mail coach and the thievery that takes place even amongst the passengers. I simply could not risk them. My books are so necessary to my work, you understand."

As she spoke, Quill noticed that her eyes were a clear green. And at her confession, something clicked into place. Of course. She was a governess. That would explain the spectacles and the books. She was likely on her way to a new position.

Before he could respond, however, Stepney bowed deeply and ignored the governess. "Very good, my lord. I'll see to it at once. Now, if you'll follow me I'll see you to your room."

And since the young woman was already directing the footman into the taproom where she was doubtless going to have a meal before she joined the rest of the passengers on the mail coach again, he gave her one last look, then followed Stepney up the stairs.

Grateful he'd thought to bring a small bag with him when he left the traveling chaise, Quill was soon bathed and wearing a fresh change of clothes. If his cravat wasn't as skillfully tied as his valet might have managed, then the clientele of the Fox and Pheasant would simply have to make do. Deciding to dine downstairs in the taproom rather than alone in his room, he was nearly at the bottom of the stairs when he heard a feminine shout. A premonition had him racing the rest of the way down and hurrying into the dining room, which took up the entire width of the building. Though it was still daylight, the lack of windows made for a dimly lit room, the only light source coming from the lamps on the tables and in sconces on the walls.

But it wasn't too dark for him to see the little governess standing defiantly before a great lummox of a man who clutched a hand against his cheek. "I'll no' take tha' from the likes o'ye," the man growled, launching himself forward and gripping the lady by her upper arms. "Who d'ye think y'are?"

In the tradition of all bystanders everywhere, the rest of the taproom seemed to settle in for a spectacle. At least that's how it seemed to Quill, who pushed his way forward, and snapped, "Unhand the lady at once, sir."

If there was one thing Quill could not abide, it was a man who laid hands on a woman. And there was something about seeing this particular lady in the other man's grip that made him particularly angry.

Not pausing to consider the wisdom of his actions, and not waiting for the fellow to obey his orders, Quill pulled her away from the ruffian and stepped between them, watching as her attacker lost his balance in his surprise and fell backward into the table behind him.

Standing over the man, lying in angry shock on the floor, Quill scowled. "Let that be a lesson to you that there are consequences for the mistreatment of ladies traveling alone. I don't know how things are done in the dark hole from whence you hail, but in the civilized world, men treat women with decency and respect. Especially when they are not noticeably under someone's protection."

Turning away from where the man sat stunned, he turned his attention to the governess, who was gaping at him with suspiciously bright eyes.

"I . . . I don't know how to thank you, my lord," she said, her voice shaking. "If you hadn't arrived when you did, I fear things would have gone very badly indeed."

Handing her his handkerchief, Quill led her to a booth on the far side of the room, where he gestured for her to take a seat.

"Why are you still here?" he demanded tersely, his residual anger making him short. "The mail coach should have departed by now." And as he quickly scanned the room, he saw that the others who had crowded into the inn with her were missing.

Wincing, she looked down. "The driver took on more passengers here, and he claimed there was no room for my trunks. When I refused to leave them behind, he left without me." As she finished this disclosure, she lifted her chin and glared defiantly at him, her eyes bright with anger. "They are necessary for my studies and I saw no reason why I should be the one to give up my trunks when there were plenty of others with far larger ones. It was grossly unfair."

"Surely you could have had them sent after you," Quill pointed out with a raised brow. From his time at university he knew that books were essential for study, but it was hardly practical for her to give up her seat for them. Any employer of merit would see the necessity of paying to have them delivered once he was informed of her situation. Which brought up another question. "Why didn't your employer make arrangements for your travel? Surely governesses are not required to travel on the common stage. I know my father always sent the traveling carriage for my sister's teachers. Or at the very least a hired carriage."

At this, she raised a brow in annoyance. "I know my gown is not of the first stare of fashion, but I hardly think I'm so drab as to be mistaken for a governess." She pursed her lips. "Not that there is anything wrong with governessing, you understand. It is a respectable profession—and one of the only ones available for a single lady of gentle birth."

Quill surveyed her appearance, taking care not to be seen doing so—a skill every young gentleman perfected in his teens lest he be forever receiving raps on the knuckles from his mama. On closer inspection, her gown, while dark gray in color, was well made. And her modest bonnet was constructed of if not the finest silk, then at the very least not the meanest. Even the trunk of books that she had lowered to the taproom floor beside her was not cheaply made. In short, he'd judged her wrongly from the start. What he'd concluded to be a lady in reduced circumstances was actually just a lady of modest tastes.

He felt his brow furrow. "If you are not a governess then, who are you?"

It was a highly inappropriate question considering they'd never been properly introduced, he knew. And it would be highly unusual for him to do the honors himself. Was she an actual governess, she'd likely read him a scold that would blister his ears. But, she didn't seem to take offense at the inquiry. "I am independent scholar," she informed him, her pride in it evident in her squared shoulders and elevated chin. And to his surprise, she offered him her gloved hand. "Miss Aphrodite Wareham, Ivy to my friends."

His hand was already clasping hers when the name registered, and it was all Quill could do to stop himself from dropping the offending extremity and turning his back on her. But good manners had been instilled in him almost from birth, and he had been taught not to be rude to a lady. No matter how grasping or conniving that lady proved to be.

He gave a quick, mirthless laugh. "I might have known we'd meet on the road to Beauchamp House. Since it is, after all, the family estate you and your cohorts wish to steal out from under my family's nose. Well, I beg leave to inform you, madam, that while my late aunt was eccentric, she was not without family protection. And we will not stand for this scheme you've concocted. No matter how you might protest your friendship with my aunt."

Her nose wrinkled in confusion. "I don't know what you mean, sir," she said with a little shake of her head. "I never met Lady Celeste while she was living. Indeed, I wish I had for I'd have offered up my sincere thanks for her generous bequest."

She frowned, tilting her head as she scanned his face. *She was quite skilled at playing the puzzled innocent,* he thought bitterly.

"I assume from your accusation that you are Lady Celeste's relation?"

As if she didn't know it already. Hell, he'd not be surprised if she'd arranged for her little contretemps with the man earlier to gain his sympathy.

He sketched a mocking bow. "Torquil Beauchamp, Marquess of Kerr, at your service." Rising to see her still maintaining her air of bewilderment, he continued with a disgusted shake of his head. "But you doubtless knew that already. Tell me, how long did it take you and your friends to choose my aunt as your target? For I have little doubt she proved a ripe pigeon for plucking given her generous nature and genuine interest in scholarship. I know there must not be much opportunity for fortune in the arts for ladies. You must have been beside yourselves with glee when you found her."

But rather than let his derision break her, she seemed to gain strength from it. "I'm not sure where you get your information, my lord, but I have never met your aunt before in my life. Nor am I acquainted with the ladies you refer to as my cohorts. As far as our scheming to somehow steal your family estate out from under you, I was given to understand that Lady Celeste owned Beauchamp House outright and that it was not included with the rest of the Beauchamp estates, which is what made it possible for her to bequeath it to us in the first place."

Her color was up and she was bristling with anger now, which Quill had no doubt was genuine. Well it might be, given that her plans were being challenged instead of what she'd likely thought would be smooth sailing on her trip to take possession of her new home.

Let her be angry, he thought with a pang of self-mockery at how quickly he'd fallen prey to her wounded-innocent act. She was probably as mean as a snake and twice as venomous.

The Beauchamps were not known for their pacifism. And as the head of the family, Quill didn't mean to let a passel of scheming harpies lure him onto a rocky shore in hopes they could take an estate that had been in the Beauchamp family for hundreds of years.

"Then, my dear Miss Wareham," he said coldly, not believing her protests for a moment, "you were sadly misinformed. And I will do my utmost to ensure that you and the other ladies who tricked my aunt are not only prevented from taking ownership, but are prosecuted for your fraud."

Chapter 2

"I might have known it was too much to ask that you were simply a kind stranger," Ivy fumed, angry with herself as much as at Lord Kerr. No man with that much polish could fail to be a scoundrel beneath his burnished exterior. She'd been a fool to let his championship against the taproom bully sway her to let down her guard. Even a little.

She'd been around enough of her father's noble pupils to recognize aristocratic good manners when she saw them. She'd seen any number of lordlings and gentlemen bow politely to her one moment, then pinch the maid on the bottom as soon as they thought they were out of sight. Lord Kerr was no different, only his grasping had been of a less crude variety.

If she was less certain of the validity of her claim upon Lady Celeste's estate, Ivy might have been more frightened by the marquess's threat to stop her and the other heirs from claiming their inheritance. But as soon as the letter from Lady Celeste had arrived, along with another from her solicitor, Ivy had asked for her father's assistance in determining whether it was legal.

Though Lord Alton Wareham, a former Oxford don who'd left the university upon his marriage, hadn't spoken to his family in some years thanks to their less-than-welcoming attitude toward his wife—Ivy's mother—he'd kept in touch with his cousin, a solicitor with clientele in the aristocracy. And upon consultation, the cousin had assured both Lord Alton and Ivy that the bequest was not only valid, but that if Ivy did not wish to risk losing her inheritance, she should travel at once to Beauchamp House and stake her claim.

As the eldest in a family of seven daughters, Ivy had been more than eager to embark on the journey. Not only because she looked forward to making use of the impressive library mentioned in Lady Celeste's letter, which was said to contain any number of Greek transcriptions that had never been made available to the academic community, but also because she was desperate to escape the mayhem of her family home.

She'd spent most of her life caring for her siblings and when that lady was subjected to yet another confinement, to her mother. Though her father had been born the younger son of the Duke of Ware, his unsupported marriage had cut off any financial assistance he might have expected from his family. And so, it had been in a modest house on the outskirts of Oxford where Ivy and her siblings had grown up. It wasn't an unhappy family. But Ivy was more than ready to strike out on her own scholarly path—to get out from under the influence of her father's tutelage and to establish herself in her own right. And if it let her also escape the responsibility of caring for her younger siblings, so much the better.

In short, she was looking forward to taking up her shared tenancy of Beauchamp House, and no amount of bullying from the Marquess of Kerr would persuade her otherwise.

"But, nephew of Lady Celeste or not," she continued, her spine ramrod straight, "you will soon find yourself disabused of these notions. You do not think I would pack my trunks and leave my home on merely the hint of an inheritance, do you?" She would indeed have done such a thing, given her desire to escape her parents' unruly abode, but Lord Kerr didn't need to know that.

He looked down his aristocratic nose at her, his blue eyes narrow with dislike. "I have no notion what a woman like you would attempt, madam," he said coldly. "You have proven yourself to be brazen enough to hoodwink an elderly lady into bequeathing a valuable family estate to you. Why should I be surprised at anything you do?"

She gasped at his words. By referring to her as "woman," he'd essentially called her respectability into question. If she were a man, and if she believed in dueling—a truly barbaric practice that was long overdue for dying out— she'd have called him out. As it was, she was a lady and would pay no attention to the slurs of a man who had proved himself to have very little claim upon the title of gentleman.

Turning her back on him, she hoisted her trunk of books with some difficulty, letting the exhale of exertion hiss through her teeth lest he realize just how much effort it took, and carried it and her valise to a table not so very far from his. (She'd have gone farther, but she greatly feared that she would drop the trunk, embarrassing herself before her nemesis.)

No sooner had she collapsed as genteelly as she could into her chair, than the innkeeper appeared at her side, his narrowed busy brows, his smile less than polite. "This taproom is for paying customers only, miss," Mr. Stepney said with a pointed look at her trunk, as if it was taking up a seat that was also meant for paying customers. "If you would like to hire a room for the night, I'll just take your payment now."

Well aware that Lord Kerr and the rest of the dining room were watching with interest, she mentally calculated the amount of money in her purse, which, she feared was not enough for even the smallest room here. Her passage on the mail coach had used the bulk of her funds, and her father had insisted that traveling with a full purse would invite cutpurses and pickpockets to prey upon her. Or so he'd said—she rather suspected it was another attempt on his part to keep her from leaving, but she'd called his bluff and gone anyway.

Smiling up hopefully at the proprietor, she said, "You seem like far too kind a man to eject a lady from your establishment, Mr. Stepney, is it? I assure you I will only be here for a little while. I am expecting a carriage from Beauchamp House near Little Seaford this afternoon." A bald-faced lie, but she was desperate. It was bad enough for a lady traveling alone to fend off the rough customers of a taproom, but if he forced her into the inn yard she didn't like her chances of surviving unscathed.

The innkeeper frowned, but before he could respond, she felt a presence at her back. "She will be traveling with me, Stepney," said Lord Kerr smoothly. "We are both bound for Beauchamp House so I thought it best to spare her the indignities of the mail coach."

Stepney's look of suspicion turned into a leer as he glanced between the marquess and Ivy. "Very well, my lord. Will you be needing another room then?" It was clear from his tone that he thought the question unnecessary.

"I don't think so," Kerr said to Ivy's shock. If the ill-tempered marquess thought she would let him get away with ruining her reputation then he was sorely mistaken.

She opened her mouth to set the innkeeper straight, but the Lord Kerr continued, "I've hired a carriage for the drive so that we can leave in a short while. My own is in need of further repair so I will leave my coachman to see to it from here. Miss Wareham may have a place in the hired coach. For propriety's sake I'll join my valet in the second carriage.."

Ivy could not have been more shocked if he'd casually announced that he drank the blood of virgins and howled at the moon. She'd judged him wrongly, she supposed. At least when it came to his desire to ruin her reputation. But as soon as Mr. Stepney had stepped away, the marquess said in a low voice only she could hear, "I'll not risk any damage to your reputation lest I find myself at the other end of your father's pistol being forced into a marriage with you. That is just what this farce needs to make it an actual circus."

She clenched her teeth, anger making her hands shake. "I wouldn't marry you if you were wrapped in gold and carrying every last missing fragment of Greek poetry," she spat.

"Then we are in agreement on something, it would seem," he sneered. "And if you are wondering why I am in such a generous mood, it's because I won't have you ruining my good name in these parts. My family has owned property here for hundreds of years and we are well known in the district. And the sooner we get to Beauchamp House and speak to my aunt's fraud of a solicitor, the sooner I can get back to London and get on with my life."

"I might have known you'd be playing dog in the manger with Beauchamp House," Ivy said shaking her head in disgust. "You don't want me or the other ladies to have it, but you don't actually want it for yourself either. Just another family property to languish empty while you and the other Beauchamps 'live your lives' in your actual homes. What a charming portrait of aristocratic generosity you paint."

"I'd mind my tongue if I were you, Miss Wareham," he said with a smile that didn't reach his eyes. "Else

I shall change my mind and leave you to the charming Mr. Stepney's care."

Recognizing the truth of his threat, she bit her tongue on the sharp retort she longed to let fly. "My apologies," she said falsely. "If the hired carriage is ready, perhaps I'd best go ahead and climb in, to spare us both further argument."

With as much dignity as she could muster, she attempted to hoist her book-laden trunk once more, only to be forestalled by Lord Kerr who wordlessly lifted it without so much as a grunt of exertion—really it was too unfair that men were endowed with such strength. Especially men like the marquess, who it was unlikely was ever called upon to lift more than a fork at his lavish dinner table. Though a quick glance at his close-cut jacket and skintight breeches showed that he must be doing some sort of exercise on a regular basis.

The villain. Why could he not be as fat as the Prince Regent and as weak as a kitten?

"Come along, Miss Wareham," he said without waiting to see if she followed. "The sooner we get to Beauchamp House, the sooner we can have you on your way back to Oxfordshire."

Rather than argue, she trudged along after him, looking forward to the moment when he'd be forced to accept just how wrong he was. About her, and about the matter of Lady Celeste Beauchamp's bequests.

There would be time enough for gloating then.

Despite her earlier upset and sparring with Lord Kerr, Ivy fell asleep almost as soon as the hired carriage departed from the inn. Her day had begun before dawn and she'd gotten little rest the night before because she was eager for her journey.

By the time the conveyance pulled to a stop some hours

later, she was awake and ready to see her new home. But night had fallen as they traveled, so all she could see was the glow of lamplight through the windows. A real look at the manor house would have to wait until tomorrow.

She was surprised to see that it was Lord Kerr who opened the door of the carriage rather than a footman.

"Don't just sit there gaping, Miss Wareham," he said extending his hand in to her after he let down the step. "You'll catch flies."

Her desire to stretch her legs after hours in the carriage was at war with her determination to be as uncivil as possible to the man who had insulted her motives so thoroughly earlier. But, she thought as she grudgingly took his proffered assistance, he had offered her safe passage to Beauchamp House—no matter how ugly the motive—so she relented.

No sooner was she standing on her own two feet than she was pulled close in a strange lady's embrace. "You must be Ivy," said the woman with a slight northern burr. "We thought you'd never arrive. We've been waiting this age. You're the last to arrive and though Lady Serena did assure us that you'd be here soon enough, I did have my doubts let me tell you, Ivy. May I call you Ivy? It's such a lovely name, though Lady Celeste's letter did say that your given name is Aphrodite, which I must say is a mouthful so I'll just use Ivy if you don't mind. Though if you insist of course, I shall call you Aphrodite, it's your name after all."

She could have continued on forever, Ivy was certain, had the young lady not glanced over into the bemused countenance of Lord Kerr. Her gray eyes grew wide and her mouth formed an O of surprise.

Taking a moment to catch her breath, Ivy glanced behind the talkative lady and saw three more ladies, a very dignified man she assumed was the butler, and a footman arrayed upon the front portico.

"Give her a moment to get her bearings, Miss Hastings" said the curvy brunette, who seemed a bit older than the other three. Smiling to soften any chastisement in her words, she continued. "That chatterbox, Miss Wareham, is Miss Sophia Hastings who along with her sister Miss Gemma Hastings, here"—she gestured to the plainer girl next to her, with beautiful dark chestnut hair in contrast to her sister's light brown locks—"is another of Lady Celeste's heirs."

"I'm Lady Daphne Forsythe," said the tall blonde, who was perhaps the most beautiful creature Ivy had ever seen. But her awkward manner kept her from the remoteness that her looks might have imbued her with. "I am a mathematician, Sophia is a painter, and Gemma studies fossils. You study ancient languages." This last was said as if an accusation, but Ivy got the feeling that there was no harm meant by the girl's brusque manner.

"Indeed I do, Lady Daphne," she said with a smile at the other girl. "But I'm sorry ma'am," she continued to the woman who'd spoken up first. "I didn't hear your own name in that list of introductions. Might you be Lady Serena Fanning?"

"She is indeed, Miss Wareham," said Lord Kerr before Lady Serena could speak up. "And I suggest we all go inside so that we can discuss this business somewhere other than the front stoop where all and sundry might listen in."

Rather than protest at the marquess's bad manners, the other ladies nodded in agreement and allowed the butler to usher them all back into the front entry, where Ivy handed the man, whom she learned was called Mr. Greaves, her cloak and asked that her trunk and valise be taken up to her room. She would have liked to wash off her travel dirt before getting into yet another argument with the marquess over the late Lady Celeste's disposition of Beauchamp House, but she'd seen the glint of annoyance in

Lord Kerr's eyes at seeing her fellow heirs waiting for her, so she knew it was coming.

"Let's retire to the parlor, shall we?" Lady Serena suggested as she led them upstairs into a well-lit chamber furnished with comfortable chairs, a couple of sofas, and a merrily burning fire.

Ivy could tell that Sophia wanted very badly to ask her a dozen more questions, but something—perhaps Lord Kerr—kept her silent until they were seated. "I had not expected you to be traveling with a gentleman, Miss Wareham," she said as if unable to keep her peace any longer. "Is he your betrothed?"

Both Ivy and Lord Kerr spoke at once.

"Good god, no!"

"Perish the thought!"

Lady Serena laughed. "Well, that was certainly heartfelt. Sophia, I can assure you that this fellow—though he does seem to have arrived with Miss Wareham, is my cousin the Marquess of Kerr, and he was likely on his way here when he met Miss Wareham on the road. Is it something like that, Quill?"

The marquess, who was looking as comfortable as a hen in a foxes' den, inclined his head to Lady Serena. "Something like that, Serena, though I must confess myself surprised at finding you here. I should have expected you to have more family feeling than to be welcoming these interlopers into Aunt Celeste's home."

"Interlopers?" Sophia asked, her nose wrinkling in puzzlement. "What can you mean?"

"The bequest is quite clearly spelled out in your aunt's will, my lord," said Lady Daphne firmly. "My solicitor made sure of it."

"As did ours," said Miss Gemma Hastings, with a firm nod. "Else we'd not have traveled such a great distance to come here."

Enjoying the sight of Lord Kerr confronted by others who were on her own side, Ivy pushed up her spectacles on her nose so that she might better see his chagrin. Of course, being Lord Kerr, he showed no such thing.

"My own solicitors are looking for loopholes as we speak, ladies," he said with a shrug. "And I fear you are all doomed to disappointment. I will, of course, do what I can to ensure you safe passage back to your respective homes."

"Quill," Lady Serena said sharply, "I think you are mistaken—both with regard to Aunt Celeste's will but also her wishes. Why do you think I am here?"

For the first time, Ivy saw a crack in his lordship's veneer of certainty. He frowned. "I don't know. I suppose I thought you brought Jeremy here to visit the seaside. And mistakenly thought these ladies were guests."

"Jeremy is her six-year-old son," Lady Daphne helpfully informed Ivy. "A bright child though not as good with maths as I was at that age."

Ivy's eyes widened, and even Lord Kerr looked shocked.

"Daphne," Sophia hissed, "that's not something you should say aloud in front of the boy's mother."

"I was only stating a fact," Lady Daphne said puzzled. "If I were Jeremy's mother I would wish to know that he is lagging behind."

Clearly Lady Daphne was lacking the ability to censor her thoughts, Ivy thought. That would make for an interesting tenure in Beauchamp House for them all.

Perhaps wishing to change the subject, Lady Serena said, "I did not bring Jeremy here to enjoy the seaside. Aunt Celeste asked me to act as chaperone for her heirs for the next year as they compete to see who will eventually become the owner of Beauchamp House."

A silence fell over the room, and Ivy could feel the shock of the other girls because it mirrored her own.

"Compete?" Lord Kerr asked, looking as flummoxed as the rest of them.

"Perhaps you'd better come have a private chat with me," Lady Serena said to the marquess. Turning to the four heiresses, she said pointedly, "And you ladies can go get Ivy settled in to her room. I daresay she'd like to rest after the journey she's had. I'll see you all in the morning."

Knowing a dismissal when she heard one, Ivy gave one last look at Lord Kerr whose frown was thoughtful as he stared at his cousin. He might have been unpleasant, but he was the last connection to her life before Beauchamp House, and Ivy found herself reluctant to leave him.

But Sophia slipped an arm through hers and smiled with understanding. "Come on," she said leading her to the doorway. "I'll ring for hot water. I know the first thing I did as soon as I got here was freshen up."

Diverted by the promise of fresh clothes and rest, Ivy went along.

Chapter 3

"You should leave, Quill," said Serena baldly as soon as the door to the parlor closed behind them. "I don't know what maggot you've got in your head about Beauchamp House, but you need to get back into your carriage and return to London."

He waited until they were safely inside Celeste's library before speaking up. Quill had never known either his aunt or Serena to fall prey to the sort of feminine whims that led other ladies to be taken in by frauds, but in this instance he was convinced that it had happened to them both. Why else would his aunt have concocted a contest that determined who would inherit a manor house that had been in the family for centuries?

"You shouldn't speak cant, Serena," he said, scowling as he opened the cupboard doors behind his aunt's desk in search of something alcoholic. "It doesn't suit you. And I'm surprised that you of all people would go along with such a ridiculous plan."

At last in the back of the cabinet, behind a stack of Minerva Press novels, he found a decanter. Pulling it out, along with the glass beside it, he held up the crystal to the light. Opening it, he sniffed. Port! He gave a sigh of relief and poured himself a glass.

Serena watched all of this in annoyance, her arms crossed over her chest. "What do you mean, me 'of all people,' cousin?" she asked sweetly. "I hope you're not referring to my late husband, else I shall be forced to toss you out on your ear myself."

Quill had the grace to feel sheepish. He also well remembered that until he'd grown strong enough to hold her off, she'd been quite good at pinching the tender skin beneath his bicep when he kidnapped her dolls or used her fans as sails for his self-constructed sailboats on the pond. Surreptitiously he slipped a hand beneath his arm at the remembered pain.

Still, even Serena had to admit that her late husband had been a charlatan of the first order. Though he could hardly say as much now. Instead, he took a sip of the excellent port—thanking the gods that his aunt hadn't been too much of a stickler not to buy her liquor from the smugglers that populated the coast.

When he saw that Serena was waiting for a response, he shrugged. "I simply thought you'd had enough of being lied to," he said simply.

"And what makes you think that I'm being lied to now?" she asked, not deigning to acknowledge his veiled mention of her late husband's perfidy.

By the time Quill had learned that his dear cousin's husband, who had spent every last farthing of her dowry, had died on his way to the continent with his mistress, it had been too late to do what he wanted— which was call out the bastard. So instead he'd seen to it that she was well taken care of and that her young son, Jeremy, was not in want of male relatives to substitute in the role of father figure. He knew all too well what it was like to grow up as the only male in a house full of women.

Grateful that they weren't going to go into the details of Fanning's bad behavior again, Quill latched on to her mention of their present problem. "Can you truly believe that Aunt Celeste would have invited four strangers into her home—where she surrounded herself with everything she loved: books, art, artifacts, academic papers—and not only given them free reign but involved them in some sort of competition for it? Our Aunt Celeste? Who disliked people almost as much as she loved books? It's laughable. She is very likely shouting at us from beyond the grave, telling us to get them out of her house and away from her things!"

Though he'd been very fond of his aunt, he knew better than anyone just how much of a misanthrope she could be when it came to interacting with people she didn't know. He'd never heard the full story, but his mother had hinted once that a failed romance had left Celeste with a sour attitude toward the *ton* and a dislike of town. It was impossible to reconcile the Celeste he knew with the sort of woman who would invite strangers into her home—no matter how lonely she might have become.

"When was the last time you actually visited her, Quill?" Serena asked pointedly. "For someone who claims to have known her so well, you weren't exactly the most doting of nephews, were you?"

"I visited," Quill protested, feeling heat creep up his neck. "I was here last summer, I think." Or was it the summer before? He'd been busy in London for the past few years with the lords and dealing with repairs and updates to the farms at Kerr Castle, the seat of the Kerr marquisate in Dorset. But he'd managed to write to her once a month like always, hadn't he? And it wasn't as if he was her only nephew. He had male cousins. Not to mention Celeste's own living sisters and brothers. There was no need for him alone to have come visit so often.

But you were her favorite, an insidious little voice whispered in his head. *You and Serena. She was here. Where were you?*

"Not enough," his cousin said flatly. "I don't blame you. You have responsibilities as the head of your family that the rest of us don't. But you cannot simply waltz in after she's made preparations and set into motion what she wished to happen after she was gone and cut up rough because you weren't consulted. You weren't here. And this competition—however crass you might think it is—is how she wanted to dispose of Beauchamp House."

It *was* crass.

That, he admitted to himself, was the part that pained him most. That his aunt—who for all her dislike of going out into company in London was as elegant as anyone he'd ever known, his own mother included—would have put up her home as the prize in a crude competition amongst a group of strange women. It wasn't anything he could ever have imagined the Lady Celeste Beauchamp he'd known doing.

"But why did she do it?" he asked Serena, who clearly had been privy to more of his aunt's thoughts on the matter than he had. If he'd ever got an inkling of such a thing from her witty letters to him over the last year he'd have dropped everything and rushed to the south coast at once. "Why these women in particular? And why give up Beauchamp House? I know grandfather gave it to her outright, but surely she was aware of its history as part of the Beauchamp properties."

Serena suddenly looked exhausted and gestured for him to give her the rest of his port. And since there didn't seem to be another glass, he poured a bit more and handed it over. Closing her eyes as she savored the wine, Serene gave a sigh of appreciation and set the glass down. Taking a seat in the well-cushioned chair across from Celeste's desk, she rubbed the spot between her brows.

"You know that Aunt Celeste was a bit of a bluestocking in her youth," she said finally, looking up at him with eyes so much like Celeste's.

"Of course," Quill responded, taking a seat behind the desk. He'd always thought it was a masculine desk for his aunt, but there was something commanding about it. And taking a seat behind it for the first time showed him why perhaps she'd kept it on moving into the house. It would be difficult to manage a household from a delicate ladies' desk like the one his mother had in her sitting room. "It was from her that I first learned about Greek and Roman myths. Not to mention Latin."

Serena laughed. "Me too. She was determined that her nieces as well as her nephews would have a working knowledge of the classics."

"Always banging on about what passed for female education in England." Quill nodded in agreement. "She was nothing if not a determined follower of Wollstonecraft. If she told me once, she told me a thousand times not to marry an empty-headed society chit."

"Which you've managed to avoid," Serena said. "Along with matrimony of any kind."

"Not for want to effort on Mama's part," he retorted with a grimace.

"Well, if you remember our aunt's views on education," Serena continued, "then you will also recall how much she prized feminine success in languages, the arts and sciences."

"So, what, these four are here to be educated according to some guidelines set forth by Aunt Celeste?" Quill asked, frowning. It made sense, he supposed. But there was the matter of Miss Wareham—she had no need for an education considering her profession.

Suddenly, it came to him. "No, Miss Wareham is the one who will teach the others. It's why she was carrying all those blasted books." He grinned. "I'm right, aren't I?"

"You really do think you know everything, don't you?" Serena asked exasperated. "Miss Wareham is the daughter of Lord Alton Wareham, former classics professor at Oxford. She's a gifted translator and scholar of ancient Greek in her own right. She is here because Aunt Celeste read one of her translations of Sappho and thought it was far more nuanced than any she'd read by the dozens of men who attempted it."

Quill frowned.

He'd known she was some sort of scholar. No woman clasps a trunk of books to her bosom with that sort of ferocity without knowing their value. And some sense had told him they weren't novels. But Sappho? He thought back to the few Greek poetess's verses he'd read and felt a spark of interest flare. Perhaps there was more to the prim Miss Wareham than he'd originally thought.

"Shall I ring for some smelling salts?" Serena asked with a knowing look. "Or better yet a block of ice to cool your heated thoughts?"

"Certainly not," he responded resisting the urge to run a finger beneath his collar. "So, Miss Wareham is a classics scholar. And she's to teach the others?"

"Hardly," his cousin retorted. "They are all experts in their own right, and that is why Aunt Celeste chose to leave the house to them. Or so I've surmised. She only asked that I come live here with them for the year while they get acclimated, and didn't tell me about her purposes in leaving it to them. Though she did praise them all as accomplished ladies whose expertise is to be commended."

"That sounds like Aunt, at least," Quill said begrudgingly. "And this . . . competition?"

He had difficulty even saying the word, the concept was so vulgar. If word of this got out, the entire Beauchamp family would be the laughingstock of the *ton*, not that he was generally given to caring what the gossips said. But as the head of the family, he did have a responsibility to prevent the sort of talk a scandal like this could cause.

"They're all to spend a year in residence here, working on some project in their chosen field," Serena said. "If any of them should move away before the year is up, she'll forfeit her inheritance. There are of course exceptions for the death of a close family member or medical catastrophe. But any or none of them could inherit according to the terms of Aunt's will, depending upon their ability to remain here. At the end of the year they should each have some new project completed that will contribute to the body of work by female scholars and artists. I suppose that, ultimately, is Aunt's purpose in choosing them."

"It's absurd," Quill said with a shake of his head. "But not, I suppose, entirely outside the realm of things I would expect from Aunt Celeste. She was nothing if not a champion of her bluestocking causes."

"So you'll agree that you've behaved like an ass and will apologize to Miss Wareham, then?" Serena's look was one he well remembered from childhood. He hated it when she was right.

"Let's not be hasty," he said raising his hands. "I didn't know the full story when we met on the road. And though I am persuaded that she is here as the result of a legitimate invitation from Aunt Celeste, I still don't necessarily condone having four strangers inherit Beauchamp House."

"Oh, give over, Quill," Serena said rising. "You're worse than Jeremy when he's trying to wiggle out of a bath. Just admit you were wrong and go back to London. There's nothing for you to do now but wait and see."

But he wasn't convinced that she was right. "Perhaps I will just remain for a while and get to know them. It would hardly be polite if the head of the family were to avoid them all. I am nothing if not cordial, after all."

"What rot." But Serena didn't try to talk him out of it. "I suppose if you're going to stay, I'd better have Mrs. Bacon prepare a room for you. Though I daresay Greaves has already done so. You always did have the servants wrapped around your little finger."

"Because I'm irresistible," Quill said with a wink.

He hoped that was still the case. Because he was going to need every wile at his disposal to convince the four potential heiresses to give up their claims on Beauchamp House.

Chapter 4

"How did you manage to meet Lord Kerr on your journey?" Sophia asked as she thumbed through the books that Ivy had just unpacked from her trunk.

Across the room, the lady's maid who'd been assigned to Ivy on her arrival was brushing out the mud-streaked traveling cloak she'd worn earlier, having already unpacked the few gowns, underthings, and shoes she'd packed. Well aware of the quality of the other girls' gowns, Ivy suspected that compared to their bags, hers had been quite sparsely packed. Even so, she wasn't one to dwell on such things. And she wasn't here to discuss fashion, she reminded herself.

At Sophia's question, however, she glanced nervously at the servant. The last thing she wanted was to be the subject of gossip below stairs. But when Sophia noticed her glance, she shrugged it off. "She's going to learn the full story from his valet anyway, aren't you Polly?"

The maid blushed. "I'm sure I don't know, miss." Turning to Ivy, she curtsied and said, "You let me know, miss, if you need help after your bath. I don't mind helping. I've never been a lady's maid before so I want to do things right and proper for ye."

"Thank you, Polly," said Ivy with genuine gratitude. It would appear that she and Polly would both be learning how to deal with new situations. "You may go now, if you like. If I have any questions, I'll ring." It was a polite lie, but she was comfortable with it. If she was going to have a maid, she wasn't going to give the girl a hatred of her on the first evening by ringing in the dead of night.

As soon as she was gone, Ivy glanced up to see all three of the other ladies looking expectantly at her.

"Fine," she said with a huff and gestured to the small sitting area in the corner of her enormous bedchamber. "But if you don't mind, I'd like to have a cup of tea while we have this uncomfortable conversation." Upon learning Ivy had missed supper, the maid had insisted on ordering a plate of cold food and a pot of tea sent up.

Despite her missishness around her new acquaintances, Ivy was starving and bit into one of the delicious watercress and cucumber sandwiches. Likely realizing that they'd not get any information until the newcomer was comfortable, Gemma played mother and poured for them all.

"The food has been excellent so far," Lady Daphne said as she picked up a lemon tart. "Lady Celeste must have employed a very skilled chef. Our own chef at home demanded five hundred pounds per annum but my father said he was worth every penny. Perhaps Lady Celeste paid more. Though this house does not seem to be as nice as ours, the food is better than even Pierre's."

Ivy exchanged looks with Sophia and Gemma who both widened their eyes at the beautiful blonde's pronouncement.

"Daphne, dearest," said Gemma casually stirring sugar into her tea, "it isn't generally the thing to discuss how much one pays one's cook. Or to speculate upon the salary of the cook in a home where one is a guest."

Quite sure the family cook at home would have retired

immediately if such a sum were offered to her, Ivy tried to imagine what five hundred pounds would look like spread out on a table, and failed.

"You keep saying things like that," Daphne said with a puzzled frown, "but if one doesn't discuss such things openly, how do they know how much they should pay? It makes no logical sense. If I were setting up a household, I would very much wish to know how much I should pay my cook. Otherwise I'd risk paying too much. And though I enjoy good food, I wouldn't want to fall prey to a schemer."

"It's not polite," Sophia said patiently. "Like telling the footman that his legs look quite strong."

Ivy choked on her tea, prompting Gemma to pound her on the back.

"But my father says that about horses all the time," Daphne protested. "I don't see what's so bad about it. Doesn't a footman need strong legs to help him carry things?"

"People are not horses," Gemma said on a laugh. "Really, perhaps it should be a good thing not to speak about anyone's . . . ah . . . parts from the waist down."

"That sounds like a sensible idea," Ivy said, wondering how on earth Lady Daphne managed to mix in polite society without saying something that would ruin her.

But Daphne waved off the warning. "I already know not to talk about buttocks and penises," she said. "I'm not a complete simpleton."

After the other three had recovered from their coughing fits, she continued. "I suppose I shall add legs to the list of things I shouldn't speak about. Really the list is quite long. It's a wonder I find anything to speak about at all. At least there is nothing about maths that can get me into trouble."

"I daresay none of us would know them if there were,"

Ivy said with a smile. It must be very hard to live life in
Lady Daphne's skin, she reflected. For she could tell it
wasn't a lack of intelligence that kept the other lady from
knowing what not to say, but a genuine lack of understanding what made it so objectionable. She herself found
societal strictures to be quite ridiculous at times.

"Perhaps we should return to my earlier question,"
Sophia said looking slyly at Ivy. "How did you manage
to arrive here in an entourage that included the Marquess
of Kerr, Miss Wareham?"

Sighing, Ivy knew she'd have to tell them or they'd speculate. "I missed my place on the mail coach at the Fox
and Pheasant, and his lordship kindly offered to convey
me to Beauchamp House. There's really nothing more to
it than that."

"He seemed quite angry when you arrived," Daphne
said. "And serious about keeping us from inheriting
Beauchamp House."

"Though from what Lady Serena said about a competition, it doesn't appear that any of us is assured of inheriting," Sophia said, her light brown brows drawn. "That
was the first I'd heard of anything like that."

"Me too," Ivy said. "I thought we each were to inherit
a share of Beauchamp House. But it sounds as if we only
inherit if we can remain here for the entire year."

"I certainly have no plans to leave before the year is
out," Lady Daphne said fiercely. "Have you seen the library? It will take that long at least for me to catalog the
mathematics collection."

"Nor do we," said Sophia, clasping her sister's hand in
hers. "I plan to paint to my heart's desire while I'm here.
You've not seen it by day, Miss Wareham, but the light is
incredible reflecting off the sea."

"The cliffs here are well known for the number of fossils

they've produced," Gemma added with a grin. "So his lordship can quite discount any notion of running the Hastings sisters off."

"And I've only just arrived," Ivy said firmly. "He might be unhappy with his aunt's decision on how to bequeath her property, but clearly Lady Celeste wanted us here, and no amount of complaints on the Marquess of Kerr's part will convince me to leave."

"Then we're agreed," Sophia said with a decisive nod. "Now, we should leave you to finish settling in."

"We'll see you at breakfast, Miss Wareham," Gemma said, giving Ivy an impulsive hug. "I'm glad you're here. Now we can begin living our year in scholarly retreat properly."

"I wish you would all call me Ivy," she said as she followed the trio to the door. "My given name is Aphrodite, of course, but my baby sister could only manage 'Ivy' out of it, so Ivy it is. And I think it suits me better, to be honest. I am far too prosaic to be an Aphrodite."

"The goddess of love, was she not?" asked Sophia with a speculative look. "I can see you that way. Do promise me you'll pose for it? I'd love to capture all that lovely auburn hair."

"Do not start that, or we'll be here all night," Gemma said tugging her sister to the door. "Good night, Ivy."

The rest of the ladies exchanged their good nights, and Ivy shut the door behind them.

Turning, she gazed around at what was to be her inner sanctum for the next year. With fine carpets and expensive wall hangings, it was far more finely furnished than her own bedchamber at home in Oxford. And for a moment, she felt a pang of homesickness that no amount of silken finery or expensive trinkets could soothe. She'd longed to escape her mundane existence for so many years that she'd never imagined that once achieving her dream she'd feel frightened by it.

She let the tears flow for a few minutes and then pulled out her handkerchief, blew her nose, and shook away her doldrums.

If she had to face Lord Kerr over the breakfast table, she'd do it after a good night's sleep so she could rebut his arguments properly.

Gathering her nightgown and underclothes, she headed for the dressing room and the hot water Polly had left for her.

Once she'd washed and prepared for bed, Ivy took one more look out at the moonlit view from her window then moved toward the large bedstead.

The bed had already been turned down—Polly again, she supposed. And as she climbed up onto the soft mattress, Ivy noticed a tidily folded missive on her pillow. Had it been there before, when the other ladies were here? Or had one of them left it?

Propping the pillow against the headboard, she settled back against it and stared at her name written in a fine copperplate on the message. Breaking the seal, she began to read.

My dear Miss Wareham,
If you are reading this, I have died under mysterious circumstances. And I must beg you to do your utmost to discover who has robbed me of the chance to meet you and the other three young ladies whom I have chosen to invite into my home, to compete for the chance to call it your own. It was my greatest wish to meet the four of you. To welcome you as fellow scholars, and to share with you my own love of language, mathematics, art, and investigation of the natural world. But for some weeks now, I have become aware that someone

near to me has wished me dead before that meeting could happen. At first I thought the accidents were merely accidents. An imagined shove as I stood on the cliffside. My own clumsiness when the heel broke off my shoe as I descended the stairs. A weak shelf that allowed books to crash down upon me in the library. But now it has become clear to me that there is someone who wishes me dead. I am quite certain I am being poisoned, and I fear each day will my last.

You will perhaps wonder why I entrust this information to you, my dear Ivy, whom I have never even met. And the answer is quite simple. I have made a study of you—of all of you young ladies whom I have chosen for study at Beauchamp House—and you have struck me as the most, how shall I put this? The most capable of managing more than one task at a time. Do not mistake me. I believe all of the others—and indeed my own niece Serena, to whom I have entrusted you in my absence—to be clever and devoted to finding truth, but you, dear Ivy, are the only one who has been forced to pursue your own studies while also assisting someone else with theirs. And that, I believe, with a father like yours, must have taken some degree of guile. I do not blame you, of course. Indeed, it only makes me admire your abilities more. For not everyone is able to maintain two tracks of thought at once.

It is for this reason that I tell you all of this. It is most unfair, I know, to saddle you with this task just as you are ready to finally embark upon your own solitary, scholarly journey, but I'm afraid it's not to be helped. There is too much at stake for me to rest easy knowing that there is a murderer so near Beauchamp House. I know at this point only that they wish to end my life. But I do not know the why of it. Perhaps there is something in the house itself that they seek, in which

*case now your own life and the lives of the other young
ladies are also in danger.*

*In thanks for your assistance in this matter, I've left
a token of my appreciation for you in the library. You
will find it inside the glass-front case on the east wall.
I've already informed Serena that it belongs to you, so
do not worry about removing it. It is yours now and I
hope it will do you some good in your studies. In return, I hope that you will confide what I have told you
in my nephew, the Marquess of Kerr. He will be quite
angry that I have left Beauchamp House to you and
your fellow bluestockings. But he is a good man, and
will do his utmost to help you in this matter. I trust him,
Ivy, and so too should you.*

*I do so wish we could have met in person, my dear,
for I've long suspected you of possessing the same
inner fire for knowledge that I myself had at your age.
But it was not to be. I shall simply have to content
myself with the knowledge that we will meet in the after-
life, where we will talk to our hearts' content about
everything and nothing.*

*Yours in scholarship,
Lady Celeste Beauchamp*

Ivy stared down at the letter. Then, more slowly, she
read it again. But no amount of rereading would dispel the
meaning of the words that Lady Celeste herself had penned
for the express purpose of informing Ivy that she'd been
murdered.

When she'd first learned that none other than the re-
nowned Lady Celeste Beauchamp had left a portion of
her South Downs estate to her, Ivy had thrilled at the prospect of using the bluestocking's famous collection of
scholarship on ancient Greek and Latin poets and philos-
ophers for her own studies. She lived in Oxford, of course,

but the Bodleian Library and its world-class collection was off limits to ladies and even if that weren't the case, she suspected her father would have forbidden her from going there. He had taught her to write and read any number of languages, but he still considered some of the works discovered in the remains of the Hellenistic world to be improper for a lady—his daughter in particular—to be exposed to. So, the hope that Lady Celeste had collected some of those forbidden works was far too tempting a prospect for Ivy to overlook.

What she had not considered was that she would find herself called to solve a murder on her first night in Beauchamp House. Or that Lady Celeste herself would beckon to her from beyond the grave.

Unbidden, the Marquess of Kerr's handsome face rose in her mind. And despite her earlier annoyance with the man, she knew that she had to tell him about this. Not only because he had clearly spent a great deal of time here at Beauchamp House and could therefore assess better than she could who was likely to have wished his aunt dead. But also because Lady Celeste was his aunt. He clearly held her in great affection and would do his utmost to find out who had killed her.

And her benefactress had asked her to tell him. That was ultimately the fact that made Ivy don her dressing gown. Hoping that the marquess was still awake and in the library, she squared her shoulders and made her way downstairs.

Chapter 5

Too wound up for sleep, Quill remained in the library after Serena had gone up to bed, wishing it wasn't too chilly for him to go for a swim. As a youth he'd spent many a summer night burning up restless energy that way. He'd been forbidden from doing so alone, of course, but when had that ever stopped him from doing something? On more than one occasion he'd been joined by his cousin, Dalton, Serena's brother, who had also been a favorite of Aunt Celeste. All three had viewed Beauchamp House as a refuge from the responsibility and strictures of their parents' houses—somewhere they could behave like typical young people rather than the children of peers, and in both Quill's and Dalton's cases, rather than the heirs to two of the oldest titles in England.

He was staring out the window into the darkness when a noise at the door to the chamber made him turn around.

"My lord," said Miss Wareham as she stepped diffidently into the room. "I hope I'm not disturbing you."

Quill was silent for a moment as he let himself drink her in. Gone was the dull traveling gown. She'd exchanged that for a perfectly respectable white night rail and robe that covered far more of her than an evening gown would have. At least that's what he told himself even as his heart skipped a beat at the idea of seeing her in such attire. And her shiny russet locks, freed now from their pins, cascaded over her shoulders in a riot of red curls that glinted in the firelight.

He'd known she was attractive—had categorized her as such almost as soon as he saw her in the Fox and Pheasant earlier that day—but even that observation hadn't led him to imagine what she'd look like in such dishabille. Well, that wasn't quite true, he amended. His mind had conjured her in much fewer clothes than this before he'd realized just who she was. But any such imaginings had been snuffed out as soon as he'd known her destination. The reality of facing her here, now, in her virginal bedclothes, however, with her lovely red hair framing her face like a halo was far more tempting than his fantasy had been.

So, yes. She was disturbing him, but likely in a way she didn't even comprehend.

Suppressing the urge to tell her just that, he said instead, "I was too restless to sleep. It takes a bit for me to settle in to a new place. So there's no harm done."

Moving farther into the room, she set her candle down on one of the large library tables and wrapped her arms across her chest. "It's chilly in here," she said frowning. "I hadn't expected it this close to the sea. I thought it was supposed to be milder here."

Wordlessly, he looked away from her and moved over to kneel before the fireplace, stoking the embers back into a blaze. "It's still early spring," he said on standing, brushing his hands together more for something to do than to remove any soot. "The breeze off the channel keeps the air fairly cool until summer."

But she wasn't paying him any mind; instead she scanned the shelves that lined the walls behind him.

"Looking for something in particular?" he asked, noting the impatience flash in her gaze before she replaced it with polite indifference. "Something to read before sleep, perhaps? Something to steal?"

Her brow furrowed at his question. He'd meant it to be playful, but her response told him that it had come off more sharply than he'd intended.

"I'd hoped you'd decided to stop treating me like an opportunist here to steal your inheritance from you," she said, pursing her lips. "I have it on very good authority that you've a great many houses as part of the Kerr estate—ones much grander and more impressive than this one. I do not understand why you cannot manage to accept the loss of this one. Unless, of course, like most boys you dislike sharing your toys."

She said this last part dismissively over her shoulder as she stepped past him and openly began to read through the shelves on the far wall.

Turning to watch her move from shelf to shelf, he sighed. "I suppose I deserve that after the way I behaved this afternoon. But let me assure you that it's no petty childhood jealousy that made me distrust you and your compatriots, Miss Wareham."

This must have surprised her, for she turned and looked at him through narrowed eyes. "No? Then what?"

He thrust a hand through his hair, fighting the urge to look away. "Have you never faced the removal of a childhood memory?" he asked, finally. "Never wished to hold onto the last bastion of somewhere that gave you comfort?"

Arrested, she tilted her head. "And that's what this place was for you?" she asked. "A bastion of comfort?"

He wasn't sure why, but Quill felt more exposed in that moment than he would have if he were stark naked. But he knew he owed her an explanation. Especially after the way he'd treated her earlier. "For me, for Serena, and for my cousin Dalton," he admitted. "Our own homes were not particularly . . ." He broke off as he tried to think of a word that wouldn't shock her. He could hardly tell her about the debauchery that had reigned in his own house before his father died. And the circumstances of Serena and Dalton's upbringing weren't his to reveal. "Let's just say that we found our visits to Beauchamp House to be a relief from our own homes."

Something flashed behind her eyes. Sympathy? Or something else? Quill wasn't sure, but he couldn't fail to note the way she squared her shoulders. As if she'd come to a decision.

Abandoning her scan of the bookshelves, she turned fully to face him, her hands clasped before her so tightly that her knuckles were white with it. "Lord Kerr," she began, her green eyes shadowed with trepidation. "There is something I must tell you."

Quill felt his stomach drop, and a pang of disappointment ran through him. Now she'd admit that she and the others actually *had* found some way to trick Aunt Celeste into leaving them Beauchamp House. The whole business of the competition had sounded like a farce, and though he'd known his aunt to possess a playful streak, he'd never guessed it would reveal itself in such a way. Certainly he'd not supposed she would play fast and loose with the disposition of Beauchamp House, where she'd spent so many happy years.

"Then by all means," he drawled, allowing every bit of the world-weary ennui that cloaked him in town to settle over him. "Tell me all, Miss Wareham. I confess I am curious to hear how you all managed it, never having set foot in Beauchamp House before. It must have taken a great deal of coordination amongst the four of you."

But if he'd expected her to surrender completely, he was to be disappointed. "What?" she asked, her nose wrinkled in puzzlement. "I thought we'd just put that behind us. And yet, here you are with accusations again. You are like a dog with a bone, Lord Kerr. Honestly!"

"If not that, then what is it you wish to tell me?" he demanded, exasperated. He'd never thought himself to be a particularly emotional man, but since he'd met this chit on the road he'd gone through more feelings than a year in London had elicited from him. He must be sickening for something. "You can hardly blame me for jumping to conclusions when we've just been speaking about my earlier suspicions."

"I can blame you all too easily," she retorted with a scowl. "But I will not because I am tired of being at cross purposes with you. And I do not believe your aunt would like it."

Indicating with a wave of his hand that she should go on, Quill waited.

"I found a letter from your aunt waiting for me in my bedchamber," she said, her fine features marred by worry. "I greatly fear that Lady Celeste was murdered."

"What the devil do you mean 'murdered'?" Quill demanded, shocked despite his foreboding at the bespectacled beauty's pronouncement. "What did this letter say?"

From the pocket of her robe, Miss Wareham produced the letter. Opening it, Quill recognized his aunt's hand at once and began to read.

When she was finished, Quill found himself shaking his head in bemusement. "I must confess, when I suspected someone of doing away with Aunt Celeste, I assumed it was one of you four heiresses," he admitted with a frown. "It never occurred to me that someone would kill her for any other reason than an inheritance. She simply wasn't the sort of person who could inspire the sort of enmity that would provoke someone to murder."

"I greatly fear that your aunt suspected otherwise," Ivy said with sympathy in her eyes. "I know it is difficult for us to see our loved ones as others see them, but was there anyone in the village or in her circle of acquaintances who might have resented her for some reason? Or even someone in the household?"

"I've been away for long enough that I may not know all of the staff she's hired in my absence. So it is possibly one of them. Though I can't imagine it. Aunt Celeste was brusque at times," he said with a sad smile, "but only with those who attempted to suggest that because she was a female she couldn't be taken seriously as a scholar. When I was a boy I recall she had a particularly scathing correspondence with the president of one of the Royal Societies about his refusal to publish the findings of one of her bluestocking friends. It was quite a scandal—well, with my mother, at any rate. She was never very supportive of Aunt's intellectual pursuits. But that was decades ago. And I cannot imagine that fellow held a grudge for that long."

"No," Ivy agreed. "That doesn't sound like something that would prompt her murder now. I must confess that I cannot imagine why someone would kill her. Though my only understanding of her is as the generous benefactor who chose me amongst dozens of classics scholars as one of her heirs. And from what you and your cousin Lady Serena have told me, she was much admired. It seems mad to think of the lady you've both described as being the victim of something so vicious."

"That's a good point," Quill admitted. "At this juncture we don't even know if she was murdered or not. After all, from what the local physician said, she died of natural causes. She was rather young, I admit, but it does happen. I wasn't here at the time, of course, and neither was Serena, so we don't know what the days were like leading up to her death, but surely if there was something untoward, the servants would have reported it."

"Perhaps they didn't know what was going on," Ivy said thoughtfully. "I believe there are any number of poisons that can act quickly and without giving away their presence in the body."

For what felt like the hundredth time, Quill castigated himself for not rushing to Beauchamp House as soon as he'd learned of Celeste's death. It had felt unnecessary, since she was the only person he'd cared about there, and her body was to be brought to Beauchamp family cemetery at Maitland Hall, the seat of the Duke of Maitland. His own mother, Celeste's sister and another daughter of the fourth duke, had been devastated at the loss of her sister—despite their differences—and had insisted upon burying her beside their parents. Now Quill realized that the haste with which it had all been taken care of had made it virtually impossible to suspect anything untoward in his aunt's manner of death. Certainly neither he nor his mother had suspected murder.

"It's too late to know now," he said with a shake of his head. "Though I could question the local physician, and even Mrs. Bacon, who was here at the time."

"What of her maid?" Ivy asked. "I know many lady's maids know their mistresses' lives even better than *they* do sometimes."

"I have no idea," Quill admitted. "I'll ask Mrs. Bacon when I see her in the morning."

The room was silent for a moment as they considered what their first move should be in investigating Lady Celeste's death.

Finally, Ivy cleared her throat. "I do not like to remind you, my lord," she said with a troubled glance. "But your aunt asked that we keep our investigation a secret from anyone else."

"Of course we must," Quill said nodding. "We don't wish to alert the killer to the fact that we've figured out it wasn't just natural causes. And besides, that it would put you in danger, which is why you must let me see to all of it. Really it's the most sensible way to handle things, you must agree."

But he was disappointed to see Miss Wareham roll her lovely green eyes. "I most certainly do not agree. I will keep things quiet, of course, but I must insist upon being part of the investigation. Your aunt entrusted this information to me, after all. Not you. If she wished for you to conduct this investigation alone, then she'd have left the letter for you."

He disliked admitting it, but she was right about that. Aunt Celeste and her silly bluestocking tendencies. Didn't she realize the danger she was placing Miss Wareham in by telling her about this? But he supposed his aunt had known what she wanted, and for all that he disliked the idea of Miss Wareham in danger, he had little doubt that she was every bit as courageous as a man would be in her place. Perhaps more.

"Fine," he said with a shake of his head. "We will work together. But you will let me question Mrs. Bacon and the physician initially. It will look more natural for me to be the one with lingering questions about her death. And I promise I'll share anything I learn with you."

She looked as if she weren't quite convinced of his sincerity, but finally Miss Wareham nodded. And with one last wistful glance at the bookshelves, she crossed the room to the door. "I'll just go back up then. I bid you good night, Lord Kerr."

Before she could open the door, however, he spoke up. "I think if we're to work together, Miss Wareham, that we'd better call ourselves by our given names. I don't think my aunt would have any objections, given her feelings about equality between the sexes."

Turning back, her hand on the doorknob, Miss Wareham gave a short nod. "All right then, my lord."

"Quill," he reminded her with a smile. "Call me, Quill."

"Very well, Quill," she said, a little breathlessly.

"Good night, Aphrodite," he said softly, liking the feel of the word on his lips, like some sort of incantation. Her green eyes widened behind her spectacles at hearing him speak her actual name. But she didn't correct him. And if he wasn't mistaken, there was a blush rising in her cheek. Perhaps there was more of the pretty scholar's namesake in her than she'd previously let on.

But then she seemed to come back to herself, straightening her spine and saying firmly, "Good night, Quill." With that, she stepped out, shutting the door behind herself with an audible click.

He stared at the door for a moment before what she'd told him returned to the forefront of his mind.

Someone had murdered Aunt Celeste.

He thought back to the last time he'd seen her, just a few months ago. How she'd teased him about his decision to put off marrying for a few years yet to, as she put it, gather his rosebuds. She'd cautioned him not to wait too long. Could that have been because she saw her own life was almost at an end?

She had confessed to feeling a bit under the weather but blamed it on the French cuisine his mother insisted upon in Castle Kerr. Had it been something more? Had someone been poisoning her beneath his roof? It was not to be borne.

If someone had deliberately put an end to Lady Celeste Beauchamp's life, then he was damned if he'd allow the miscreant to run tame as if nothing had happened.

And something else occurred to him, now. If the motive for Celeste's murder had been something related to Beauchamp House, then the ladies who stood to inherit the manor were in danger too.

He trusted Serena, his valet York, and those servants who'd been at Beauchamp House since his boyhood, but that was the extent of it. If he was going to learn more about his aunt's poisoning, he'd need to have someone here he could trust. Someone who had loved Celeste as much as he did.

Searching the desk for writing materials, he quickly scratched out a message. Finding some sealing wax in the drawer, he melted it and quickly pressed his signet ring into the crimson liquid.

When he reached his bedchamber, he found York waiting for him. "I'd like this to go to London first thing tomorrow," he told the man he trusted with his life. "If you cannot find someone to go, then I'd like you to go yourself."

The other man's surprise showed in his raised brows, but that was the only sign he gave of recognizing his master's agitation. "Very good, my lord." After pocketing the missive, he went back to brushing out Quill's greatcoat.

Feeling somewhat more sanguine about his task, Quill readied himself for sleep that did not come.

Chapter 6

Despite her difficulty sleeping, Ivy awoke at her usual early hour the next morning and was pleased to find that Lady Daphne and Miss Gemma Hastings were seated at the breakfast table when she arrived.

"How pleasant to find that I am not the only early riser amongst our little band," she said as she returned from the sideboard with a plate of eggs and toast and took a seat next to Lady Daphne. "I presume, Miss Gemma, that your sister does not share this proclivity?"

Biting into a piece of toast, Gemma shook her head. "No," she said with a frown. "Sophia tends to stay up quite late and as a result ends up sleeping late too. It made for many a schoolroom battle when we were younger, I can assure you. She could never understand why she should keep regular hours when she felt more alert in the evenings. She was always falling asleep during our lessons."

"It can hardly be considered an aberration," said Lady Daphne returning her teacup to its saucer, "when so much of society spends the season keeping those kind of hours. It is really only the lower classes who value regulated schedules such as you describe, Gemma, and that's mostly because they tend to work in factories which require it. Is not your father an industrialist? You are surely aware of this as his daughter. I'd think anyone who makes their fortune in such a manner would be."

Ivy had thought perhaps she'd imagined the mathematician's excessive good looks the night before, but the bright light of day only proved Lady Daphne Forsyth to be more beautiful than Ivy had first thought. Taller than the other ladies, her figure was not so buxom as to be vulgar but not so svelte to be thought unfeminine. And her golden hair, arranged in fashionable ringlets that perfectly framed her face, was like something an actual Greek goddess would possess—which made Ivy feel rather inadequate to her given name.

The girl's lack of tact, however, she had not imagined, and after posing her question to Miss Gemma Hastings, Lady Daphne simply sipped her tea, as if she hadn't just called the Hastings family common. Or at the very least, called attention to their position in a class lower than her own family hailed from.

Given that her own family was often made aware of its fall from the exalted heights of society by ladies of a similar rank to Lady Daphne, who sought to depress any pretensions Ivy and her sisters might have to raise themselves through marriage, Miss Hastings was maybe more sensitive to such pointed comments. And lord knew she'd been insulted in far subtler ways than Daphne had just done. Even so, Ivy was unable to stop herself from coming to Gemma's defense.

"If you are suggesting, Lady Daphne, that Gemma is vulgar for valuing the merits of maintaining a regulated sleep schedule," she said tightly, "then you must surely call me vulgar too, for I am also someone who values waking before the morning has passed."

At Ivy's annoyed tone, Lady Daphne frowned in puzzlement. "I didn't call Gemma vulgar," she said with real confusion. "I merely pointed out that people of her social standing tend to value such sleeping regularity. I fear I am an aberration to my own class, for I also would rather not sleep the day away. But then, I can get by on only a few hours of sleep without much trouble. Sophia, it would seem, is far more suited to the life of an aristocrat despite her being born the daughter of an industrialist."

Gemma placed a hand over Ivy's but said to Daphne, "I understand what you meant, my dear. I fear Ivy hasn't got used to your plain speaking yet. It will take her a bit, as you well know." Turning to Ivy, she continued, "She means no insult, I can assure you. And Sophia, the wretch will likely be quite pleased to know she is suited to the life of an aristocrat. God knows Papa has told her that often enough."

"I seem to lack the ability to make my words fit into the sort of polite chatter that is needed to converse without insulting my listeners, Ivy," said Daphne with an apologetic smile. "I hope you won't hold my clumsy speech against me. By all accounts you are considered to be a brilliant linguist and I should hate to think we will live together in Beauchamp House for the coming year and you will hold me in dislike all the while. I truly did not mean offense."

Despite herself, Ivy was touched by the apology, which seemed heartfelt at least. "Do you truly not recognize it when your own words could be construed as insulting?" she asked, curious about the other girl's deficiency.

Daphne's beautiful features twisted in unhappiness. She nodded. "I never mean it, but I am always saying the wrong thing to someone. I tend to avoid polite company because of it. Which is quite acceptable to me, since I would rather spend my time working on calculations and constructing proofs. It can be lonely at times, but so few people are able to understand my work that it is not all that interesting for me to converse with them anyway."

Ivy certainly wouldn't be able to say the first thing of

sense about mathematics. What a lonely existence Daphne must have. And yet, she didn't seem particularly unhappy. Indeed, she was sanguine about her situation. Ivy was sure of it.

"I wonder," Daphne continued, "why Lady Celeste included me in this group at all, given how different my own talents are from yours. If any of us is the odd woman out, it is I. Though for that matter, why did she choose any of us?"

At the mention of their benefactor, Ivy recalled to mind her own task set forth by that lady. "Did any of you know much about Lady Celeste before you received word of your inheritance?" she asked. "I know that I had never met her before, but it seemed as if she knew quite a bit about me, and my studies."

Sophia's appearance in the doorway of the breakfast room delayed their discussion for a moment while they waited for her to fill a plate and join them at the table.

"We didn't move in the same circles," Gemma said with a wry smile given Daphne's earlier statement about the Hastings social placement. "But I was aware of the brief pieces she contributed to a small journal a few of her blue-stocking friends published about her findings amongst the fossils of the South Downs. We shared a friend in common. But we never met. And I certainly didn't expect to be invited to remain in her home for a year so that I could excavate the cliffs myself."

"And she was quite well known amongst the fellows of the Royal Society," said Sophia with a shrug. "Though I never met her either. Not even when my painting was shown. She apparently didn't make the journey to town very often. Especially not this last year."

Ivy frowned. "What was different about this past year?" she asked. Had word of Lady Celeste's poison-induced illness made its way to London? And if so, who had spread the word of it?

* * *

"The first night we were here, Mrs. Bacon told us that Lady Celeste was ill for much of this past year," Daphne said. "The local physician was never able to learn what the cause was, but it seemed to come and go. And the unpredictability of it made her reluctant to travel given that she never knew when an attack would overtake her. I should have thought such an illness would prompt her to seek out a Harley Street specialist, but she allowed sentiment to keep her loyal to her local physician. Which is quite maddening when one considers that her foolishness may have caused her untimely death."

Biting her tongue, Ivy reminded herself that Daphne was not being purposefully insulting about Lady Celeste. And her frustration mirrored Ivy's own. Especially since determining the cause of her demise was something she—a classics scholar for heaven's sake—had been entrusted with. What on earth did she know about investigating crime? She might as well have been asked to solve one of Daphne's mathematical equations.

"So, the servants were aware of Lady Celeste's condition?" Ivy asked, stifling her self-doubt for the time being.

"Certainly," Gemma said with a nod. "And when you consider it, they often know far more about our lives than we know about one another. I know our maids have been privy to more of our scrapes and misdeeds than our parents have been."

"Which is all for the best," Sophia said with a grin. "Else we'd neither of us been allowed to travel to the south coast at all. Mama and Papa are sadly rigid about their ideas regarding feminine behavior. Much more so than the upper ten thousand if Daphne is to be believed."

Having only one maid who served all five of the Wareham sisters, Ivy was perhaps not as familiar as the other ladies were about life with personal servants. But even in their small household, with just a handful of servants, there were certain things about the Warehams that their maids knew better than those with whom the family socialized.

"Why are you so curious about Lady Celeste's illness?" Daphne asked. "It is unlikely to have been something that would linger in the household, as by all accounts she was the only person in Beauchamp House to suffer from it."

Mindful of her agreement with Lord Kerr to keep their investigation of Lady Celeste's murder to themselves, Ivy shrugged. "I was merely curious. Never having met the lady, I was foolishly wondering if there may have been some way of preventing her death. Which is silly now that I consider it. Especially since there is nothing to be done about it now."

"But hardly unusual," said Sophia gently. "When someone you love dies unexpectedly I think there is always a tendency amongst the mourners to wish it hadn't happened. And we, all of us, owe so much to Lady Celeste. I know neither Gemma nor I would have been able to devote an entire year to our passions without our benefactor's generosity. And I dare say it's the same for both of you."

Ivy nodded in agreement, but Daphne shook her head. "My father allows me to do as I please so long as it doesn't bring ridicule on the family."

Sophia bit her lip, stifling laughter. "Most of us, then," she amended with a wink at Ivy. "And even Daphne would wish to be able to thank Lady Celeste."

Before Daphne could object—and her mouth opened as if she was going to—Ivy broke in. "Of course she would. No matter how pointless it is to wish something that happened in the past hadn't occurred. Isn't that right, Daphne?"

"I suppose so," said Daphne with a frown. "But really it is not realistic to dream of the fantastical. It will only lead to disappointment. It is far more sensible to acknowledge a bad thing has happened and then to move on."

Smiling ruefully, Ivy decided a change of subject was in order. "Have any of you seen Lord Kerr this morning?" Knowing that the inquiry would lead to speculation from the others, she added, "One of his bags was brought to my room by mistake so I wished to let him know."

"I feel sure you could have your maid take it to his valet," Sophia said raising her brows.

"If you wish to engage in an affair with Lord Kerr," said Daphne baldly, "then you would do far better to summon him to your bedchamber to retrieve the bag."

Sophia and Gemma covered their startled laughter with coughs. Ivy felt her face turn red with mortification. "I most certainly do not wish any such thing, Daphne. I truly only wished to return his bag, I can assure you." Though the notion of what an affair with Lord Kerr—Quill, as he'd asked her to call him—would entail gave her a moment's pause as she considered it. Even so, she would hardly admit to it here in the breakfast room.

"I believe I saw him headed toward the servants' quarters on my way here," Sophia said once she'd managed to stifle her laughter. "Perhaps he was in search of his bag."

But Ivy knew precisely what his lordship was in search of and it wasn't his fictitious missing bag. He was beginning the investigation into Lady Celeste's murder without her, curse him, which was not the plan that they'd agreed to. She might have known that all his promises to work together with her to find his aunt's killer had been mere pretense. He was distrustful of her from the start so it should come as no surprise that he didn't trust her enough to include her in the questioning of the servants. No matter that his aunt had asked *her*—not her high-handed nephew to find out who killed her.

Rising, she threw down her napkin. "I shall simply have to seek him out downstairs, then. Pray excuse me."

Chapter 7

"You still make the best scones in the county, Mrs. B," Quill said, fighting the urge to pat his stomach after consuming three of the housekeeper's famous pastries. It was unusual for a housekeeper to undertake such a task, of course, and many cooks would not condone an interloper in their kitchen. But since Mrs. Bacon only made one thing—scones—the cook at Beauchamp House, a no-nonsense woman named Mrs. Mason, overlooked the irregularity when the chatelaine came in search of flour and butter.

When he was a boy, Quill had spent many a happy hour at the broad kitchen table where the servants took their meals. There was something about the easy manners of the servants—a family, though none of them were related—that offered him a welcome reprieve from the stifling formality of his own home. Of course, Beauchamp House itself had been less formal too, but he'd never have managed a trip to the kitchens in Kerr Castle without receiving a swift reprimand. Here he knew that there would be no repercussions, no matter how his aunt might chide him when she found him wiping crumbs from his mouth.

"You're the only one who ever said so, my lord," said

the housekeeper with a fond smile. "You and his grace, the Duke of Maitland, that is. Though it wasn't a great mystery since the pair of you could eat a kitchen's worth of food in your day."

"In my day!" Quill raised a hand to his chest. "You're not saying I'm an old man, now, are you? I confess I'm pained to hear you say so."

"But you are old, cousin," piped up Jeremy from the chair beside Quill's where he was doing his best to consume his third scone. "Least, to me you are. Though Mama says I shouldn't call old people old."

"That's because when one is old, young Jem," said Quill wryly, "one doesn't like to be reminded of it. Certainly not by young rapscallions who declare they're going to break one's scone-eating record."

"Uncle Dalton says records are made to be broken," said the boy, chewing unrepentantly.

The marquess would have responded, but Mrs. Bacon's curtsy toward the doorway made him turn.

Her expressive green eyes narrow with suspicion behind her spectacles, Miss Wareham—or Ivy, he corrected himself, though it was a devilishly prosaic name for such a fiery creature—stepped into the kitchen warily. "I do apologize for intruding Mrs. Bacon," she began, "but I was told I could find his lordship down here."

Having stood as soon as he saw her, Quill nudged Jeremy, who had missed the lady's entrance so wrapped up in his scone was he. "Mind your manners, Jem."

The look of chagrin on the child's face would have been comical if Quill weren't sure the panic had been seeded in some sharp word from Jeremy's late father.

"It's all right," he told the boy in a low voice. "You stood as soon as you knew." He placed a comforting hand on Jeremy's shoulder, and they both bowed to Miss Wareham.

"I didn't realize you were not alone, my lord," she said

looking somewhat deflated. "I had heard you were in the servants' hall and . . ."

And she'd suspected him of questioning them without her, he guessed. But the opportunity that presented itself when he'd found Jem lingering in the kitchen waiting for Mrs. Bacon's scones to come out of the oven had been too much to resist. The presence of Ivy, a newcomer, would likely inhibit the older woman from speaking frankly.

Even so, he wasn't about to help her reprimand him. One had to take advantage of opportunity when it came to call.

"And, Miss Wareham?" he asked, brows raised.

"And," she said with a speaking look, "I thought perhaps you were searching for your missing bag. The one that inadvertently was left in my chamber. I suppose when the bags were brought in yesterday one of yours got mixed in with mine."

Her eyes told him not to correct her, and it was rather good as reasons for seeking him out went. Though a more correct lady might have had her lady's maid perform such a task by having her converse with his valet. But something about the simplicity of her gowns and the self-sufficiency she evinced made him suspect that Miss Wareham did not enjoy the services of an abigail. At the very least not one all to herself. "Ah, yes," he said with a nod. "I am glad you spoke up. I noticed its absence last evening, but didn't wish to disturb you by sending my valet for it."

Looking ill at ease, Ivy bit her lip, causing a host of less-than-polite thoughts to flood his imagination.

"Would you like a scone, Miss Wareham?" said Jeremy, very effectively puncturing Quill's wanton imagination. "There's some left ain't there, Mrs. B?"

"I'll just get you a plate, miss," said the housekeeper bustling around as she set a place at the table for the interloper—as if she entertained parties in the kitchens every day.

"Oh, I . . ." Ivy began, but when Jem stepped forward and took her hand in his, she gave one helpless look at Quill before giving in to the child's tug and following him. "I suppose I could have one. Though I've just had breakfast."

"You won't let a little thing like that keep you from the county's best scones, will you, Miss Wareham?" Quill asked with a grin. "I thought you were bolder than that."

"Do you have scones at your house, Miss Wareham?" Jeremy asked, watching avidly as Ivy spread butter followed by gooseberry jam on her scone. "They're my favorite."

Ivy smiled indulgently at the boy, revealing a dimple in her left cheek that Quill hadn't noticed the night before. "Indeed I do, Jeremy," she assured him. "Though I must confess that my absolute favorite confection from our cook is her lemon tart."

"You surprise me, Miss Wareham," said Quill, biting back a grin. "I shouldn't have thought you would have a taste for tarts." It was juvenile of him, but he found himself fighting a boyish impulse to tweak her pigtails, or in this case, to tease her with double entendres. "It is unusual, I think, for a lady to express such a desire."

Her lips twitched, and he had no doubt that she'd understood the jest. "There's a great deal you don't know about me, my lord," she said guilelessly. "Indeed, I must confess myself surprised that you prefer scones to tarts yourself. I was given to understand that men of your social station possessed an insatiable appetite for them. At least, that is what I hear from the gossip." It was clear from her expression that she didn't approve of it, either.

"Well, we don't *all* enjoy tarts," he said feeling as if he needed to defend himself against her censure. "I will grant that a great many titled men seek them out. But that doesn't mean that we all do. Some men, myself amongst them, are more selective about the . . . desserts we choose."

"I like all kinds of sweets," Jeremy offered helpfully. "Biscuits, cakes, tarts, Christmas pudding."

At the mention of pudding, Ivy covered her mouth with her hand, and her cheeks turned red with the suppression of laughter.

"I think perhaps we've bored Miss Wareham enough with talk about ways to quench her sweet tooth, Jem," Quill said, clapping the boy on the shoulder even as he exchanged a wry grin with Ivy. "If you're finished with your scone, why don't you go see if York will let you assist him with polishing my boots. I know you enjoy it."

"I like to see my face in them," Jeremy said with a grin, pushing his chair back from the table at once. Then, mindful of his manners, he gave Ivy a very correct bow. "Good day, Miss Wareham."

When the child was gone, Ivy gave Quill an exasperated look. "You should be ashamed of yourself speaking like that in front of a child." Though it was clear from the ghost of a smile that still lingered on her pink lips that her ire wasn't serious.

"You're the one who brought up tarts," he said defensively. "I was merely expressing my surprise. Surely there is nothing wrong with that."

"Certainly not," she conceded with a shake of her head. "If, that is, you do not then imply that I enjoy spending time with ladies of ill-repute. Which, I should inform you, is not far off from what that villain in the Fox and Pheasant said to me."

At the mention of the man he'd rescued her from at the inn, all humor fled from Quill. "What do you mean?" he asked, wishing he'd beaten the villain when he had the chance.

"Calm down," she said, tilting her head in puzzlement at his sudden change of mood. "I shouldn't have said anything. It's long gone anyway."

"What did he say, Ivy?" he pressed her, his eyes pinning her in place with their intensity.

"Just something about how I shouldn't be surprised at being treated roughly if I kept such low company," she said, looking down at where her hands lay clenched on the table. "He saw me speaking to one of the women lingering in the taproom. I suspected she might be . . . in need of help. Sometimes there are circumstances so desperate that a woman has only the choice between virtue and survival. And I thought perhaps I could assist . . ."

Quill cursed under his breath. "So he thought you were working together. That's why he put his hands on you."

Nodding, Ivy said angrily, "It infuriates me that the same men who use women like that will turn around and shame them as if the men themselves are innocent of any sin. I work sometimes at a home for unfortunates near my home in Oxford, and the stories I've heard there would make your hair curl."

"An inn in a town you've never been to is not the same as a home in Oxford, Ivy," Quill said with a shake of his head. "A home which I daresay your father has visited to ensure it's safety so that you can go there with no harm to your reputation."

But Ivy's pained expression told him it wasn't so easy as that. "He doesn't know you go there," he guessed.

"No," Ivy admitted with a shrug. "If I'd informed him he would forbid me from going at all. And those women need help. My help."

"Oh, they need to be able to translate ancient Greek?" he asked with a sarcasm he regretted almost immediately. His dislike of her putting herself in danger was just so consuming that he had trouble filtering his words.

"No," she said with a scowl. "I teach them how to read so that they might better themselves. Perhaps get a job as a clerk in a shop. Or maybe a copyist if they are able to learn to write their letters. I won't be ashamed of it, my lord, so you needn't try."

Sighing, Quill wiped a hand over his face. "I apologize. I was rude. I simply do not like to imagine you placing yourself in danger like that. Certainly if I'd known that was what precipitated the actions of that man at the inn I'd have dealt much more roughly with him."

"It wasn't perhaps a wish to keep me out of danger that led you to start questioning the servants without me this morning, was it?" Ivy asked, her eyes knowing. "Because I cannot help but think that's what made you come down here this morning. But thankfully for me, Jeremy interrupted. Else you'd have spoken to all of them before I even got a chance to come below stairs"

"I was only thinking of your safety," he said scowling. Lowering his voice, he leaned forward. "Someone *murdered* my aunt. If you think for one minute I'm going to allow you to place yourself in similar danger then you are sorely mistaken."

"I know she was murdered," Ivy hissed. "I was the one she chose to tell, and I hope you won't forget that. Your aunt obviously thought I was capable enough to handle the task, so kindly let me do it. Indeed, it was I who invited your assistance. Not the other way round. So I will thank you to remember that."

"My aunt was just as pigheaded as you are when it came to her thoughts on the role of ladies in society," Quill argued. "And I loved her. But that doesn't mean I always agreed with her."

"In this instance," she said haughtily, "you have no choice. I will investigate this matter. Whether you wish to assist me is entirely up to you."

And as if the matter was settled, she rose from the table, brushed off her hands, and turned to exit the kitchen.

Despite himself, Quill was impressed with her determination. But that didn't mean he would let her risk her own safety. He'd simply have to find a way to protect her. Against her will if necessary.

Wordlessly he stood and followed her.

Chapter 8

Ivy found Mrs. Bacon in the dining room, overseeing two of the housemaids as they polished the enormous cherry wood table. She felt Quill's presence behind her but chose not to remark upon it. If he were going to assist her in this matter, then he would have to follow her lead.

As soon as the trio became aware of their presence, they dropped into curtsies.

"Mrs. Bacon," Ivy began, "I wonder if I might have a word?"

But to her frustration, the older woman looked to Quill first, who nodded, before turning back to Ivy. "Of course, Miss Wareham," she said with a smile. "Would you like to step into my parlor?"

"If it's not too much trouble, Mrs. B," Quill responded, "that would be ideal. It's a matter for some discretion."

Biting back a sharp retort at having him intrude upon her task, Ivy nodded, and shook her head silently at Quill when he gestured for her to precede him.

Once inside the tiny room, which the housekeeper had made cozy with embroidery, a few bits of mismatched furniture, and a comfortable-looking chair, they declined to sit as Ivy thought it best if they got straight to the point.

"Can you tell us a bit about the servants employed by the house at the time of Lady Celeste's death?" she asked, trying to sound both authoritative and kind. No easy task, she realized.

At Mrs. Bacon's frown, Quill spoke up. "We only wish to know if there has been anyone who gave my aunt any trouble. Or who perhaps felt slighted upon her death. I know many of the servants here have been at Beauchamp House since I was a boy.

"What's this about, my lord?" Mrs. Bacon asked, her brow furrowed with worry. "Has someone been complaining because they didn't receive a bequest in her ladyship's will? For I won't stand for that sort of behavior from any of my staff. Just let me know who it is and I'll have him out on his ear at once."

Before Quill could jump in, Ivy hastened to reassure her. "No, no. It's nothing like that. I simply wondered, whether it might be worth finding out some of the history of the people who have kept Beauchamp so well these last years. And to find out who might have caused your mistress trouble. I should hate to think one of us might inadvertently invite them back, not knowing their history here."

"That might not be a bad idea, Miss Wareham," said Mrs. Bacon approvingly. "It would be a shame if someone tried to ingratiate himself with you young ladies in such a way. But aside from her ladyship's maid, who left because there was no lady for her to serve anymore, and the steward, who retired to live with his daughter, we haven't lost anyone in the past several years. We tend to keep the same staff on for years at a time. Which is why it's such a shock to lose someone. Or for that matter to hire someone new."

"I should imagine so," Ivy said with a nod. "Well, I can assure you that the other ladies and I have no plans on dismissing or hiring anyone anytime soon."

Rather than appearing reassured by this pronouncement, Mrs. Bacon only looked uncomfortable, as if she
felt Ivy was trying a bit too hard to win her over. "I . . .
that is to say . . . very good, Miss."

Clearing his throat, Quill spoke up. "Mrs. B, I know it's
perhaps a difficult subject, but might we talk for a moment
about the particulars of my aunt's illness? I wasn't here for
her, you know, and it pains me to think that she was suf-
fering."

Ivy was relieved that Quill had decided to ask the question himself, for the housekeeper's entire manner softened
as she took in his genuine grief. "I wish I could tell you it
was quick and painless, my lord, but I'm afraid it was anything but. She suffered for several months before it finally
took her. And indeed it was hard for all of us. I think it
preyed upon Dr. Vance's mind the most, though. He was
so helpless, you see. Everything he tried failed. Until one
day my lady just slipped away. And there was naught any
of us could do."

Quill, Ivy noticed, had to struggle to keep his composure.
"Why didn't she tell me, Mrs. B?" he asked with a sigh.
"Any of us? If we'd known she was ill, I know I would have
been here at a moment's notice."

With a soft look, Mrs. B shook her head. "That's just
what she didn't want, my lord. Your aunt was a proud lady.
And she didn't wish for you to remember her like that. Ill,
and looking nothing like her vibrant self. I did ask more
than once if she'd like me to contact her family—for I
knew that you, and Lady Serena, and his grace would wish
to come—but she would never agree. Said you all had your
own lives and that besides, she wanted you to remember
her as she was before the illness."

Wishing she could touch him, Ivy had to content herself with standing at his side, hoping her presence would offer some kind of comfort.

"I suppose you're right, Mrs. B," he said with a shake of his head. "I just can't help but think of what might have been."

"You and I both, my lord," said the housekeeper. "And, as I said, Dr. Vance was most troubled of all."

"You never said what her illness was," Ivy said tentatively, not wishing to impose upon Quill's grief, but also wishing to know if Dr. Vance had any suspicions.

"That's because none of us knew, Miss Wareham," said Mrs. Bacon. "Dr. Vance could never discover exactly what it was that ailed her. He thought at first it might have been something she'd eaten. But by the end, he was convinced it must have been a wasting disease of some kind. But he never said what."

"Is his office still in town, Mrs. B?" Quill asked, exchanging a look with Ivy. "On the same street as the blacksmith's shop?"

"Aye," the housekeeper nodded. "And I know he'd be happy to see you, my lord. If only to relay his sympathies in person. I've known him for many a year now and I don't mind telling you that he took your aunt's death quite hard."

"Thank you so much for your assistance, Mrs. Bacon," Ivy said, hoping the conversation might have thawed relations between them. But she had no such luck.

"I'm happy to help, Miss Wareham," Mrs. Bacon said stiffly. Then turning to Quill, she offered a broad smile. "If there's anything you need at all, my lord, I hope you won't hesitate to ask."

"Of course I won't, Mrs. B," said Quill, breaching their formality to buss the older woman on the cheek. Which made her blush like a giddy schoolgirl, Ivy noted. Were there no lengths to which this man would not stoop to sway people to his side?

Allowing him to guide her from the room and up the servants' stairs, she would have spoken as soon as they reached the main floor but he shook his head and indicated she should wait. Only once they were safely in the little study Lady Celeste had used for handling household business did he give her a nod that indicated she could speak.

"What on earth did I do to make that woman detest me so?" Ivy demanded with a huff as she stalked over to the fireplace. "You would think I'd burst in demanding she hand over her most prize possessions at gunpoint!"

Quill, easy as ever, strolled over and bent to stoke the fire, standing far too close for Ivy's comfort. When he did not respond immediately, she glared at him. "Well?"

Straightening, he shrugged. "I've known Mrs. Bacon and Greaves and many of the other servants since I was in short coats. You cannot expect to be in Beauchamp House for one day and have them treat you like a treasured friend."

"I did not expect that," Ivy insisted, though a small voice in her head reminded her that perhaps she had. "At least," she amended, "I didn't expect her to simply tell me everything. But why did she look on me with such suspicion? I wasn't rude. Or demanding."

"She lost her employer, whom she has served for almost thirty years just a few months ago," he reminded her quietly, not mentioning that he too had lost his aunt. "And now she has to accustom herself to not one, but five new mistresses including my cousin and the four of you bluestockings. Can you blame her for being a bit stiff with you?"

When he put it like that, Ivy was forced to agree that perhaps she'd not been altogether fair to Mrs. Bacon. "I suppose that is a great deal for one to take in," she conceded. Then, not wishing to dwell on the housekeeper's obvious dislike, she asked, "What did you think about the physician? Might it be worth a visit to the village to see what he has to say?"

His jaw tight, Quill nodded. "If he knew my aunt was being poisoned and did nothing to find the culprit, I warn you now that I will not be answerable for my actions."

Ivy fought the urge to lay a consoling hand on him. What was it about this man that brought out her protective instincts? It wasn't as if he was a weakling who needed it. And he certainly wouldn't thank her for it. His posture projected strength where any other man would seem vulnerable. Was it just a product of his position as a peer of the realm with the weight of generations bolstering him? Or was it something more personal? Like his upbringing? Cursing her own dangerous curiosity, she kept her hands to herself.

"Then perhaps you had better let me pay a call on the good doctor," she said. "That way you won't be tempted to do something rash."

"Like hell," Quill snapped, then recalling to whom he spoke perhaps, he sighed. "My apologies, Miss Wareham. I seem to have forgotten my manners."

But Ivy, who had grown up in a household where young men in need of tutoring ran tame, was hardly offended. "It's nothing I've not heard before," she assured him. "Or said myself from time to time. Though I hope you won't tell my mother. She has corrected me for my unruly tongue more than once."

If she'd expected him to be surprised by her confession, she was disappointed. Instead he gave a quick grin. "Why am I not surprised?" he asked with a laugh.

The diversion lightened the mood somewhat and it was with a bit less ferocity that Quill said, "Why don't we both go to the village to see the doctor. That way you can keep me from doing anything rash."

"And what purpose will *you* serve?" she asked with a raised brow, unable to keep from baiting him.

"I'll keep you from doing anything your mother would find improper," he said, extending his arm to her.

"I look forward to seeing you try," Ivy responded taking his arm. "I can swear in several languages."

"But that's no impediment to me, Miss Wareham," he said as he shut the library door behind them. "So can I."

Chapter 9

To Ivy's frustration and disappointment, however, Lady Serena had scheduled a tour of Beauchamp House and the surrounding grounds that morning.

"Now that you're all finally here," she explained to Ivy and Lord Kerr as they stood near the door to the servants' quarters, "I can show you just what it is that Lady Celeste built here. Beauchamp House is more than just its magnificent library and scholarly collection. It's also a working farm, and boasts a pottery staffed solely by women."

Despite her vexation at not being able to question the doctor, Ivy's interest was piqued by Serena's mention of the pottery. "I had hoped to go into the village today—" she began.

"But surely that can wait, Miss Wareham?" asked the marquess with a speaking look. "I know I said I'd accompany you, but perhaps it would be better if we go another day."

Recalling how he'd attempted to question Mrs. Bacon without her, Ivy was skeptical. "You would be willing to wait, my lord? And will promise not to travel into the village on your own without me?"

Lady Serena frowned, looking from Ivy to her cousin and back again. "Clearly I've missed something here."

Holding Lord Kerr's gaze, Ivy raised a brow in question.

After a moment, he let out a breath. "Fine, Miss Wareham. I will promise not to go into the village without you. Though I must warn you that our errand is a time-sensitive one."

"What errand?" Serena asked, her brows snapping together in suspicion.

"Nothing mysterious, cousin," Lord Kerr said holding up his hands to protest his innocence. "I merely offered to escort Miss Wareham into the village to purchase some ink."

"Ink?"

Before his lordship could elaborate, Ivy interjected. "I prefer to use a very particular brand of ink for my translation work. And I realized upon unpacking that I'd left my own behind. But it can wait."

The other woman looked skeptical, but didn't argue. "So you'll join the rest of us, then?"

After one last speaking look at Lord Kerr, Ivy nodded. "I would like to very much."

"Then take yourself off, Quill," said Lady Serena, slipping an arm through Ivy's. "This outing is for ladies only."

It was only after they were out of earshot of the marquess that Lady Serena continued. "I hope, Miss Wareham, that you will accept a word of advice."

Still unsettled by the hasty reversal of her plans for the day, it took Ivy a moment to realize she was expected to respond. "About what, Lady Serena?" Though she had some idea about whom it might pertain to.

They had just reached the double doors leading into the library, when the chaperone turned to face Ivy before she continued. "My cousin is a very handsome man, Miss

Wareham, but he is a notorious flirt. He is an honorable man, but like all men, he doesn't always think before he acts. I should hate to see you come to harm because of it." She paused, and Ivy saw a shadow cross her face.

"Lady Serena?" Ivy asked, concerned. "What is it?"

But whatever it was had passed, and the chaperone shook her head a little. "Nothing, my dear. I am doubtlessly being overprotective. Just promise me you will not take Quill too much to heart."

Thinking back to the pull of attraction she'd felt between herself and the marquess, Ivy nevertheless waved away Lady Serena's warning. "I can assure you, my lady," she said firmly, "that I'm in no danger of succumbing to your cousin's charms. He may be handsome, but he's also stubborn and not just a little arrogant."

Serena narrowed her eyes, as if trying to discern the truth of Ivy's denial. Then, biting back whatever retort she'd been about to make, she opened the library door and pulled her charge into the chamber that would never stop setting Ivy's heart to beating faster.

If she was in danger of losing her head, it was over the first-class collection of manuscripts, books, and artifacts in this room, she thought as her eyes scanned the floor-to-ceiling shelves with something like wonder.

"Were you able to find Lord Kerr, Miss Wareham?" asked Sophia, looking up from where she stood perusing one of the cabinets where Ivy knew the art books were shelved.

Feeling Serena's gaze on her, Ivy tried to look nonchalant. "I did, thank you, Sophia." Stepping farther into the room, she crossed to glance out the window looking out over the gardens. "I wish you would call me Ivy. It will be a tiresome year if we all stand on ceremony with one another for the duration."

"I can see nothing objectionable in that," Serena said from where she'd moved to remove a thick, bound leather volume from one of the shelves. "And as I said before, you must call me Serena. I am serving as your chaperone of course, but we're of an age, I think. And I hope we can become friends."

Before any of them could reply, Lady Serena continued. "Now, are you all ready for a tour of the house and gardens? My aunt left strict instructions about what areas and features she most particularly wished for you all to see." She held up the volume in her hand to emphasize her words.

Daphne looked up from where she was seated at one of the large library tables with a stack of books before her. "Must I go too? I've only just started in on this fascinating account of the Goldbach conjecture . . ."

"And I'm immersed in this history of Dr. Harvey's dig at Stonehenge," Gemma added looking vexed. "Perhaps you should take only Sophia and Ivy for this first tour, Lady Serena. After all, we don't wish to disrupt the household with a large party traipsing here and there."

But Lady Serena would have none of it, much to Ivy's relief. Despite her wish to begin investigating the circumstances of Lady Celeste's death, she too wanted some time alone with the contents of the library and the idea of being off on a tour while the others had free reign in the magnificent room sent a pang of outright jealousy through her.

"Come along, Gemma and Daphne," Sophia said, reluctantly turning from the art books. "If Lady Celeste wished us to see these parts of Beauchamp House, then I daresay it was important to her. The least we can do for the poor woman's sake is to do as she wished. Without her we'd not be here at all."

"I hate it when you're sensible," Gemma groused,

though she stood and tugged a still-reluctant Daphne from her chair.

"I suppose it will still be here when we return." Daphne gave one last longing look at her chosen tome.

Without any sort of preplanning, the four ladies stood in a row before Lady Serena, who smiled approvingly. "Excellent. Now, you've seen the library, so let's go downstairs and start in the entrance hall."

As they made to follow her through the double doors, Sophia took Ivy's arm. "You don't suppose Lord Kerr will make an appearance do you? I should very much like to study those cheekbones a bit more. He'd make a very good Mars for my study of the war god and his lady."

"Why don't you just ask him to sit for you?" Ivy asked pettishly. Something about the other lady's interest in the marquess set her teeth on edge.

But Sophia shook her head, and slipped her arm through Ivy's companionably. "Men are the most wretched models I've found. They are impatient as can stare, and don't take orders very well at all. Much better to just get the details in the usual course of things and use my imagination for the rest."

The artist had a point, Ivy conceded. Lord Kerr was nothing if not headstrong.

"I have no idea what his plans were for the rest of the day," she said with diffidence.

Was it her imagination or was Sophia smirking at her?

Really, she thought, if she'd known her tenure at Beauchamp House would entail so much scrutiny from her fellow bluestockings, she would have remained home.

But as they reached the second-floor landing she saw the portrait of Lady Celeste and immediately felt a pang of guilt.

Not only had her benefactor chosen her to share Beauchamp House, she'd also, for some reason Ivy hadn't figured out yet, deemed her trustworthy enough to solve her murder.

If she had to endure some teasing from the other ladies, then so be it. She'd endured worse from her brothers at home.

And besides that, she was hardly some wilting violet who couldn't stand up for herself.

She was made of sterner stuff than that.

Aloud, she said, "Enough about the marquess. This is part of our inheritance, Sophia."

At Sophia's look of surprise, Ivy raised a speaking brow. "For bluestockings only."

Gemma and Daphne, who were just ahead of them, turned.

"Bluestockings only," Daphne said with a nod. "I like it."

"As do I," said Gemma grinning.

"I believe we've got our motto, ladies," Sophia said with a laugh. "Beauchamp House, for Bluestockings Only."

And, however reluctantly we might accept them, Ivy added silently, *relations of Lady Celeste Beauchamp.*

Despite his instinct, which was to make his way to the village posthaste to meet with his aunt's physician, Quill curbed the impulse and decided to take Jem out to see his horses.

Starved for male attention, the boy was elated when his older cousin appeared at the nursery door and requested his company for a trip to the stables.

"Since you've not seen his lordship in a long while, Master Jeremy," his nanny, Mrs. Ellis said firmly, "I will allow it. But no more sneaking down to the kitchens without asking first."

Trying and failing to look contrite, the boy nodded vigorously but couldn't conceal the grin that overtook his face.

"She seems like a good sport," Quill said as they made

their way down the back stairs to the door leading out to the stableyard. "Not at all like my old nanny, who'd have skinned me alive for a stunt like the one you pulled this morning."

Jeremy shrugged. "I suppose so. Mama thinks I don't know, but I heard her telling Mrs. Ellis not to be too hard on me. On account of Father."

The boy spat out the last word, as if it left a foul taste in his mouth.

Yet another sin to lay upon the grave of the late unlamented Lord Fanning, Quill thought grimly. "Is that so? Does it bother you?"

The boy pondered the question for a moment. "I don't know 'xactly. On the one hand I like not getting into much trouble."

"Who wouldn't?" Quill bit back a smile.

"But I don't like it that they treat me like a baby." He looked up at his cousin, a fierce look in his countenance. "I'm *not* a baby."

Knowing it would be exactly the wrong thing at this moment, Quill suppressed the urge to ruffle the boy's hair. Even after the difficulties he'd faced when Fanning had terrorized both the boy and his mother, Jeremy managed to maintain a sort of quiet dignity that the marquess couldn't help but be proud of.

"Certainly not."

They were crossing the side yard now, and the stables were just in sight.

"I know Mama thinks I need coddling because of what he did," Jeremy said, a note of frustration in his young voice. "But I don't. I can take care of myself. And her too."

He paused, and Quill waited for him to finish.

"I couldn't when he was alive, you know." His expression was that of someone many years older. "I was too little then. But I'm not now. I'll never let anyone hurt her again."

Placing a comforting hand on the child's shoulder, Quill said, "Of course you won't. You're a good man, Jem. I'm sure your Mama knows it."

"I let her down, Uncle Quill," the boy said with a sigh. "But I won't do it again."

Unable to let the boy continue in this vein, Quill knelt before him. Looking into eyes that were so much like Serena's, he said firmly, "You have nothing to be sorry for. You were no match for a man like your father. And I know beyond a shadow of a doubt that your mother believes the same thing."

"But he hurt her, Uncle Quill," Jem pressed on. "And I couldn't stop—"

Hoping that Fanning was roasting in Hades, the marquess interrupted his small cousin. "Do you blame your Mama for not defending herself better? Do you believe that she should have been able to stop him?"

That gave the boy pause. His brow furrowed. "What? Of course not. She's just a lady and—"

"I'll stop you right there, boy," said Quill with a laugh. "Never let your Mama or any of Aunt Celeste's heiresses hear you call any of them 'just a lady' if you know what's good for you."

He stood, and they resumed their trek to the stables.

"But they *are* ladies," Jem said, puzzled.

"True enough," the marquess agreed, "but that doesn't mean that they're defenseless. You certainly wouldn't like it if they were to call you 'just a child' would you?"

"Of course not," Jem said heatedly, as if someone had called him that. Then, Quill could almost hear the realization come to him.

"Oh."

"Yes," Quill agreed. "Oh."

"So that's what Auntie Celeste meant about not treating ladies like children?"

"Something like that," Quill agreed. "So, let's have no more lamentations from you over your helplessness in the face of a man three times your size. You and your Mama did your best in a difficult situation. And there's an end on it."

Looking thoughtful, Jeremy nodded.

Then, as if the discussion had allowed him to cast off a heavy cloak of guilt, he brightened. "Do you think Graham in the stables will let me brush out your grays?"

Relieved that he'd managed the conversation with some degree of success, Quill clapped the boy on the shoulder. "I think that can certainly be arranged."

Chapter 10

"It's a shame we weren't able to visit the pottery today because of the rain," Ivy said that evening as the residents of Beauchamp House sat in the drawing room after dinner.

To her surprise, she meant the words. Though she'd been reluctant to pause her investigation into Lady Celeste's death with something as seemingly trivial as a tour of the house, the hours spent in the company of her fellow heiresses had proved to be both informative and entertaining. And Lady Serena had proved to be quite knowledgeable about all the considerations her aunt had put into the decoration and improvement of her estate.

"Unfortunately, Miss Wareham," said the marquess from where he stood with one shoulder against the sitting room mantle, "you'll find that this part of the country is prone to unexpected showers at this time of year."

"If we're reduced to discussing the weather," Sophia said with a shake of her auburn curls, "then I shall simply be forced to do something scandalous in order to alleviate my boredom. Pray, do not make me do it."

There was a hint of the absurd in her tone, but Ivy got the feeling that the artist would not be above making good on her threat.

"There is no need to resort to drastic measures, Miss Hastings," interjected the marquess with a staying hand. "I will change the subject immediately. I shouldn't like my cousin's first foray into the realm of chaperonage to be a failure, you know."

Serena gave him a speaking look. "I will thank you very much to mind your own business, Kerr. I am quite able to handle whatever attempts at scandal these ladies attempt to dish out." After a quelling look in Sophia's direction, she turned to Ivy. "Perhaps you can tell us a bit more about your translation work, Ivy."

Feeling all eyes turn on her, Ivy felt herself flush. "Oh, it's not very interesting to talk about," she demurred. "Just a process of reading the original, then trying to capture the essence of it using our own language."

But she wasn't to be let off so lightly.

"A great deal of Greek poetry is rather shocking, isn't it, Ivy?" Gemma asked, her blue eyes glinting with slyness. "At least, that's what one of the essays I read about the Elgin marbles said."

Before Ivy could confirm or deny the question, Daphne spoke up. "I was quite disappointed by the marbles when I was finally able to view them. I was expecting the male mem—"

"Daphne, dear," Serena interrupted, "it's not the done thing to discuss such things in mixed company, you know."

"Or any company," said Sophia in a low voice that only Ivy, seated beside her, could hear.

Unable to stop herself, Ivy looked up to see how the marquess had reacted to Daphne's slip up. To her surprise, he was looking right at her.

Their eyes met, and she felt a zing of awareness run through her before she quickly looked away.

But Serena's next words diverted her attention away from the marquess.

"Perhaps you can recite one of your translations for us, Ivy?" Seeing the entreaty in her chaperone's eyes, she gave an inward sigh.

She hated reciting poetry above all things.

Not because it was difficult. But because it had been a regular evening entertainment in her father's house for the children to recite. And her father had been nothing if not demanding when it came to the ability of his offspring to recall every cadence and emphasis of a verse.

When she was very young, Ivy had suffered from a slight stutter, and it would resurrect itself, it seemed, only at those times when she most needed to be able to speak with confidence and ease. Which, during her childhood, had been those evening recitations.

Still, she could see that Serena was desperate for some way to divert attention away from Daphne and her inappropriate chatter. And she'd long ago managed to rid herself of the impediment.

"I suppose I can recall a few of them," she said, inclining her head toward Lady Serena. "Perhaps a bit of Sappho's song to Aphrodite."

A hush fell over the room, and Ivy felt the attention of the others in the room like a tangible thing. The weight of it almost took her breath away, until she managed to shut everything out but the words, and began to speak.

"Splendour-throned Queen, immortal Aphrodite,
Daughter of Jove, Enchantress, I implore thee
Vex not my soul with agonies and anguish;
Slay me not, Goddess!"

And so she began to recite her own translation of the celebrated poet's only complete work—the rest had been discovered in mere fragments, their complete sentiments left to the ravages of time and the abyss of imagination— which she had laboriously worked on for nearly a year. She'd debated whether the first word was *poikilothron* or *poikilophron*—something that hadn't ever been settled amongst those who had transcribed the lyrics from the original Greek—finally deciding on the latter, which meant "many-colored throne" rather than "many-colored mind." After all, she'd reasoned, it was far more likely for a throne to be multicolored than a mind.

As she said the words, aware as she did so of her own role in bringing thoughts and ideas that had first been sparked in the ancient world, she felt a small shiver run through her. As if Sappho herself was bestowing some otherworldly approval from the ether.

When she'd finished, the room was once again silent, only this time it was a lull before the other occupants erupted in praise and applause.

"My dear, Ivy," said Sophia, hurrying over to give her a brief hug, "you must never try to speak of what you do as dull again. It's breathtaking to think that you were able to wrangle those beautiful sentiments out of the unintelligible squiggles that make up the Greek language."

"Sophia was never very fond of languages," said Gemma wryly as she kissed Ivy's cheek. "But she's right. I can actually read Greek but I sincerely doubt my own translation would be anything but workmanlike and prosaic at best. You've made the words spring to life."

"Shall I ring for some tea?" asked Daphne, standing awkwardly on the other side of the room. Clearly she had not been as moved as the Hastings sisters, Ivy thought wryly. At least she could always count on the mathematician to keep her from becoming too full of her own importance.

From where she stood beside Lord Kerr, Serena gave the blonde girl a look of exasperation. But rather than chide her, she simply said, "That would be lovely, Daphne. Thank you."

The spell broken, they drifted into different corners of

the room, and Ivy soon found herself standing with the marquess near the fire.

"I hadn't thought about Greek poetry since I was at school," said Lord Kerr with a wry smile. "And then it was not for the beauty of the language."

Ivy felt her cheeks pinken. She knew quite well what this marquess and his schoolmates had found of interest in ancient poetry. There was quite a bit of it—much of which Ivy had read herself in the original—that could be called licentious.

"I understand that is how many young men become acquainted with the classics," she said primly.

He tilted his head. "But not young ladies?"

"Since the vast majority of young ladies are not taught either Greek or Latin," she said tartly, "then I would say, no. Not young ladies."

"But you were taught both, weren't you, Miss Wareham," he said with a grin. "So, perhaps you too spent some time with the *classics*." He said the last word with an emphasis that left her in no doubt of what he meant.

"My father was not very keen on it," she admitted, not meeting his gaze. "But I was able to convince him that it was impossible to gain a true understanding of the classics without having read everything Catullus has written. Even that which might be considered prurient."

She had, in point of fact, made her father's daily life miserable until he agreed to let her read Catullus. But they had agreed that neither of them would tell her mother about it—ever.

"How clever," the marquess said with an approving nod. "And unlike most schoolboys who claim to read Catullus merely to improve their fluency in Latin, you have bolstered your own case by actually becoming a Latin scholar."

"Yes." Ivy fought the urge to roll her eyes. "Years of study and hard work were simply a ruse to allow me to achieve my actual goal—reading the naughty verse of the most celebrated Roman poet of all time. Which, by the by, isn't even his greatest work."

"When you put it like that," Quill said with a shrug, "it sounds absurd. Which is likely why it isn't a scheme employed by more people. Far too much trouble."

Unable to stop herself, Ivy laughed. Then, thinking about what he'd said, she asked, "You weren't, by any chance, speaking of your own excuses for reading classics, were you? That explanation seemed far too well-rehearsed to have been invented on the spot."

For a fraction of a second—so quickly that Ivy wasn't even sure it had happened—the marquess's gaze rested on her mouth. Then he met her gaze with his own. "I was a schoolboy once, Miss Wareham," he said with a half smile. "Perhaps you can test my knowledge of Catullus some time."

It was said in an unexceptional tone. The same way that he might have suggested they go for a ride in the park, or take a turn about the room.

But his eyes told a different tale, and Ivy felt the blush that had rested in her cheeks for most of their conversation spread to her chest. And lower.

Before she could respond to his words, they were interrupted by the arrival of Lady Serena, who looked between them with suspicion. "Did I miss something?"

"Not at all," Lord Kerr said to his cousin with an easy smile. "We were just discussing various methods of teaching the classics to schoolboys."

Ivy could have kicked him.

At the mention of schoolboys, Lady Serena's eyes lit with interest. "Oh, indeed? I should very much like to hear your views on the matter, Ivy, since I am considering how best to settle Jeremy's education. Though he is a bit young yet."

"I've just remembered I need to speak to York about something," the marquess said before Ivy could respond. "I'm sure Miss Wareham will be able to steer you right, cousin. She is well versed in the matter."

Ivy stared at his retreating back for a moment. She wasn't quite sure what had just happened, but it had been unsettling.

"You don't mind, do you, Ivy?" Lady Serena asked, frowning a little. "I wouldn't wish to impose."

Seeing that the chaperone was, indeed, looking troubled, Ivy sought to reassure her. "Of course not, Lady Serena. Now, what do you wish to know?"

And the two ladies discussed how best to prepare Jeremy for the rigors of classical languages.

But a part of Ivy's mind was still thinking of that moment of heat in Lord Kerr's eyes.

Mindful of the danger in spending too much time in the company of a certain classics scholar, Quill spent the next several days immersing himself in estate matters. Aunt Celeste had left the day-to-day operations of the farm and the rest of the estate business in the hands of a very capable steward. But there was always hard work to be found if one was looking for it. And aware that any more suggestive conversations with Miss Wareham might lead him down a path he wasn't quite ready for, Quill took advantage of that fact.

Repairing fences and visiting tenants kept him busy. But not too busy to think about the circumstances that had brought him to Beauchamp House in the first place.

Now that he'd met and spent some time in the company of all four of the lady scholars his aunt had chosen to bestow her estate upon, he wasn't as angry about the situation as he'd been when he first set out for Beauchamp House.

All four ladies were, so far as he could tell, knowledge-able about their areas of study and, far from being the social outcasts or tight-lipped scolds he'd been afraid of, would not embarrass the Beauchamp name—excepting Lady Daphne, perhaps, but she was quite lovely, so she would probably not face too much censure in the *ton* for her plain speaking.

Lady Celeste's decision to leave her home to strangers still rankled, however. And he could not deny that the fact she'd asked Miss Wareham to find the person who killed her stung.

Then again, he'd known her his whole life yet failed to notice she was in trouble. It was no wonder she'd decided to ask a young woman she'd never even met for help in-stead of her self-absorbed family.

He might have kept on avoiding the ladies of the house under the guise of manual labor were it not for Miss Ware-ham, who found him one afternoon almost a week later, brushing out his grays in the stables.

"I would have thought a marquess might not wish to dirty his hands with work better suited to a stable lad," she said from the other side of the stall door. "Though your horses seem to think you do a good job."

"You might be surprised at the sort of work a marquess is required to do from time to time," Quill said without looking up. "I would not ask one of my servants to do something that I myself wouldn't be willing to do."

He felt her gaze on him, and wondered what she saw when she looked at him. A pampered aristocrat playing at being a servant for a day? Or perhaps she saw a man who had been too caught up in his own life to pay attention to his dying aunt? Either way, he had a feeling she wasn't im-pressed by him. Which was just as well, since there was no need for them to be friends. There might be some attraction there, but he had a feeling she'd value her independence too much to get entangled with any man. And of all the ladies he'd ever met, she was the least likely to be swayed by his title. It was intellect she valued, and though he wasn't a simpleton, nor was he the kind of man who spent his days with his nose buried in a book.

"Even emptying chamber pots?" she asked with gentle skepticism.

She had him there.

Unable to resist looking up, he did and saw that her rosy lips were curved in a smile.

"Perhaps not that," he amended, standing up straight and giving the horse one last pat before turning to exit the stall.

As he neared her, Miss Wareham watched his progress, stepping back as he reached the latched gate and allowing him to open it.

"You've been avoiding me," she said when he'd latched it back and turned to face her.

It wasn't a question, and he didn't condescend to her by pretending it was.

"Perhaps," he agreed, crossing his arms over his chest. "Though there has been plenty to keep me busy."

"Shall I take your behavior as a confirmation that you won't help me find out whether your aunt was actually murdered?" she asked, not sugarcoating the question.

Quill was grateful for her forthrightness. It would make his refusal to work with her that much easier to deliver.

"You may," he said with an air of finality he didn't feel. "My aunt may have chosen to confide her suspicions to you, but I have only known you for a week or so. That is hardly enough, in my book, to prove your trustworthiness. For all I know, you and the other three benefactors conspired to have my aunt killed as soon as you learned you stood to inherit her estate."

She looked as if he'd slapped her.

"You don't believe that, surely?" she asked, her eyes wide with shock.

Relenting a little, he shook his head. "I don't believe it, no. But it's possible. And until I know you well enough to judge with my head and not my . . ." He paused, realizing what he'd been about to say. "Until I know you better," he amended, "I can't trust you."

Miss Wareham looked nonplussed.

"Is there something about me that you don't understand?" he asked, growing impatient with her refusal to see reason.

"Yes," she said, standing up straighter and stepping closer. "I don't understand how a man who purports to have loved his aunt more than anyone in the world could possibly stand by and let her murderer go on about his merry way."

She took another step.

"I also don't understand how, if getting to know me enough to find me trustworthy is your goal," she continued, her eyes flashing, "you can spend almost an entire week avoiding me."

He opened his mouth to respond, but Miss Wareham poked him in the chest with her forefinger. "If you want to know what I think," she said with a toss of her head, "I think that you, Lord Kerr, are behaving like a spoiled little boy. Your aunt didn't leave her estate to you, and so you're punishing her by refusing to search for the person or persons who killed her."

"Now just a minute, Miss Wareham," he began, her words sticking like a barb in his chest, "I won't allow you to—"

"Oh, do not tell me what you will or will not allow," she said with disgust. "You've made it clear that you have no interest in finding your aunt's killer. So, I will simply have to do it myself. Which is hardly a surprise, since if you want anything done well, it's best to call a woman."

She turned and, before he'd judged the wisdom of such a move, he grasped her by the shoulder. "Stop."

Turning to face him, she glared. And to Quill's surprise, there were tears glistening in her eyes.

"What?" she demanded, holding herself back from him, their only contact, his hand which was now resting softly on her shoulder.

They were silent for a moment. He reached up, and with his thumb, stroked away the tear that had fallen onto her cheek.

"Why do you care so much?" he asked hoarsely. "You didn't even know her."

"Because she chose me," she said in a low voice. "She believed in me. In my abilities." She looked up and he realized she was utterly sincere.

"Perhaps you don't know what it's like to move in a world where your every decision is scrutinized, questioned, doubted," she continued. "Where even your father, who taught you himself, doesn't believe you're good enough to be a real scholar. Where the associations and societies who should welcome you, keep you out because you weren't born with a certain ridiculous appendage. But I do. And the one person who believed I could make a difference was murdered. Not only that, but she asked me to find out by whom.

"Yes, I care," she said, her voice stronger now, her eyes lit with determination. "Because I owe her a debt of gratitude. I had thought perhaps you did, too, but as with many things, I can see I was wrong."

She turned to go.

"You weren't wrong, damn it."

Once more, she turned back to him, her brow raised in question.

"I owe her, too," he admitted with a scowl. He thrust a hand into his hair, feeling more flustered than he could ever remember. "And I want to find out who killed her. But you have to understand, from the time I was a small boy, family loyalty has been drummed into me. And it's the way of the world. Family inherits from family. The fact that Aunt Celeste chose to leave her estate—where I and my cousins spent the best months of our childhood—to four women I'd never heard of before the reading of the will, well, it has been difficult to swallow."

At his admission, her gaze softened. "I'm not unsympathetic, my lord," she said, lifting her hand as if she'd touch him, then letting it fall. "I understand how difficult this must be. But don't let your disappointment about the inheritance keep you from finding out why your aunt died in the first place. As you say, you owed her a debt of gratitude as well. Don't make the mistake of failing the one person you should honor above all."

Suddenly exhausted, Quill let his shoulders slump a little. "Where do you want to start?"

The flash of triumph was gone from her eyes before he even realized he'd seen it.

"As we were going to before the rain set in," she said firmly, "I would like for us to pay a visit to your aunt's physician in the village, Dr. Vance. I have an actual letter home to post now, so it won't even be a prevarication when we give it as our reason for going."

"Anyone who underestimates you, Miss Wareham," he said with a shake of his head, "does so at their own peril."

Waving off the compliment, she said, "I would like to set off within the hour. Meet me in the entry hall after you've had a chance to clean up a bit."

Leaving him to stare after her in exasperation, she hurried off.

Chapter 11

"I would rather remain here organizing the collection of mathematics books," said Lady Daphne in response to Miss Wareham's invitation that the other ladies join them on their trip to the village. Quill and Ivy had decided that inviting the others to accompany them would go a long way toward alleviating any suspicions that they had any other purpose for visiting the village than posting her letter and purchasing ink. Once there, Ivy would recall that she needed headache powder and Quill would offer to introduce her to the local doctor.

"There are any number of valuable contributions to the subject, but it is impossible to find them when they are interspersed with inferior scholarship that would better be put to use as kindling." Not looking up from her position seated on the library floor where she was surrounded by uneven stacks of books, Daphne punctuated her remarks by tossing one rather thin volume in the direction of the fireplace.

Which was also where Sophia happened to be curled up in a chair before the fire, her sketchbook in hand. "Have a care, Lady Disdain," the artist said with a frown at the floor where the thrown book had landed. "Ducking from flying objects is not one my best skills while I'm drawing. And I'll thank you to remain in the same general pose, otherwise your portrait will be a complete failure." Turning to Ivy, who stood at Lord Kerr's side, she added, "I'm trying to do a study of each of you, to commemorate our first week in Beauchamp House. Perhaps for use later as a series on the Muses. But perhaps not. I don't know that I will be able to keep Daphne still for long."

The marquess stepped forward to peer down at the sketch. "That's quite good, Miss Hastings," he said before he could stop himself. Of course it's good, he thought. His aunt would hardly have invited Miss Hastings here if she were a mere dabbler.

"My thanks, Lord Kerr," Sophia said, sharing an unreadable glance with Ivy. "For the compliment and the invitation. But I believe I'll stay here and capture Daphne while she is somewhat still. She's given me to understand that once she begins concentrating on the contents of the books themselves, she'll be a whirlwind of chalk and slate and calculations. Which does not sound conducive to being captured in pencil."

Thus far, the subterfuge they'd worked out had proved unnecessary since no one had agreed to come with them.

"Where is Gemma?" Ivy asked, scanning the chamber as if the second Hastings sister was lying prone on the library floor with a book in her hands. "No, let me guess. She's searching for fossils on the shore."

"Of course she is," Sophia said, not looking up from where her pencil flew across the page. "She was off almost before she'd finished her breakfast. Apparently the tide is out just now so she will be able to examine the cliffs without drowning. Which I must say is a prudent choice. I am not quite convinced she'd have held back from her quest even if the tide was in. My sister on the trail of a fossil sighting is not someone you'd wish to step in the way of."

"I daresay that holds true for any of you and your chosen field of study," Quill said dryly. "I suppose I'm fortunate that Miss Wareham has agreed to give up her first full day at Beauchamp House to accompany me." He turned to Ivy. "Perhaps you'd rather remain here and explore the various titles and fragments my aunt gathered during her trips to Greece?"

Ivy gave him a hard look. "You won't shake me off that easily, my lord. After the past week of rain, I am quite ready for a long walk." Her silent glance of rebuke told him that she was not amused at his attempt to leave her behind.

"Where are you planning to go, Miss Wareham?" inquired Serena from the doorway behind them.

Of course Serena would choose that moment to come upon them, Quill thought with an inward sigh. Which in the general course of things was perfectly fine. But this particular chaperone had known him from childhood. And Serena had suffered enough of her own tragedy that he wanted to protect her from the knowledge that their beloved aunt might not have died of natural causes. It was bad enough to see her stricken look every time Fanning was mentioned. He would not add to her sorrows with the news that her beloved aunt had been murdered until it was absolutely necessary. He'd sent for his cousin Maitland for precisely this reason. If anyone could distract Serena it was her younger brother.

"Just a trip to the village to post a letter to my family, Lady Serena," Ivy said brightly. "I know I could send it from here, but I'd like to get to know the village if I'm to be here for a year. And Lord Kerr has kindly agreed to accompany me."

Serena cast a knowing glance at her cousin, and Quill found himself feeling guilty for things he'd not even properly imagined yet. Not that he *would,* he reminded himself firmly. Whatever spark of attraction he might feel for Miss Wareham and her sharp wit was something that he had no intention of acting on—no matter how tempting her habit of biting her lower lip might be.

"Has he indeed?" Serena asked with raised brows. "How kind of you, Kerr. I had no idea you'd developed such a chivalrous streak."

"You pain me, cousin," he retorted with mock dismay. "I hope I have always behaved like a gentleman, which includes rescuing ladies in need. I seem to recall a couple of times in our youth when I came to your aid when you had need of a champion. Particularly when Lord Henry Threadgill snubbed you at the local assembly."

At the mention of Threadgill, Serena's eyes widened with amused shock. "What a heartless rogue you are to bring him up!" she hissed. "I was desperately in love with Lord Henry Threadgill."

"For all of two weeks when you were seventeen," Quill said with a laugh. "Didn't he throw you over for Miss Madeline Staynes?"

"Yes, the lout," she said with a shake of her head. "And she professed to be my friend. It was a particularly dreadful evening for me. But you saved it by diverting the attention of the tabbies by making a cake of yourself over some local widow."

A widow whom he'd bedded not too long after, Quill recalled with wry amusement. Not that Serena had known that.

But somehow Ivy's knowing glance at him upon the mention of the widow made Quill feel as if the whole of his youthful affair had already been revealed.

"Never let it be said that I am not loyal to a family member in distress," he said with a slight bow. "Now, unless you wish to accompany us, Serena, I think Miss Wareham and I had better set off before the day has got away from us. We don't wish to miss luncheon, do we Miss Wareham?"

"Perhaps you'd better have the cook pack you a basket just in case your trip takes longer than you anticipate," Serena said wryly. "It is already gone eleven. And I do know how you hate to miss a meal, cousin."

"An excellent idea," Quill said. "Why don't you fetch your cloak and hat, Miss Wareham, and I'll see about provisions."

"Very well," Ivy responded, looking as if she wanted to say something more. But shaking her head a little, she left and headed toward her chamber.

"I hope you know what you're doing," Serena said in a low voice as Quill moved to leave the library.

"Always, cousin," he responded. Though in this particular case, he wasn't as self-assured as he proclaimed himself to be. There was something about Ivy Wareham that set him off-balance.

And he'd better figure out a way to keep from falling, else they'd both be facing the consequences.

"You seem to be quite close with your cousin," Ivy said once she and Quill had set out away from the coast and inland toward the village of Little Seaford, a basket of sandwiches and biscuits swinging from Quill's arm.

It was impossible not to notice the resemblance between the cousins. Whereas on Quill the strong nose and dimpled chin were utterly masculine, on Serena they were muted, more delicate. And there was something else there. There was the ease that came of kinship. The same sort of bond that Ivy had with her own siblings.

"We were close when we were younger," Quill said as he assisted her up and over a stile. The path from Beauchamp House to the village crossed several fields that were sectioned neatly off with rock walls. "Unfortunately, we lost touch when she married Fanning."

Ivy noted the troubled look in his blue eyes as she stepped down and let go of his hand. "Was he as bad as I suspect?" she asked quietly. "I could not help but notice that she goes a little pale every time his name comes up. And your jaw hardens."

In her work with the women at the home she'd spoken of earlier, Ivy had become all too familiar with the signs that marked a woman as having endured some kind of abuse. Whether he'd laid hands on her or not, she suspected that the late Lord Fanning had not been kind to his wife.

"Likely he was worse than you suspect," Quill said darkly. "He took a vibrant, amusing, lovely young woman and turned her into a shrinking, tentative creature afraid of her own shadow. That he managed to get himself killed before either Dalton or I was able to do anything about it was his good fortune."

Despite her suspicions, it was difficult for Ivy to image the calm, poised Lady Serena as Quill described her. She had shadows around her, true, but she must have healed a great deal to reach her current level of self-possession.

"Aunt Celeste spent a great deal of time bringing her back to life," Quill said, guessing at her thoughts. "She invited Serena and Jeremy to stay almost as soon as Fanning was in the ground. And since Beauchamp House had always been a haven for us, she came. Thank god, for I don't think more time in the Fanning dower house, trapped in isolation, would have done her any good."

It was hardly a surprise that Lady Celeste had been instrumental in her niece's recovery. Every layer that Ivy managed to uncover of the Lady Celeste enigma seemed to reveal another way that the woman had done good. Not for the first time, she regretted that meeting her benefactor had only become possible after her death, through the recollections of others. And Lady Celeste's own written words. She had no doubt that had she met Lady Celeste in person, she would have admired her even more than she did posthumously.

"How difficult it must have been for you to stand by while she was mistreated," Ivy said, knowing instinctively that Quill would not find it easy to let anyone—even her husband—harm someone he loved.

"If I'd known half of it while he was still alive, I'd have killed him myself," Quill said grimly. "That is, I'd have killed him after Serena's brother, the Duke of Maitland, killed him first. Unfortunately, we knew nothing about it for the first several years of their marriage. He was no fool. He hid her away in Yorkshire where we would see nothing amiss. And Serena's letters were full of happy nonsense. It was only when Aunt Celeste paid a visit to them on her way to Scotland that she learned how bad things were. And by that time Fanning was on his way to the hunting trip that led to him getting shot."

"An accident?" Ivy asked.

"Only if you think it a coincidence that the bullet came from the gun of a man Fanning was cuckolding." Quill smiled but there was no joy in it. "I suppose Jackson spared us the trouble of calling him out. And because they were hunting at the time, the magistrate ruled it an accident. Though I have my doubts."

"I suppose Lady Serena was lucky to have such concerned family," Ivy said, reflecting that most of the women she knew in Oxford who suffered at their husband's hands had no such recourse for escape. "And I hadn't thought Lady Celeste could rise any higher in my estimation, but every new thing I learn makes me wish again that she had invited us here while she was still alive."

"She would certainly have liked you," Quill said with a fond smile. "Which I suppose she knew, otherwise why leave her home to you. Though I dislike her decision, of course, I can understand it somewhat more after getting to know you a little better."

Ivy looked up and saw that he was being entirely serious. "Is it possible that Lord Kerr has decided to stop fighting against his aunt's wishes?" she asked, with playful astonishment. But though she was mocking him a little, she was surprised that he'd come around so quickly.

Not looking at her, Quill squinted across the field before them. "Not precisely," he answered, his eyes serious. "I don't believe I will ever forgive her for bequeathing the house outside the family."

At his words, Ivy felt a pang of disappointment. She'd been foolish to think that he'd change his mind so precipitately.

"I cannot ignore my aunt's decision to inform you of her suspicions about being in danger, however," he said grudgingly. "For some reason, despite the kinship I felt with her thanks to the summers I spent here as a child, she chose to tell you rather than me." His jaw clenched and Ivy felt a pang of compassion for him. It must have been hard for him to know that in her time of need his aunt had not come to him for help.

Neither had Serena, come to think of it.

She suspected he was not a man to take such matters lightly. His next words confirmed it.

"I may not like what my aunt did in leaving Beauchamp House to you all, but what's done is done. And since I was unable to help her while she was alive, I must do whatever I can to do so now she's gone. And if that means working together with her chosen one, then I will do it. I must, if I do not wish to fail her again."

Ivy was silent for a moment, the anguish in his eyes making her own burn with emotion. Not only had he failed to protect his own sister from her husband's abuse, he hadn't even known that his beloved aunt was in trouble until it was far, far too late. In his position, Ivy would have been wracked with guilt too. And with resentment for the usurper his aunt had chosen in his place.

It was a wonder he'd agreed to work with her at all.

"I'm sure she valued your relationship as much as you did," Ivy said aloud, unable to hold back the impulse to lay a light hand on his arm. At the contact, his eyes flew to hers. She felt her breath catch at the flash of fire there. But just as quickly it was gone, and by the time she'd pulled her hand back he was looking ahead of them again.

"I know she did," he said tightly as they neared another stile. "And I daresay she chose not to tell either Dalton or me about her fears because she didn't wish us to do something rash. As you might have guessed, we can be a little ferocious when someone we care about is endangered."

"I hadn't noticed," Ivy said with a wink as she glanced down from atop the stile. He stood on the other side, waiting for her to descend, and for a moment she wondered if he would catch her if she jumped. He must have read the thought in her eyes, for he extended his arms at the ready.

Before she could check herself, Ivy leapt, and found herself pulled up close against a hard male body. Closing her eyes, she inhaled his intoxicating scent of sandalwood, grass, and fresh sea air. Opening her eyes, she saw his face only inches from hers. And noted those tiny details only this sort of closeness revealed: the shadow of his beard, which was dark despite the lighter hints in his windswept hair, and the tiny lines that fanned out from the outer corners of his eyes. Eyes as blue as the sky above them, and looking at her with what she knew instinctively was not simple friendship.

"Easy," he said, his breath soft on the skin of her cheek as he pulled her closer infinitesimally before just as quickly setting her firmly back onto her own two feet. "You shouldn't take risks like that. What if I hadn't caught you?"

But she knew from the way his eyes twinkled that he would have sooner cut off a limb than let her fall. This man, for all his faults, took his role of protector quite seriously. For whatever reason, he'd decided it was his duty to protect her. And despite her innate sense of self-sufficiency, Ivy found it a little intoxicating.

"But you did," she said with a cheeky grin.

And stepping out ahead of him, she followed the path forward, able to see the village just over the next rise.

Chapter 12

The village of Little Seaford was situated to the east of Beauchamp House, farther inland. The office of Dr. Henry Vance was indeed near the blacksmith, and as they passed that establishment, they could hear the sound of metal striking metal.

"It does not look as if the good doctor is hurting for business," Quinn said dryly as he noted the newly painted exterior of the row house where the physician's office made its home. In addition, a shiny new plaque hung by the door, informing them that they were in the right spot.

A brisk knock on the door produced a mobcapped maid, who upon learning Quinn's identity informed them that the doctor was indeed in and invited them inside. If the exterior was impressive, that was nothing when compared to the interior, which boasted carpets at least as fine as those in Beauchamp House and, if Quill wasn't mistaken, a small seascape by Turner hanging prominently in the little parlor where he and Ivy were shown.

"I'm not sure what I expected," Ivy said, holding her hands before the fire burning merrily in the hearth, "but I had thought a village doctor so near the coast would be used to a more democratic clientele. I cannot imagine the local fisherman find all this finery comforting."

"I daresay he has another space for seeing patients," Quill said, examining what looked to be a primitive medical instrument hanging on the wall. "And of course his more-elevated patients he doubtless sees in their own homes, as he did with Aunt Celeste."

The walk had left Ivy with pink cheeks, and her russet hair, which had been neatly coiled around her head when they set out, was desperately trying to escape its pins. He watched, transfixed, as she rose from the fire and attempted to tidy herself, smoothing a hand over her hair, pulling down the cuffs of her hunter green pelisse.

Sensing his scrutiny, she glanced up, and they locked eyes for a moment. If possible, her cheeks turned even redder, and to Quill's anguish and delight, she bit down on her lower lip before she seemed to snap out of it and looked away. "I must look a fright," she said tersely, turning away from him to look out the window that overlooked the street below.

He opened his mouth to correct her, but was forestalled by the opening of the door to reveal the maid with a tea tray. "Dr. Vance will just be a few minutes longer, my lord," she said, curtsying once she'd set down the heavy tray. "He asked me to bring up some refreshments for you and the lady while you wait."

"How lovely," Ivy said with a warm smile. "It was a bit cooler out today than I'd anticipated and a hot cup of tea is just what I was wishing for. Thank you so much . . . I'm sorry but I don't know your name?"

Dropping a slightly shallower curtsy, the maid said, "You're very welcome, miss. And it's Daisy."

Quill stepped forward and took the cup Ivy offered him,

and hid a smile as she began to question the little maid under the guise of being new to the area.

"Oh"—the maid's eyes grew round upon hearing that Ivy was one of the four heiresses up at Beauchamp House— "I hadn't thought to meet one of you so soon." Her tone implied that the four bluestockings had been much talked about in Daisy's social circles. "Is it true that one of the ladies likes to paint folks without any clothes on?" This last was said in a low whisper as if saying the words too loudly would conjure Sophia who would demand that everybody get naked at once. Before Ivy could respond, the maid continued. "Or that another one arrived with a gentleman who wasn't her husband?"

Ivy blinked, then exchanged a wide-eyed look with Quill as if to ask whether she should respond. Clearly Daisy wasn't all that bright if she were asking the latter lady about herself. But that didn't mean her inquiry wasn't alarming for Ivy. Taking pity on her, he said, "I can assure you, Daisy, that there have been no such displays while I've been up at Beauchamp House. And while it's true that Miss Wareham and I arrived around the same time, that doesn't mean we were traveling together. Perhaps one of the servants has been telling tales to make them seem more exciting. For I can assure you, all I've seen so far is a great deal of reading. And some organizing of the library shelves."

Though he said this with the same polished ease with which he would chat with any of the villagers, inside Quill was fuming. Rumors were to be expected with new arrivals, of course. It was bound to happen when so little occurred in the area to divert the townspeople that didn't involve the local fishing harvest or the rhythms of the tides. But he was furious that someone at Beauchamp House had been spreading tales about the bluestockings. It was irregular enough that Lady Celeste had chosen to leave her home to four strangers, but if they were going to be here for any extended length of time—and he was now resigned to the fact that they would be—then they would have to be welcomed into the close-knit community. Which was less likely to happen if their reputations were ruined before they even had a chance to meet their neighbors. Not to mention the fact that such tales often found their way to London. It was one thing to wish them gone from his aunt's home, but it was quite another to wish them to be utterly ruined.

At his denial of the rumors, and the revelation that he was the gentleman in question, Daisy's eyes grew alarmingly wide. "Oh, my lord!" She clapped her hands on either side of her face. "I'm that sorry. I didn't know it was you." Dropping into another curtsy, this one so low she was almost unable to get up again, she muttered another apology before hurriedly excusing herself and fleeing the room.

"Well," Ivy said staring after her. "I suppose it's comforting to know that gossip is the same wherever one goes. Though I'm rather shocked at how quickly word of our arrival has made it here. There must be quite a healthy network of gossips between Beauchamp House and the village."

"Dashed busybodies," Quill said with a grimace. He didn't like how falsely bright Ivy's expression seemed to be, as if she were hiding her true feelings on the matter. "Hopefully Daisy will set those particular rumors to rest. Though you might wish to tell Sophia that she should refrain from painting nudes for a bit."

"I was unaware that she'd painted any at all," Ivy said with a twist of her lips. "I am guessing that rumor might be just that. Unless she perhaps brought some of her paintings with her. Indeed, I rather think that must be the case, for I cannot imagine her asking Lady Daphne to pose for her. And though they are sisters, Gemma does not strike me as someone who would willingly pose for any painting, let alone a nude one."

Quill pinched the bridge of his nose, wishing Ivy would stop using the word "nude."

"Ah, I see Daisy has brought you some refreshment," Dr. Vance said, poking his head in the door before opening it all the way and stepping inside. "I do apologize, Lord Kerr. I was consulting with the local apothecary and was unable to get away."

"It's good of you to see us, Vance," Quill said, grateful for the distraction. "May I present Miss Aphrodite Wareham. As you may have heard, she is one of the four young ladies to whom my aunt left Beauchamp House."

At the mention of Lady Celeste, the doctor's face fell a little. Then he rallied and moved to bow over Ivy's hand. "It is delightful to make your acquaintance, Miss Wareham," he said with a warm smile. "I know Lady Celeste was quite eager to make her home a haven for scholarly ladies such as yourself. What a comfort it is, as her friend, to know that you are just as delightful as she had hoped."

Quill blinked. "Do you mean to say that you knew about my aunt's plans, Vance?" he demanded, unable to keep the note of annoyance from his voice. It was one thing to be blindsided by his aunt's plans if everyone else close to her had been too. But hearing that she'd confided her plans to her local physician was a little bit galling.

But if the doctor was abashed by Quill's question, he didn't show it. "Your aunt was ill for some months before she died, my lord. And as her physician I spent a great deal of time with her before she passed. Something that gave her much comfort over those weeks was the knowledge that her passing would make it possible for four intelligent young ladies to make their homes in Beauchamp House and to make their marks in a way which Lady Celeste could not."

"How wonderful that she was able to have not only her physician by her side," Ivy said, after a quelling glance at Quill, "but also a dear friend. For I'm sure she must have counted you so if she confided her plans to you. I hope that knowing how much you helped her gives you comfort."

To Quill's surprise the other man's eyes welled and he was forced to pull an enormous handkerchief from his pocket to wipe his eyes. "I do apologize, Miss Wareham," Vance said with a grimace, his bushy gray eyebrows almost touching in his distress. "But you are quite right that I counted Lady Celeste as a friend. And it was quite hard to lose her. Especially when I still don't know precisely what caused her death."

Mindful of their reason for being in the doctor's offices, Quill spoke up, watching with narrow eyes as Ivy patted Vance's hand. "That's just why we've come, doctor. Miss Wareham and I were curious about what it might have been that took my aunt away in her prime." Improvising to explain why Ivy might have accompanied him, he continued. "Miss Wareham has a fear of illness in general and she could not rest until we confirmed with you that whatever it was that killed my aunt is not, in fact, something that could pass on to others living in Beauchamp House."

Far from flinching at his mischaracterization, Ivy nodded at Quill's description of her phobia. "Indeed, Dr. Vance. I had a rather weak constitution as a child, so I am quite careful about ensuring I don't needlessly place myself in harm's way. When I learned upon my arrival at Beauchamp House that Lady Celeste died of a mysterious illness, I could not help but fear that it might be something that even now lingers within the house. I simply cannot go about my usual business if I'm constantly worried that touching this book or wandering that corridor will bring on one of the attacks I suffered so often as a child."

On hearing Ivy's explanation, the doctor at first looked troubled, then relieved. "I can assure you Miss Wareham that there is no indication that whatever Lady Celeste suffered from was in any way catching. No one else in the house fell ill, and indeed no one in the village did either. If it was something that might be shared between patients, then it is long gone from Beauchamp House."

"What a relief, Dr. Vance," Ivy said with a heaving sigh. "But if you don't mind my asking, what was your best guess at what might have caused her illness? I know Lord Kerr hasn't said so, but I do know how hard it is to lose a loved one. And one wants to know why, don't they?"

She was a little too good at playing the concerned former invalid, Quill thought wryly as he watched Ivy blink up at Vance with her big green eyes. She'd best be careful if she didn't wish to receive a proposal from the man. He was looking quite bowled over by her attention.

Shaking his head, Vance turned so that he could face both Quill and Ivy. "As I told your lordship in my letter," he said glumly, "I was never able to pinpoint her cause of death. I did suspect perhaps that she suffered from some sort of stomach ailment. A cancer perhaps, but that didn't explain all of her other symptoms. In the end, I fear her heart simply could not support her any longer and gave out."

"I do not wish to press you," Ivy said into the silence that followed, "but might her illness have been brought on by something she consumed? I do not like to speculate, but my dear aunt Jane fell ill after she began taking a tonic she purchased while in London. I fear she was rather too zealous about taking it and ended up quite ill as a result. It's just that Lady Celeste's symptoms as Mrs. Bacon described them to me sound so similar."

It wasn't a bad guess, Quill thought, impressed despite himself at Ivy's suggestion. Though he'd never known his aunt to be particularly prone to relying upon the sorts of tonics and tinctures that could be had in any apothecary shop, instead choosing to take whatever her doctor chose to have made up for her. But it did offer a possible means of transmitting poison.

But Dr. Vance shook his head. "I asked her, of course, about what remedies she might have been taking on her own before she consulted me," he explained with a dour expression. "But she assured me that she was taking nothing out of the ordinary. I do know that her maid was fond of giving her herbal tisanes for her headaches, but those were only occasionally, and I questioned the maid thoroughly about the ingredients. None of which would cause the kind of illness that Lady Celeste suffered from."

"If you'll indulge me, however, Dr. Vance," said Quill firmly, "is there something that in usual quantities isn't dangerous but might be if it is taken too often? Or in too large a dose?"

Dr. Vance's eyes narrowed. "Are you asking me if I think your aunt was poisoned, Lord Kerr?" he demanded, his gaze traveling from Ivy to Quill and back again.

"That is precisely what I'm asking," Quill said baldly. "My aunt suspected that someone was trying to kill her. And what I wish to know is, did you suspect it as well?"

Chapter 13

Ivy couldn't take her eyes off Quill.

Despite his wind-ravaged hair and relaxed country attire, the Marquess of Kerr was every inch the aggrieved nobleman as he waited for Dr. Vance to answer his question. And the doctor was well aware of it too, Ivy could see. Though his jaw clenched at Quill's sharp tone, he didn't wave off the question or give an easy platitude that might have worked with one of his less highly ranked patients' families.

She was always aware, of course, that Lord Kerr came from a different world than her own. But it was not difficult to imagine he was just like other men beneath the beautifully tailored clothes when he was teasing her and striding across the countryside. His posture and steely tone now told her just how much of a mistake it was to forget his privileged existence.

"I suspected it, yes," the doctor said, his mouth tight with anger. "But I had no way to prove it short of having a coroner conduct the sort of posthumous examination that I know your aunt would have despised." He looked down, clearly trying to get hold of his temper. "I knew your aunt for decades, my lord. And held her in some affection. We were friends. And I wanted more than anything to find out what was slowly killing her. For myself as much as for her own peace of mind. But she made me promise not to conduct any kind of invasive testing on her after she was gone."

He looked up and Ivy could see that, far from the coolly detached physician she had at first thought him, Dr. Vance was truly grief-stricken over Lady Celeste's death. They were of an age, she realized as she took in the doctor's trim physique and not unattractive salt-and-pepper hair. Could Dr. Vance and Lady Celeste had been more to each other than friends? If so, how painful must it have been for him to watch her wither away?

Quill must have wondered the same thing, for his next words were a bit less sharp. "But you must have tried to stop the source of the poison, surely? If you did indeed suspect that was the culprit?"

"So many stomach ailments have the same symptoms as many poisons," Dr. Vance said. "And without an autopsy there was no way of knowing for sure. So yes, I did go so far as to attempt to control what she consumed. Her maid, whom she trusted implicitly, personally oversaw what she ate and drank for the last month of her life. Which did not make her popular in the servants' hall, I can tell you. And indeed she did seem to improve for a time. But not long after she suffered what was her last attack of illness and only days later she was gone."

"And you didn't think to send for me," Quill said, clearly angry. At the situation or Dr. Vance, Ivy couldn't tell. "I might have removed her from Beauchamp House to London where she could have seen the best physicians Harley Street had to offer." He began to pace, his agitation impossible to contain now.

Though he might have taken offense at the mention of Harley Street, to Dr. Vance's credit he said, "I tried, my lord. As I said, your aunt was my friend, and I wanted to see her well. But she thought she would be able to figure out who was responsible. And by the time she was ready to admit defeat, she was too far gone to travel. Believe me when I say I did everything I could to persuade her to leave. But you know as well as I do that Lady Celeste Beauchamp was as stubborn a woman who has ever lived. And she was unwilling to listen to reason. One of the downsides of a woman with a keen intellect, I suspect."

At his last words, Ivy bristled but chose not to argue. Though, honestly, she thought, no one ever complained of stubbornness in intelligent men. Because they assumed that a smart man was always right. Indeed, when the contest was between a man and a woman, the man was always right no matter how inferior his intellect might be.

"For whatever reason," she said coolly, "Lady Celeste chose to conduct her own investigation. Did she happen to share her suspicions with you, Dr. Vance?"

He shook his head. "She refused to blacken anyone's name when she had no proof. And when it came down to it, I don't believe she had any idea who it was. She certainly had no concrete suspect, else she'd have accused them. Or at the very least dismissed them from her household, which she did not."

Seeing that there was little more they could learn from the doctor, and not wanting to overstay their welcome lest they need to question him again, Ivy was trying to catch Quill's eye to indicate they should take their leave, when a sharp knock sounded on the door.

A pretty lady, about a decade older than Ivy, stepped inside and smiled inquisitively. "I am sorry to intrude, my dear, but you've received a summons from the Granthams. Their eldest boy has fallen from a tree and broken his arm and they need you at once."

To Ivy's surprise, Dr. Vance's face transformed for a

moment as he looked at his wife—for that must surely be who the lady was. Unless his housekeeper called him "my dear," which would be highly unusual. "Come in, dearest," he said with a smile that made him look years younger. "Lord Kerr, Miss Wareham, may I present my wife, Mrs. Marianne Vance. Mrs. Vance, this is Lord Kerr, the Marquess of Kerr, and Miss Wareham of Beauchamp House."

The doctor's wife made her very correct curtsy to Quill and smiled warmly at Ivy, taking her hand in her own. "You must be one of the ladies that dear Lady Celeste left Beauchamp House to. How lovely to meet you. I had no idea that any of you were in residence yet, else I'd have paid a call by now."

"Oh, I only arrived yesterday," Ivy assured her quickly. "And my compatriots only a couple of days before that. Though I look forward to welcoming you, of course."

"Perhaps once you're all settled," Mrs. Vance continued, "we can hold an assembly to welcome you all to the neighborhood. For I know the rest of our little circle will be desperate to meet you all."

At her effusive words, Ivy laughed. "I'm not sure anyone should be desperate to meet any of us, though I appreciate your enthusiasm, of course."

"Well, I must admit that we were a little worried when we learned of Lady Celeste's bequest," Mrs. Vance said with a confiding smile. "We are a close-knit community and no one knew what to make of the notion we'd be getting a sudden influx of bluestockings in our midst. But you seem like a normal young lady and not at all the sort of dour creature full of her own importance I imagined you'd be."

Ivy leaned back a little, shocked despite herself at the other lady's description of her expectations of her. She supposed villages were not as used to mixing with intellectually inclined ladies as cities like Oxford or London were. But even so, it was hard not to be offended by the assumptions Mrs. Vance had made.

"I can assure you, Mrs. Vance," said Quill, perhaps interpreting Ivy's silence correctly, "I have met all four of the young ladies my aunt left Beauchamp House to and they are all delightful. Not a hint of the radical amongst the lot of them."

This last annoyed Ivy. She didn't need him reassuring women like Mrs. Vance about her political proclivities. His words made her desperately want to spout off some outrageous philosophy or casually ask when the village anarchists held their meetings.

"Oh, I can see that for myself, my lord," Mrs. Vance said beaming. "Though I am grateful for your assurances. I should hate to think that Little Seaford was in danger of being overrun by Amazons." She laughed merrily and didn't seem to notice that Ivy didn't join in. "I am so pleased to meet you, Miss Wareham, and will definitely pay a call on the four of you before the week is out."

"Do not forget our chaperone, Lady Serena Fanning," Ivy said wryly. "She at least will lend the rest of us consequence if our own good behavior does not."

Perhaps sensing the undercurrents, Dr. Vance jumped in. "If I am to reach the Grantham farm in good time, I should take my leave. My lord, Miss Wareham, I hope you will come to me if you have any more questions."

And before his wife could ask any impertinent questions about their reasons for the visit, Ivy slipped her hand into Quill's arm and stepped back out into the street, where a glance at the sky was enough to tell her that the fine weather they'd enjoyed earlier had changed. Now a dark cloud hung low on the horizon and looked to be headed back the way they'd come.

"Damn it," Quill said under his breath. "I knew I should

have sent the coachman ahead to wait here in the village for us. The weather here is apt to change at the drop of a hat. Which I well know."

"I'm sure if we hurry we can make it back to Beauchamp House before the storm," Ivy said, not necessarily believing her words but not wishing to wait it out in the village when she wanted to get back to the manor so that she could reread Lady Celeste's letter to see if there were any clues she might have missed.

To her relief, Quill seemed to agree with her. "Let's get started then before it overtakes us."

They'd only got to the edge of the village, both of them walking briskly in an effort to outrun the coming storm, when Quill heard a carriage rumbling toward them.

There was plenty of room for it to pass, thanks to the width of the carriageway at that point, but nevertheless, he said, "Perhaps we should move to the side to let him by."

Lost in thought, Ivy gave a start but allowed him to guide her to the roadside. When she glanced behind them, however, her eyes grew wide. And when Quill looked back, he saw that rather than taking advantage of the area they'd ceded to him, the driver of the cart was barreling toward them.

Without thinking, he threw himself against her, just before the horses followed by the careening vehicle sped past where they'd just been standing.

"What on earth?" Ivy gasped from beneath him, her breath coming in gasps as she tried to regain her composure. "Were his horses out of control?"

His own breath in short supply, he shook his head. "I don't know. I don't think so."

Turning to look down at her, he realized he was sprawled on top of her, and scrambled to his feet. Taking advantage of the moment, he gave her a hand up. They busied themselves

in brushing off their clothes, and Quill retrieved his hat
from where it had fallen in the grass a few feet away.

"Are you all right?" he asked, looking at her at last and
seeing that she seemed more annoyed than hurt.

"I'm fine," she said with a frown. "But I'd like to know
why that man just tried to run us over."

"I didn't recognize him," Quill said with a frown as he
looked in the direction where the cart had sped off. "It was
very likely just some tradesman in a hurry to reach his next
stop."

"Well, I've lived in Oxford my whole life," she said, still
frowning, "and it is far more congested than this village,
and I've never once been in danger of being trampled by
a runaway cart."

Realizing she was likely far more upset by the incident
than she let on, Quill refrained from minimizing her reaction. Instead, he calmly tucked her arm into his elbow
and started them off in the direction of home.

"I fear we'd best discuss this as we walk, for it looks as
if this storm is about to be upon us," he said. It was a mea-
sure of how unsettled she was that she had allowed him to
lead her without so much as a murmur of protest.

Despite their best efforts, the storm did, in fact, overtake
them about halfway back to Beauchamp House, pelting
them with a deluge of wind and rain.

"Now is not the time for missishness," he said to Ivy,
who despite her shivering, was attempting to accept the
shelter of his coat without touching him. "You won't give a
hang about your reputation when you're dying of the ague
in your solitary bed," he snapped, pulling her roughly
against him even as they hurried along the path.

"I'm not . . ." she began to protest, then, perhaps thinking better of it, stopped herself. "Fine," she muttered in a
voice he strained to hear over the sound of the rain, "but

don't blame me if we're spotted and someone forces us into a betrothal."

Quill could think of worse things than to find himself leg-shackled to a curvaceous beauty with a sharp tongue, but wisely chose to keep his own counsel on the matter. Now was not the time to raise her ire. If his memory served, there was an empty cottage up ahead used by shepherds moving their flocks, which though likely to offend his companion's sensibilities, was at the very least dry and, if they were lucky, boasted a fireplace.

"This way," he said, unabashedly holding her against him as he led her down a side path toward the cottage, which he spotted—thank god—just as he began to think his memory had deceived him with a remembered mirage.

Fortunately, she didn't question his diversion, and when she saw the weather-beaten shack, she cried out with relief.

"I've never been so happy to see an abandoned cottage in all my life," she said as she pulled out of the shelter of his arms and began to remove her ruined hat.

Not pausing to reflect on how strangely bereft he felt at their separation, Quill removed his greatcoat and handed it to her. "Take off your pelisse and put this on while I start the fire. There should be some blankets in that chest. The shepherds generally keep a few things in these cottages for those nights when they're forced to remain here."

Relief swept through him when she did as she was told. He would never forgive himself his foolishness at getting her into this predicament if she caught her death of a cold. And a missish refusal to get out of her wet things would have risked just that. But Ivy was more sensible than that, thank god.

Confident that she was on her way to drying off, and aware that his blood was still up thanks to the near miss on the road, he knelt before the fireplace and concentrated on lighting the kindling and logs left there by the cottage's last occupant.

"How did you know about this place?" Ivy asked from behind him. "I didn't see it on our way into the village."

"I remembered waiting out rain storms here when I was a lad," Quill said, brushing his hands off on his breeches before standing. "I'm surprised it's still . . . here." When he'd turned it was to see that not only had Ivy removed her soaked outer garment, but she was seated on the little cot unlacing her boots, which revealed an impressive pair of bestockinged calves. Fortunately, she was too intent on her task to notice his hot gaze.

Or maybe she was too cold to care.

Despite his suddenly desperate wish to watch as she unrolled those stockings, Quill turned his back on her unconsciously seductive actions and began to remove his soggy coat. Once that was off, he set to work on his own boots, which he feared were beyond hope. He never traveled without extra pairs, but it almost made him weep to see Hoby's handiwork so utterly demolished.

"It's lucky you remembered it, else I know I would have crumbled in a heap on the side of the path," she said with some relief. "I can endure many things, but cold and wet is my Achilles' heel. I could withstand the heat of the desert or the tropical forests described by travelers to the southern regions of America without incident, I think. But unrelenting rain and cold I simply cannot abide."

"How unfortunate that you should be born in England, then," Quill said with a laugh. "For I do not think you could find a colder, wetter climate if you tried."

"I'm just lucky that way, I suppose," she said with an answering note of amusement.

Her laugh did something to him, Quill realized. Touched some part of him that admired her indefatigable spirit.

Despite her discomfort and distress at being drenched, she was in possession of the sort of temperament that did not allow the petty annoyances of life to dampen her spirit. He could not think of a single other lady of his acquaintance who would meet such a situation with such equanimity.

"If you wish," he said over his shoulder, "you may remove your gown and wrap up in one of the blankets . . ."

He trailed off as he saw that she was already in the process of doing just that. He swallowed at the sight of her breasts outlined by the wet fabric as she tried to reach behind to unbutton her gown.

"I am trying to do just that, but I'm afraid this gown requires the assistance of another pair of hands." In another woman he might have suspected her of flirtation, but there was a sort of shy diffidence in the way she spoke that told him she was not trying to be coy. It was a refreshing change from the cynical seductions he was used to in London.

But when he looked up, their eyes caught, and he muttered a curse. She might be an innocent, but she had a wellspring of natural sensuality that just might do him in.

Completely unaware of the direction of his thoughts, she asked, "Would you mind helping me?"

He was crossing toward her before she even finished speaking, and when he moved to stand behind her, he was almost jealous of the wisps of damp hair that kissed the nape of her neck. "Move your hands," he said thickly, unable to say more in case he'd tell her what he was truly thinking.

As he bent his head a little to see the buttons, Quill was assailed by the scent of woman mixed with rosewater rising from her warm skin. He fumbled a little as he set his fingers working against the fastenings, unable to resist dragging a little against the smooth skin of her back as one by one he pulled the bindings free. It was near impossible for him to breathe as he watched inch after inch of her gown part to reveal first the almost transparent fabric of her chemise, then neatly threaded laces of corset below.

As if she sensed his hesitation, she said quietly, "That's good enough. I think my gown bore the brunt of it."

The danger of the temptation she posed suddenly making its way into his brain, Quill pulled his hands back as if they'd been licked by flames. "I'll go have a look at the fire," he said pointedly as he turned his back to her and placed one hand against the wall beside the stone fireplace and gazed down into the actual flames below.

Perhaps it would have been safer for them both if they'd pressed on to Beauchamp House, he reflected as he tried not to listen to the rustling of her clothes as she slipped out of them. It had been years since he'd felt the sort of uncontrolled desire that held him in its grip now. It was impossible to forget every luscious detail of her. From the smooth skin of her bare back to the flush in her cheeks.

He'd also been cursed with a healthy imagination when it came to his carnal desires, which now unhelpfully flooded his mind with all the delicious ways in which two adults could put a rainy afternoon in close quarters to good use.

"You may turn around now," Ivy said finally, after several fraught minutes of him trying to think of everything but the woman undressing just feet away from him, and failing miserably.

When he turned, he saw that the thick wool blanket that covered her was about as unflattering a garment as it could be. But even that did nothing to quell the effect of her loveliness on him.

"You may sit beside me if you like," she said tentatively, her green eyes perhaps seeing more of his discomfort than he was comfortable with. "There's no other chair here, and it would be ridiculous for you to sit on the floor when there is a perfectly good seat here."

His expression must have shown his skepticism as he looked pointedly at the empty place beside her on the small bed.

"Do not be missish, my lord," she said, echoing his own words to her as they huddled beneath his greatcoat. "We are both sensible creatures. I can sit beside you without unleashing my base passions on you and offending your delicate sensibilities."

Despite his misgivings, Quill bit back a laugh. "I believe that is supposed to be my line," he said with a grin. "You must think me a poor figure of a man if you think I will collapse in a fit of the vapors." As he spoke, he walked the few steps to the other side of the cottage and lowered himself gingerly to the cot beside her.

"Hardly that," she said holding her blanket at the neck while extending her other hand toward the heat of the fire. "You looked so serious, I thought to relieve the tension a bit, that's all."

"You use humor like that frequently, don't you?" he asked, unfastening the diamond stick pin from where it nestled in the now-crumpled folds of his cravat.

Before she could respond, he said, "Let's use this to hold that," holding up the pin.

Nodding, she shifted a little to face him, lifting her chin so that he could duck his head and see what he was doing as he stabbed the pin through the thick blanket. Pulling back a little, he looked up to find her green gaze lingering on his mouth. And unable to stop himself, he gave in to the temptation that had dogged him ever since they set out together that morning.

Pulling her against him, he covered Ivy's mouth with his own, and kissed her.

Chapter 14

Ivy wasn't sure when the moment changed. Perhaps when he leaned in so close that she could feel the warmth of his body and smell the clean scent of his cologne mixed with something intoxicatingly male. Or maybe it was when he looked up at her from beneath his impossibly long lashes and their eyes met just before he glanced at her lips.

She wasn't sure because instinct made her close her eyes just before he brought his mouth up to press against hers.

And she was flooded with nothing but sensation.

His lips were soft. Softer than seemed possible. But more seductive than the most eloquent of Sappho's lyrics.

And when she kissed him back, opened her mouth and leaned into him, Quill took full advantage of the invitation, stroking into her in a tangle of tongues that was more carnal than she'd imagined a kiss could be. He pulled her closer, and Ivy slid her arms up over his chest and into the silky hair at his nape. The press of her breasts against the hard wall of his chest combined with the heat of their mouths was almost her undoing, and she moaned a little as he nipped at her lower lip. She'd been kissed before, of course.

There had been one overeager suitor who'd managed to maneuver her into an alcove during a local assembly, but that had been years ago, and she'd been more surprised than flattered since she suspected he was only using her to make another girl jealous. But she could hardly remember what it had felt like. Certainly it hadn't filled her with the sort of breathless wonder that now threatened to overtake her completely.

"May I kiss you, Aphrodite?" Quill asked, and she felt the low rumble of his voice all the way to her toes.

"A bit late for asking permission, my lord," she murmured against his mouth. "Does not lack of protest indicate consent?"

He kissed a path down from her mouth over her chin, saying as he moved, "Not always. And I have a strong desire"—he sucked lightly in a spot beneath her ear—"to hear you say yes."

"Then, yes," she said leaning back a little to give him more access to her collarbone. "Kiss me, Quill. Please."

Something relaxed in him. Ivy could feel it in the set of his shoulders as he moved against her. "Since you asked so nicely." She felt his smile as he moved back up her body and took her mouth again, this time with a demanding hunger that called out to some unnamed yearning she hardly recognized as her own. She only knew that she had to get closer, press harder, open herself to his every unspoken request. Struggling against the rough wool of the blanket, she shrugged, the stickpin holding the neck together unfastening as it fell from her shoulders onto the bed behind her.

The relief at feeling the skin of her chest and shoulders against the fabric of his shirt and waistcoat was almost palpable, and when his hand caressed her breast through the fabric of her stays, Ivy felt it in her core. The combination of the heat of their mouths and the stroke of his thumb over her hardened nipple was enough to make her jolt, and Quill pulled back a little from her mouth, whispering, "Easy, sweet. Easy."

And for reasons she could not say, she trusted him. Even as the ache his touch wrought made her move against him, seeking some relief in that restless place where only she had ever touched.

As if sensing her need, Quill pressed her back to lie on the little cot, taking a moment to glance down at her with eyes dark blue with desire just before he set his mouth over the tip of her breast beneath the thin fabric of her chemise. It was both pleasure and pain to feel the pull of his mouth on her, and when his hand slid slowly up her knee toward her aching center, it was only by biting her lip that she didn't cry out for him to move faster. But she must have made some sort of sound because he huffed out a laugh and pulled back a little to use his teeth on her sensitive breast. "Soon enough, sweet Aphrodite."

But she couldn't stop herself from lifting her hips in a silent plea for relief, and when he finally, finally stroked a finger over the bare flesh at the heart of her, Ivy's gasp of pleasure was loud over the pounding of the rain outside.

"I have to see you," Quill muttered, all amusement gone from his voice. And without removing his hand from where he caressed her, he shifted to kneel between her bent legs. Ivy widened them so that when he lifted her chemise he could look his fill of her.

She had no notion of why this man had managed to get past her defenses, but she had no wish to contemplate such things while she watched desire sharpen the lines of his austere face.

Her clothes no longer in the way, he shrugged out of his coats, and Ivy inhaled a sharp gasp of anticipation. She watched breathlessly as he made quick work of his cravat, and in one fluid motion pulled his shirt over his head and tossed it aside. Unable to look away, she only had time for an appreciative glance at his naked chest before he leaned down and took her mouth again. The sensation of skin to skin was nearly her undoing.

"Is this comfortable?" he asked after a moment, and she realized that she was clinging to him like a limpet, her hands skimming over the warm skin of his back almost without her knowing it.

Unable to find her voice, Ivy nodded, but when he stroked a finger over the sensitive flesh between her legs, she gave a gasp of pleasure. And soon she was moving restlessly against him again, only this time she felt the added sensation of his hardness through the nankeen of his breeches. Rocking against him, she brought her calves up around his hips, and pulled him closer. He mimicked their movements with the hot thrust of his tongue into her mouth.

Unable to stop herself, and driven by curiosity and a need to feel more of him, she slipped her hands between them and set to work at the buttons of his breeches. Quill hissed at the touch, and put a staying hand against hers. "I am trying like the devil to be gentle with you, Ivy," he said through gritted teeth. "If you don't release me, I can't be answerable for the consequences."

"But I want to feel you," she said, punctuating her words with a lift of her hips. She'd certainly read enough erotic classical poetry to know how the mechanics worked, but she also knew that she wanted to give him as much pleasure as he seemed intent on giving her. "And I want you to feel as good as I do."

He closed his eyes as she brushed his hand away and continued to unbutton his falls. She smiled in triumph at his surrender, and when his body sprang forth, she stroked a hand from root to tip, eliciting a groan of relief from him. And almost before she knew what he was doing, she found herself pressed back against the cot with her hands clasped above her head, imprisoned by one of his.

When she made to protest, he stifled her with his mouth. "You are undoubtedly one of the most brilliant ladies I've ever met," he said to her with a chiding look, "but I have more knowledge in this particular area. So let me lead."

She was robbed of the ability to respond by the feel of his eager body, hard and ready against the bare skin of her thigh. Suddenly she felt her chest flood with emotion as she looked up into his all too serious gaze. Kissing her softly, he said, "I'll take care of you, Ivy. I promise." It was a gentle kiss, and she trusted him despite the butterflies of nerves fluttering in her stomach. And as if they'd never paused, she felt the passion between them rise again as Quill's clever fingers stroked over her and, as she silently begged for more, thrust into her. First one, then another, which he rhythmically moved within her. The sound of their breathing rang in her ears as she shifted her hips faster and faster to meet his thrusting fingers.

She was nearing some peak she'd never scaled before when he suddenly pulled his hand away. "Come back," she ordered in a desperate voice she barely recognized as her own. "Oh, please Quill, come back."

And before she could even finish her protest, he replaced his fingers with the hot hardness of his body. And she sighed with relief as she urged him forward silently with a tiny thrust of her hips.

"Be still, Ivy," he said in a strained voice as he let go of her imprisoned hands and used his own to hold himself over her. "I'm trying to do this slowly. I don't want to hurt you."

Which was utterly noble, she knew, but her body wanted him now. "I don't mind pain," she hissed. "I just want you. Now."

And she used her heels and hands to pull him into her,

gaining another delicious inch that stretched her beyond what was comfortable. Even so, she wanted more, and with another strong pull against him, she felt Quill surrender and with one swift thrust he was fully seated within her.

Ivy gasped as he moved over her.

Quill touched his forehead to hers, and asked in a strained voice, "Is it too much?" If she said yes, he was prepared to withdraw, but it was hard to imagine doing so when he was clasped in the hot, tightness of her sweet body. Still, he had no wish to give her pain, and the last thing he wanted was to give her a fear of coupling. Because he damned well intended to do this with her again. And again.

"No," she said with a little shake of her head. "No. Just . . . different."

Offering up a silent prayer of thanksgiving, he pulled back slowly then just as slowly pressed in again. This time her gasp was one of pure pleasure, and he let himself go a little, moving against her in a rhythm that pleased them both if the clench of her body around his was any indication. Soon they were both too consumed by the slick slide of their bodies against each other to speak. Dipping his head down to kiss her as he thrust, he growled out a groan as he felt her hands slide up into his hair, pulling his face closer as he moved against her. But she pulled her face away when he reached down to touch her just above where their bodies joined, and he felt some part of her uncoil with abandon as her body gripped him where he moved inside her.

"Oh Quill," she gasped as he gritted his teeth against the feel of his own completion nearing. "I. Oh. That's . . ."

Closing his eyes in relief, he felt her quicken her hips and in turn the pulsing grip of her around his cock as she gave herself over to her orgasm. And like a stallion let off its lead, only now did he give himself permission to let himself go, unable to hold back his need any longer. He pressed into her soft body with a desperation he'd not allowed himself to feel in decades, if ever. It was as if Ivy with her eager kisses and open sensuality had bewitched him into revealing some part of himself he'd long kept hidden from view. And the result was a mad hunger that made him grind into her without any thought for finesse or chivalry, but instead unleashing a raw need that had him pounding into her with abandon until finally, joyfully, he felt that telltale tingle in his spine before he gripped her buttocks and with a harsh cry went over the edge with her.

When he came back to himself, Quill realized he'd collapsed on top of her like a selfish oaf, and with a muttered apology he turned over onto his back, a barely successful maneuver given how narrow the cot was.

With the return of awareness, also came a sense of the gravity of what he'd just done. Not only had he compromised Ivy beyond repair, he'd done so after not even a full twenty-four hours of knowing her. That must be some sort of record. At least it was in his family, where as far back as he could recall betrothals had all been conducted with the attendant pomp and circumstance that accompanied marriages made within the elite circles of the beau monde.

Beside him, Ivy lay silent, and he wondered if she was regretting the rashness of their actions. If he were assessing her likely reaction to being compromised into marriage by a marquess when he'd first learned her identity yesterday, he would have assumed she'd be tickled pink. The woman he'd assumed had come to Beauchamp House with no other goal than to steal his family's inheritance out from under them would have been smiling like the cat who licked the cream as she lay beside him. But it had only taken a few more minutes' conversation with Miss Aphrodite Wareham to know that she cared only about the inheritance insofar as it would allow her to continue her studies. And even that she'd set aside today in favor of investigating the circumstances behind his aunt's death. A woman who thought only of her own well-being would have ignored the letter from Celeste and stayed behind in the library with her fellow scholars.

"It's stopped raining," she said from beside him, though she made no move to rise. "We should be getting back to Beauchamp House if we don't want them to send out a search party. I daresay the fact that we're so late will be scandal enough. Especially given the fact that I neglected to bring a maid along."

"The proprieties are a bit more relaxed in the country than they are in town," Quill responded curtly, the consequences of their missing lunch the least of his worries. In one fluid motion, he sat up and stood, turning his back to her as he refastened his breeches and bent to retrieve his cravat, shirt, and waistcoat from where he'd tossed them onto the floor. Folding his own garments over his arm, he picked up Ivy's gown and handed it wordlessly to her, not daring to meet her eye lest he see the censure he deserved in them.

He'd done a number of foolish things in his life, but this might be the worst of them. Because he knew without asking her that Ivy would not marry him without protest. And yet marriage was the only way in which he could honorably repair the damage this interlude sheltering from the storm had caused.

"I suppose you're right," she said, scrambling off the cot and taking her gown from him. From within her gown, which she had pulled on over her head, she continued, "But I don't wish to upset your cousin. She seems like such a conscientious lady, and she will see this as some dereliction on her part, I fear."

Chapter 15

Tying his cravat in as tidy a fashion as he could imagine without a mirror, he said wryly, "I think she will be less bothered by your absence from luncheon than by the fact that I spent the time waiting out the storm taking your virginity, Ivy."

Blushing, she thrust her arms into the sleeves of her gown, and turned to offer him her back. Having finished pulling on his own clothes, he stepped behind her and began doing up the tiny buttons, steeling himself not to touch the soft, pale skin above her chemise, which he'd only minutes before caressed with his bare hand.

"We need not tell anyone about that," Ivy said in a hopeful tone.

Did she honestly think he could forget what they'd just done? If so she was sorely mistaken. And not just because it had been the single most intoxicating experience of his adult life.

"There is every need," Quill said, his self-recrimination making him short. "Or rather, we needn't tell everyone the reason why. But when we return to the house we will announce that we have decided to marry. I will leave this afternoon for Oxford so that I can inform your father, and

I have a friend with an uncle who is a bishop from whom I can get a special license. It will not take me above a couple of days. And I'll send a note to my secretary and have him send a notice to the papers. We can be married within the week if things are arranged properly."

He'd just finished the last button at this point, and when Ivy turned there was fire in her eyes. And not from passion.

"Were you going to consult me about this, or just issue a set of orders to me along with the rest of your minions?" she asked, her cheeks and neck flushed red with anger. Before he could respond, she continued, "I am not one of your meek society ladies who will take direction from you without so much as a by-your-leave. Has it occurred to you that I might not even believe in the institution of marriage? Or that perhaps my decision to give myself to you had nothing to do with anyone but us?"

While Quill understood her anger—he hadn't started the day with a desire to get married in a week's time either—he disagreed with the rationale behind it. "I would not have thought a lady with as much scholarly knowledge would be so naive about the way the world works. You and I might wish to keep this slipup between the two of us, but these things have a way of getting out. Certainly there could be rumors in the servants' quarters about us. I daresay they began as soon as the table was laid for luncheon and we still had not returned. Have you considered what it might do to your reputation to be dogged with such whispers? What having that kind of reputation might do to your ability to move freely in scholarly circles?"

At the mention of her scholarly reputation, Ivy's eyes widened, and despite feeling petty for it, Quill felt a stab of triumph. Perhaps he should have begun with the threat to her scholarly reputation rather than her societal one. After all, from everything he'd seen about her, she cared far more for her ability to do her work than she did about moving in society. He suspected some of that had to do with her father's estrangement from his family. It certainly wouldn't endear him to the *ton* if he'd been raised by someone who'd been purposely kept out of it.

Her jaw tight, Ivy gave a small nod. "You may be correct about scholarly circles. It is difficult enough as a woman to gain recognition for one's work. I can only imagine how much more difficult it would be to do so with a reputation for libertine behavior. It's all well and good if one is married." She gave a moue of distaste. "But as an unmarried lady I have already seen how narrow-minded male scholars can be when it comes to accepting my work without ascribing silly female illogic and foolishness to it. I'm damned for innocence when it comes to certain lyric poetry because I am unmarried, but I can guess that I'd be damned for being too knowing if I were to lose my good name."

Despite his relief that she was beginning to see reason, Quill was not so foolish as to let his triumph show on his face. Besides, were not ladies known for changing their minds? Aloud he said, "So, you agree that our marrying is the sensible course of action? I do think that you might be able to get a bit further in your quest for recognition as the Marchioness of Kerr than as Miss Wareham, if it's any consolation."

But her mouth was still tight with disapproval. "I can see the rationality behind your arguments, my lord. Indeed, I even agree with some of them, but I cannot think it will do either of us good to leap into a hasty marriage. Not only does it seem precipitate, but we are both overlooking the fact that there may be no gossip after today's excursion. It would be a shame to make such an important decision based on fears that might be unfounded."

He could see her point, but by this point Quill was already decided. It was just a matter of persuading Ivy. And if his own pleas fell on deaf ears, he had little doubt that her father would see things his way. He could not imagine that a man who had suffered banishment from the society he'd been born into would allow something similar to happen to his daughter.

Still, he had one more arrow in his quiver, and he had no qualms about using it. "Have you considered that you might already be with child?" he asked, not happy about the fact that he was the one who had put the flash of alarm in her emerald eyes, but knowing it was entirely necessary. "This is about more than the two of us, Ivy. I certainly will not countenance having a child born out of wedlock—or waiting until it becomes apparent that it's the only reason for our marriage."

"I hadn't thought of that," she admitted. "I hope you don't think I am so selfish that I would choose my own freedom at the expense of my child. Though in fairness, we do not even know yet if there is a child."

"But we must behave as if we know there is, Ivy," he said quietly. "We can avoid scandal, but only if we do the sensible thing and marry."

Seeing that she still didn't seem appeased, Quill stepped closer and took her hands in his. "I know things are moving quickly," he said, wishing he could kiss away her doubts. "But that doesn't mean we need to fight each other. And you need not think that I will be a demanding husband. I know already how much a part of you your studies are. And I would do nothing to take that away from you. I give you my word."

If he thought she would simply capitulate in the face of his gentle persuasion, however, he was quite mistaken.

Not backing down, she said, "May I have a day or two to think things over?" There was a plea for understanding in her gaze, which despite the urgency he felt about settling things between them, he could not deny.

"Of course," he agreed, with more ease than he felt. He was grateful that she was willing to consider his proposal at all, but he couldn't help a pang of impatience at her resistance. Even so, he was well aware that she was quite capable of digging in her heels and telling him to go to the devil if she chose. So he told himself to be patient and give her the time she needed. No matter how much his inner brute wished to override her objections and bend her to his will.

"Thank you," she said, her obvious relief stinging his conscience at his boorish thoughts. However he might chafe at her resistance, it was genuine and she deserved to be given some latitude in the matter.

"Now," she continued with a sheepish smile, "before we are discovered alone here, I suggest we start back for Beauchamp House. Otherwise there will be no question of which action we take. Your cousin will see to it that we're wed whether we agree to it or not."

Suddenly, he was reluctant to leave the little cottage that had served as a refuge from the rest of the world for a few short hours.

But, she was correct that they needed to get back, and the sooner the better.

With one last look over his shoulder into the little house, Quill shut the door behind them and followed Ivy toward the path back to Beauchamp House.

Far from the quiet return Ivy had hoped for, as soon as she and Quill stepped inside of Beauchamp House they were greeted as if they'd disappeared on an Egyptian expedition rather than simply disappeared for a few hours in a rainstorm.

"Oh, dear," said Sophia, giving Ivy an impulsive hug. "You look as if you could use a cup of tea and a hot bath. As soon as we saw the clouds threatening we began to worry, but I thought you would at least remain in the village until it passed." She shot a baleful glance in Quill's direction, but to Ivy's relief, he didn't betray a hint of guilty conscience. She supposed if she were going to choose a man to ruin herself over, she'd done well to pick one who would fall on his sword before he betrayed her to anyone.

Well, anyone who wasn't her father, she amended, recalling their earlier argument. Just the thought of her father hearing about this afternoon's events made her stomach flip in anxiety. She was brave enough when it came to forging her own path as a scholar, but as the eldest daughter she'd come to appreciate her father's guidance when it came to her scholarship. And she'd prided herself on not behaving like the sort of ninny she'd always thought could get herself into a situation like the one she now found herself in. The idea of disappointing her father was far worse than any fears she had about society's response to her transgressions.

"I'll tell Mrs. Bacon to have hot water brought up to both of your rooms," said Lady Serena with a cryptic glance at Quill. "I'll have some soup and sandwiches sent up as well. I daresay you're both starving after missing luncheon."

"That would be most appreciated, cousin," Quill said with a short bow. He turned to Ivy as if he wanted to say something to her, but perhaps thinking better of it, only gave her a nod and hurried up the stairs. Ivy wasn't sure if she was relieved or disappointed.

"I'll go up too," she said after a pregnant pause in which she felt as if all four ladies were staring at her.

To her dismay, Daphne, Sophia, and Gemma followed behind her and without asking permission, filed in through the door to her bedchamber.

Polly was there watching two footmen like a hawk while they filled the slipper tub in Ivy's dressing room.

Turning when she heard the door though, she rushed forward. "Miss, I'm glad to see you're well. The rains came upon us sudden-like, and I just knew you were caught up in it."

Once the footmen were gone, and Ivy's fellow scholars had seated themselves around the room, the maid led her like a child into the dressing room and helped her out of her wet clothes, *tut-tutting* and *tsk-tsking* all the way when she saw how wet her pelisse and gown were, and pronounced that her boots needed a thorough cleaning. "I'll take these down, and you get into that hot bath at once."

Thanking the girl, and grateful for the chance to be alone after her ordeal, Ivy slid into the hot water, her cold skin stinging a little at the change in temperature. She closed her eyes and breathed in the lavender-scented steam, and was once more in the little cottage, Quill's warm body heavy on hers. How could a few hours have changed her whole life so utterly? For though she hadn't agreed to anything yet, she had a feeling that one way or the other Quill would get his way. From the moment they'd met she'd known he was a man accustomed to getting his way. And though she'd since learned that he didn't lack the capacity for compromise, he was certainly not quick to change his mind. Or to admit defeat.

A knock on the door broke into her reverie, and she called out for them to come in—for she had little doubt who had knocked.

"Surely you didn't think you could just hide away in here and escape us," Sophia said cheerily as she stepped in, followed by Daphne and Gemma.

"She's relentless," Gemma said to Ivy with an apologetic smile. "It is far easier to concede defeat in the face of her inquiries."

"How unloyal you are, Gem," her sister chided. "I am

perfectly reasonable. I simply have an inquisitive nature. That is all."

"That is what I try to tell people about me," Daphne said, aggrieved. "But I am forever being called rude and impertinent. But why should I not ask questions when I have them? It is how one learns, after all."

Having grown up with a houseful of sisters, Ivy was used to a lack of privacy and to being interrogated. So she wasn't particularly worried about her ability to keep her own counsel. Still, there was something familiar about being surrounded by inquisitive ladies that made her feel at home, and for that she was grateful.

While they chatted amongst themselves, she washed her hair, and finally warm and ready to talk, she said, "If you'll hand me that towel, Sophia, I'll get out of the tub and we can go see if the sandwiches have been sent up." As if to emphasize her words, her stomach gave a low growl.

"By all means," Sophia said, handing her the towel. Ivy stood and wrapped herself up in it and used another for her hair.

Once she'd dried off and wrapped herself in a thick robe, she led the other three into her bedchamber, where a pot of tea and a plate of sandwiches had been laid out on a little serving table near the fire.

Bless Mrs. Bacon, she thought as she took a seat and bit into one of the sandwiches.

Gemma, meanwhile, poured each of them a cup of the steaming tea.

"I must confess that I thought for a while on the trek back that I'd never be warm again," Ivy said after a few fortifying sips. "I've never been so happy to be indoors in my life."

"Did you get your letter posted?" Sophia asked with an ease that made Ivy suspicious. "It must have taken quite a bit of time, for you were gone for several hours."

"We looked in on the local physician so that Lord Kerr could thank him for all he did for Lady Celeste while she was ill," Ivy said in what was not precisely a lie—Quill had thanked Dr. Vance. It was just that it hadn't been *all* they'd talked about. "That took quite a bit, for his wife came to look in on us and we chatted for quite a long while."

"That was kind of his lordship," Gemma said with approval. "I gather from what Lady Serena has said, he and his aunt were quite close."

"Then one would think he would respect her wishes and not be so difficult about her leaving Beauchamp House to us," Daphne said, her lips pursed in disapproval. "It isn't as if he is destitute without this house. According to Lady Serena, the Kerr marquisate counts seven estates and manor houses amongst its holdings. And that's not counting Kerr Castle and the London townhouse."

Ivy felt her heart beat faster at hearing the extent of Quill's estates. If she were to accept his proposal, lacking in finesse as it had been, she would be mistress of all those places.

Never in her life had she longed for the sort of wealth generations of Kerrs had likely taken for granted. Oh, on occasion she'd wished her family had enough to own their own carriage or to buy some hat that had taken her fancy. But that wasn't the same as wishing she could become a marchioness and move in wealthy circles. She found most social evenings tedious and would rather speak with a hundred impoverished scholars than one society fribble. The idea of being forced to do so for the rest of her life was disconcerting to say the least.

"I suppose he has a sentimental attachment to it," Gemma said with a shrug. "I'd be the same if strangers were to inherit our family home."

"They will," Sophia said wryly. "Though we can hope

that Papa will live for a very long time before Cousin Everett can even dream of inheriting."

"We can only hope," Gemma said "It's not the same as what's happened here with Beauchamp House, of course, since he has his own estate, but I can understand somewhat his reluctance to accept his aunt's decision."

"You're quiet, Ivy," Sophia said, her gaze intent. "And you've spent more time than any of us in Lord Kerr's company. What do you think about his reaction to learning we'd inherited Beauchamp House?"

Ivy blushed, hoping that her changed attitude toward Quill wasn't as obvious to them as it was to her. "I can see why he would be disappointed, of course," she said after a moment, with what she hoped was a careless shrug. "But I think he's resigned himself to it. At least, that is what he implied this afternoon. We didn't really talk much about it."

"What *did* you talk about, then?" Gemma asked, her curiosity making her eyes bright. "For I must confess I find him handsome as the very devil."

"Don't swear, Gemma," Sophia said reflexively as if used to correcting this impropriety on her sister's part.

Gemma rolled her eyes, confirming Ivy's suspicion that this was a common argument between the sisters.

Wishing she could latch onto their quibbling instead of answering Gemma's question, Ivy decided that a direct response would likely be less suspicious.

"We spoke about all sorts of things," she said breezily. "He told me a little about how he and his cousins spent childhood summers here. And he told me quite a bit about Lady Celeste and her championing of bluestocking issues."

"You must have had a long time to talk waiting out the storm," Sophia said with a speaking glance as Ivy realized that she'd been far less clever about hiding her feelings than she'd thought.

"I suppose so," she responded with a nervous laugh. "I didn't really notice."

"Hmm," Gemma said, her eyes narrowing with suspicion. "An afternoon alone, a convenient rainstorm. Just what *did* happen on the road from the village, Miss Wareham?"

Chapter 16

Ivy was saved from replying to Gemma's question by Daphne, though perhaps "saved" wasn't quite the right term.

"Your gown was almost dry when you arrived back," Daphne declared into the silence that followed Gemma's query. "So you must have waited it out somewhere. The air is far too wet for it to have done so while you walked back. Therefore, you must have got wet, gone indoors with a fire, then set out once the rain stopped. Either that or you never got wet in the first place."

Ivy bit back a frustrated sigh as she felt all three ladies staring at her with varying degrees of curiosity. So much for keeping the interlude in the little cottage a secret, she thought.

"As it happens," she said raising her chin in defiance at her companions' raised brows, "we did take shelter in a little cottage the shepherds use. It was quite rustic, but it was at least dry. Lord Kerr built a fire and that helped to dry our clothes."

"How cozy," Gemma said with a twinkle in her eyes. "I might even go so far as to call it romantic."

"I do not know why ladies are so intent upon calling what is a perfectly rational response to being caught in the rain romantic," Daphne argued. "We do not call it romantic when the wild animals seek out shelter from a storm."

"But we are not animals, Daphne," said Sophia with a tilt of her head. "Indeed, such an interlude could be called scandalous in some circles. I certainly do not think Lady Serena would be pleased to know of it. I wonder if Lord Kerr will tell her. For it behooves him as a gentleman to do so."

At this idea, Ivy sat up straighter. Surely he wouldn't. He'd promised.

"However," Sophia continued, "I suspect he will not. Unless something untoward happened while you were there."

Ivy's guilt must have shown on her face, for Gemma clapped her hands. "It did! Did he kiss you? Of course he did. A man like that would never let an occasion like that—being holed up with a pretty girl—pass by without taking some sort of liberty."

Despite herself, Ivy felt the need to defend Quill. "You must have a very poor opinion of Lord Kerr," she said with a frown.

But far from being abashed, Gemma shrugged. "Not particularly, but he is a man who seems to know what he wants. And one would have to be blind not to notice how he looked at you last night."

"And how was that?" Ivy asked, half-dreading the answer.

"As if he wanted to bed you," Daphne said baldly.

At the collective gasp from the other ladies, Ivy scowled. "It was obvious that was what he wanted. Men are quite transparent about that sort of thing at times. Ridiculous society rules mean we cannot speak openly of such things, but I thought you were all too smart to fall prey to those things."

"Daphne, dearest," said Ivy after a muffled laugh, "we might all of us think that society rules are silly at times, but that doesn't mean we should speak whatever crosses our minds. It might prove uncomfortable for one's companions. And one doesn't wish to make others uncomfortable, does one?"

"I can hardly be held responsible for how another person feels," Daphne said with a shake of her head. "For one thing, I have a very hard time knowing what others feel to begin with. But I will agree that I do not wish to make others unhappy. I simply cannot seem to figure out why plain speaking is so wrong. If we are to understand one another, why not be as precise as we can be?"

"It's all right, Daphne," said Sophia, squeezing the other girl's arm. "We are private here, so you haven't offended anyone. And your assessment of Lord Kerr's looks at Ivy is accurate. I would have put it more delicately, but that's beside the point." Turning to Ivy, she continued, "I find it very hard to believe that a man who gets what he wants most of the time would not take the opportunity to steal a kiss at the very least while you were all alone together."

Knowing that if she did not tell them, they'd continue to harass her until she confessed, Ivy sighed. "Yes, he kissed me. Are you happy now? You have winkled out my secret."

"I knew it!" Gemma said with triumph. "Especially when the two of you could barely look at each other when you returned. A word of advice for the next time this situation befalls you, my dear. Do not avoid the gentleman's gaze. It quite gives you away when you do that. You have to behave as normal no matter how much you might balk at the thought."

"I'll keep that in mind for the next time I must take shelter from a storm with a handsome gentleman, Gemma," Ivy said wryly. "I thank you for the advice."

"It is unlikely that such a thing will happen again," Daphne said. "The odds are quite steep."

Ignoring the other two, Sophia eyed Ivy with a suspicious eye. "Men have been called out for less, Ivy. Unless of course he offered to make things right."

Not liking the direction Sophia's enquiry was taking, Ivy changed the subject. "I almost forgot the most frightening part," she said, hoping that the others would forget about her confession about Quill. "We were almost run over by a runaway cart."

That had the effect Ivy had been looking for.

"In the village?" Gemma demanded, her brow furrowed.

"Was this before or after you were caught in the storm?" Sophia asked, looking concerned. "Either way, it's no wonder you were out of sorts, you poor thing."

"I was once almost trampled by a horse," Daphne offered with a sympathetic nod. "It was quite unpleasant."

Grateful that her subterfuge had worked, Ivy couldn't help but recall that the incident *had* been unsettling. "Lord Kerr was able to get me out of the way in time, but it was a near thing."

Speculatively, Sophia tilted her head to look at Ivy. "That explains the kissing, then," she said with an air of one who knows.

"What do you mean?" Ivy asked.

"Danger," Sophia said firmly. "It brings out the baser passions."

Thinking about just how passionate Quill had been in the little cottage, Ivy couldn't help but agree. Still, she didn't want to go down that conversational road again. "I find myself quite exhausted after this morning's ordeal," she said, and was then overcome by an actual sigh of exhaustion. "Do you mind very much if we discuss this later?"

Sophia shook her head in disappointment, but did not press. "I can only imagine," she said softly, and Ivy was quite certain that Sophia had guessed the truth.

Her sister, meanwhile, rose and gave Ivy an impulsive hug. "I'm quite jealous, you know," she said with a grin that removed any sting from the pronouncement. "If he weren't obviously dazzled by your beauty, I would have tried to catch his eye myself. But I don't think he would be the sort to enjoy digging around in the sand for fossils, so I'll concede gracefully."

"You are pale," Daphne said, eyeing Ivy as if she were one of Gemma's fossils. "And there are dark circles beneath your eyes. You should rest."

After Gemma's praise of her beauty, Ivy almost laughed outright at Daphne's plain speaking. "Thank you, Daphne. I will endeavor to rest so that I will look better at supper."

"Don't think this is over," Sophia said into Ivy's ear as she gave her a hug. Then, with a saucy wink, she followed the other two from the room.

Ivy shut the door behind them and fell back against it with a sigh.

It seemed years since she'd gone down to breakfast this morning. But rather than dwell on everything that had happened, she padded on bare feet over the thick carpet and climbed into her bed, which Polly had turned down for her before she had slipped out.

She was asleep almost before she could pull up the coverlet.

After he'd had a bath and changed into dry clothes, Quill made his way downstairs in search of Serena. He might not divulge the whole of what had passed in the little cottage, but he would at the very least let her know that he meant to offer for Ivy. Let her make of that what she would.

He found his cousin in her private sitting room going over the household accounts with Mrs. Bacon. As soon as he stepped into the room, however, the housekeeper rose and gathered up the ledger she and Serena had been looking through.

"I'm pleased to see you're none the worse for wear after your soaking, my lord," she said with the ease of someone who had known him since he was younger than Serena's boy. "I'll just come back later to finish up with these, my lady," she said to Serena before leaving the room with a curtsy.

"I hope that Ivy, too, is none the worse for wear," Serena said wryly after the door had closed behind Mrs. Bacon. "For I had the feeling when you both returned that something more than just being caught in the rain had occurred. Of course, that may have been my imagination. Please tell me that is the case."

Moving to stand before the fireplace, where he made a closer-than-necessary examination of a fatuous-looking shepherdess figurine, Quill was silent for a moment before turning around to meet Serena's eyes.

"Perhaps," he said with a slight shrug. "But that is between Miss Wareham and myself."

Serena's eyes narrowed. "Since I have been entrusted with her care while she is under this roof," she said with raised brows, "then I believe that is not quite true."

"And because you are her chaperone," he said calmly, "I have come to tell you that I mean to offer for Miss Wareham's hand. So the particulars of this afternoon are not the point."

But rather than being placated, Serena was so annoyed she rose from her chair and began to pace. "I should never have agreed to let her go with you this morning. I knew one of them would likely get into some scrape while I was in charge of them, but I never imagined it would happen in the first few days of their residency. In Ivy's case, it's only her first full day in Beauchamp House. That must be some sort of record!"

"Do not take on so, Serena," Quill said, stepping in his cousin's path to stop her agitated trek across the carpet. "It's no reflection on you as a chaperone. These things happen. You could hardly predict that a storm would force us to take shelter alone in an uninhabited cottage."

"Oh god," Serena groaned. "Could you be any more of a cliché? A cottage in the rain, Quill? It might have been penned in a Minerva Press novel, it's so trite. I might have expected it from you. But I thought Miss Wareham was much more sensible than to fall prey to your charms. And you, as the head of the family, know better."

Something about her dismissal rankled with him. Perhaps it was a cliché, but it had been damned cozy in that cottage. *A damned sight more than this room at present,* he thought. "I will thank you not to speak about my betrothed's sense—lacking or otherwise," he said through clenched teeth. "And I am well aware of what my duty is. Which is why I intend to marry her."

Pinching the bridge of her nose, Serena struggled to get hold of her emotions. "You are right. I apologize. I was overset." She collapsed into the chair she'd so recently vacated. "But do you have feelings for Ivy, or is this something you are doing out of honor? For I will not force the girl into a loveless marriage. Especially when the only people who know that you were even alone with her are the two of you."

He knew all too well what Serena's own marriage had been like, and while he understood her desire to shield Ivy from such a union, he also was a little offended that she would put him in the same category as Fanning. He certainly had never raised his hand to a woman as that monster had done.

"I am not Fanning," he said, trying not to let his hurt color his voice. "And though I do not claim to love Miss Wareham, there is a certain affinity between us that I think might grow into something deeper."

At his denial, Serena reached out and touched him on the arm. "I am sorry, Quill. I know you are cut from a different cloth entirely. I just . . ." she paused, as if searching for the right words.

"You don't have to explain," he said gently. "I understand. Truly. And you needn't worry. I promise to treat her well."

"I know you will," she said with a smile. "Of course you will. I am being silly."

"You are being a mother hen, which is exactly why Aunt Celeste chose you to chaperone her girls," Quill said with an answering smile. "She knew what she was about."

At the mention of Celeste, Serena's eyes softened. "She did, didn't she. Though I doubt even *she* could have predicted that Ivy would fall prey to your charms so soon into her residence."

Quill laughed. "No, though she did tell me once that my charm would be my undoing. I daresay this is as swift a comeuppance as she'd have wished."

"Will you ride to Oxford tomorrow to speak to Ivy's father?" Serena asked, already thinking ahead to all the tasks necessary for seeing her charge settled.

At her query, Quill smiled sheepishly. "If I were pleasing myself, that is indeed what I'd do tomorrow. But I have agreed to give Ivy a few days to make up her mind about things."

Serena's brows drew together. "What is there to decide upon? She is compromised. You must marry."

He could not help but say, "Just a moment ago you were vowing to save her from a loveless marriage."

"But that was before I realized whom I was speaking of," Serena said with a wave of her hand.

"What is that supposed to mean?" Quill asked, not quite sure he wished to hear her response.

"Come, Quill," she said with a roll of her eyes. "When have you ever done anything that you didn't wish to do? Ever? I certainly cannot think of anything."

"You make me sound like a very selfish fellow," he said stiffly.

"No," she said, "quite the opposite, in fact. You are generous to a fault because it pleases you to please others. But you are hardly someone who does things out of only propriety. If not following the rules will make someone unhappy, then you will follow them. But if no one would be the wiser, you do what you want."

"And?"

"And, no one but you and Ivy knew about your afternoon together, yet you sought me out to tell me you intended to marry her," Serena said with a triumphant grin. "A man who did not wish to marry Ivy would have kept his mouth shut and prayed no one ever found out."

Which was likely true. He would not ruin his cousin's impression of his romantic nature by telling her that he'd chosen to tell her because he might need an ally should Ivy prove recalcitrant when it came to accepting his proposal. And that far from asking for Ivy's hand out of affection, though he did feel fond of her, it was the fact that she might be carrying his child that made him reveal their tryst to his cousin. Because he would not allow his child to be born out of wedlock.

Keeping his own counsel on the matter, he said instead, "You seem to know me better than I know myself, cousin."

"Of course I do," she said, beaming. "Now, I will say that I think it is a mistake to give Ivy too much time to think this over. But you must make up your mind I suppose."

"I thank you for your permission," Quill said. "Most kind."

"If that is all," Serena said with a speaking look, "I need to finish going over the accounts with Mrs. Bacon."

Knowing when he'd been dismissed, Quill took his leave of her and went in search of Aunt Celeste's brandy bottle.

Chapter 17

Ivy awoke some hours later and for a split second had no idea where she was, what time it was, or why she felt so oddly sore.

Closing her eyes again, the events of earlier in the day came rushing back in a flood of memory and awareness and for a breath she could feel Quill's weight pressing down upon her again, could smell his sandalwood and clean male scent.

This would not do at all.

She'd never been one to wallow in her emotions, and one morning's passion was hardly reason to begin now. Yes, Quill was a handsome man, and he had been all that she could have wished for in a lover. Of course she had no one to compare him to, but she had found their encounter pleasurable enough. Certainly she understood now why so many of the women in the reformatory she worked with back in Oxford fell prey to such desires. It had been a heady feeling indeed to share that nearness, that vulnerability with him.

But thankfully, Quill had agreed to give her time to decide if it warranted a betrothal. She was well aware that a man so accustomed to having his own way in everything did not generally have the inclination to grant such a demand. That Quill had done so spoke to the inherent fairness in his nature. A sign, no doubt, that he would perhaps make for an agreeable husband.

Still, she was not going to spend every waking moment between now and two days from now thinking only of what she should do.

She'd learned long ago that the mind had a way of working things out while one did other things. And the "other thing" that was most important at the moment was discovering who had so callously murdered Lady Celeste. A woman who, as far as Ivy could tell, had never harmed anyone in her life and should be alive and well to share the finer points of her impressive collection of books and artifacts with the four young women she had chosen to share them with.

Tossing back the covers, she reached for the bell pull to summon Polly and was soon dressed for dinner.

"There, miss," said Polly, putting the finishing touches on Ivy's upswept hair. "The gentlemen won't know what hit them."

Staring at her reflection in the glass of the dressing table, Ivy had to admit that she was looking well. She would miss Polly's skill with a hairpin when she returned to Oxford. *If* she returned to Oxford, she amended, trying to accustom herself to the notion with some difficulty. Which surprised her given her eagerness to escape the little house where she'd shared a single maid with five sisters. Perhaps Pope was right and familiarity did breed contempt.

Then, Polly's words filtered through.

"Gentlemen?" she asked, turning to face the maid. "Has someone else arrived besides Lord Kerr?"

And to her surprise Polly blushed. "Oh, yes, miss. Lady Serena's brother, the Duke of Maitland, arrived in his high perch phaeton while you were sleeping."

"His grace is handsome, then?" Ivy asked with a teasing smile. It was amusing to see the serious maid all atwitter. Clearly, Ivy thought wryly, Polly was impressed with the duke.

"It is impertinent for me to say so, miss," Polly said with a grin, "but, yes. Quite handsome. And dashing."

"And dashing," Ivy repeated. She supposed high perch phaetons were rare in this part of the country, but clearly the Duke of Maitland was something out of the ordinary to make Polly grin like a lunatic.

"Then I suppose I'd best make my way downstairs to see this paragon for myself," she said rising. She wished suddenly she'd been able to bring a better evening gown with her. She knew the deep green silk was striking with her hair and eyes, but it was hardly as fine as anything Daphne or the Hastings sisters had. When she packed her things to travel to the south coast, she'd assumed she would spend most evenings with her fellow scholars. If she'd known she would be rubbing shoulders with dukes and marquesses, she'd have been more careful about what she brought.

As a general rule she wasn't overly concerned with fashion, but she had no wish to look a dowd either.

Quill hadn't seemed to notice, and if he did mind, he'd simply have to come to terms with it, she thought grimly. She might wish for finery on occasion, but in this instance he would have to take her as she was. Outmoded gown and all.

"You're as fine as five pence, miss," Polly said to her as she opened the door into the hall for Ivy. "The duke won't be able to look away," she said in a conspiratorial tone.

But Ivy was more concerned with the gaze of a certain marquess.

When she reached the first landing, where a tall clock ticked away the minutes, she realized she was a few minutes early. On impulse, when she reached the first landing she kept going to the ground floor and made her way into the servants' hall.

If Dr. Vance's assertion that Lady Celeste's maid had brewed herbal tisanes for her mistress was correct, then the cook must have seen her doing so.

As soon as she stepped into the kitchen, however, she realized that it was not the best time to question the cook or any of the upper servants who would be involved in serving dinner. The room was a beehive of activity, but as soon as Mrs. Mason saw her, she set down the heavy tureen she carried and bowed.

"Miss Wareham," she said with a curtsy. And everyone else, from kitchen maid to Greaves, the butler, bowed or curtsied.

"Is there something you need, miss?" Greaves asked with formality.

"I am sorry," Ivy said with a shake of her head. "I've come at a bad time. I'll return later when you aren't so busy. Though I must say, this smells so delicious I look forward to sampling it at dinner."

Turning, she saw Mrs. Bacon standing behind her. Before the lady could curtsy, Ivy stepped forward and said, "Mrs. Bacon, will you walk with me a little?"

Not betraying a hint of surprise or question, the housekeeper nodded and walked beside Ivy toward the terminus of the servant's hall in the front entrance of the house.

"I was hoping you might be able to tell me where Lady Celeste's personal maid went after her ladyship died," Ivy said without preamble. She did not elaborate on why she might want such information, but Mrs. Bacon didn't seem to think it an odd question. Or if she did she did not say so.

"Elsie was able to secure a place as maid to Squire Northman's wife, miss," said Mrs. Bacon. "Mrs. Northman is a bit of a social climber, if you don't mind my saying so, miss. And I suspect she was quite pleased with herself to steal away Elsie from Beauchamp House. Even if there was no longer a lady here for Elsie to serve once poor Lady Celeste died. Lady Serena brought her own maid, you see and there was no call for Elsie anymore. So it was a good move for her. A step down, if you ask me. Her family is from around here, though, so she was pleased to keep a situation in the same neighborhood."

It was far more than Ivy had expected from the taciturn housekeeper. And learning that Elsie was nearby was good news, indeed, since she wished to ask her about the tisanes the maid had brewed for her mistress. There were few people who controlled what a lady consumed on a daily basis more influential than a maid. From her morning chocolate to her hot milk before bed, a maid brought everything but meals served at table to a lady. It would be difficult to poison meals as a maid because a maid had no reason to go near the meals. But things served in the bedchamber were another story.

"Thank you so much, Mrs. Bacon. You have been most helpful. I had heard that Elsie was quite enterprising when it came to concocting medicinal tisanes for Lady Celeste's headaches. I was hoping to get the recipe."

At that the housekeeper sniffed. "I'm not sure she'll deign to give it to you, miss," she said tartly. "She was quite secretive about those tisanes of hers was Elsie. Wouldn't give the recipe to any of us, that's for certain."

Interesting, Ivy thought. Now she was even more eager to speak to Elsie.

Before she could take her leave of the housekeeper, Mrs. Bacon said with some diffidence, "I heard about what happened in the village yesterday, Miss Wareham."

For one brief moment, Ivy thought she was speaking of the interlude in the cottage and felt a jolt of real fear run down her spine. But Mrs. Bacon's next words made her sag with relief. "Yes, his lordship told one of the grooms about the runaway cart on the road back from Little Seaford. I am glad neither of you was hurt, Miss. I don't know what this world is coming to with such reckless drivers on the roads at all hours."

Touched by the normally starchy woman's genuine concern, Ivy thanked her.

Just then, they reached the front hall. Bidding the housekeeper good evening, Ivy headed back upstairs toward the drawing room where the household gathered before dinner. She was almost to the doorway, and deep in thought, when she collided with a hard male chest.

"Oh, I do apologize," she said as the gentleman reached out to grasp her by the shoulders. Looking up, and then up again, into a pair of twinkling gray eyes, she surmised that this must be the Duke of Maitland who had set Polly's heart aflutter.

"The fault is all mine, my dear girl," said the duke with a sweeping bow. "I am forever tripping over these feet of mine. They're quite large as you can see, and if they didn't get me from one place to another I'd get rid of them all together."

"That would be quite inconvenient, I would imagine," Ivy said wryly in response to this absurdity.

"I daresay you are right," he said easily as he walked beside her into the drawing room where the rest of the house was already gathered.

Before Ivy could step over to where the other bluestockings were chatting, the man beside her addressed Lady Serena who was in conversation with Quill.

"Serena, you must introduce me to this beautiful creature at once," the duke said to his sister. "For I nearly knocked her down just now and a proper apology demands a proper name, doesn't it?"

Ivy was quick to note Quill's scowl at the other man, and the way he looked from Ivy to the duke and back again.

Lady Serena, however, seemed accustomed to her brother's odd manners, and as Ivy and the duke stepped closer to them she said, "Dalton, I vow you are the clumsiest man I've ever met. And that includes Father who fell off his own horse I don't know how many times."

The duke shrugged, as if to ask what one could do.

"This creature, as you so suavely call her," Lady Serena continued, "is Miss Ivy Wareham, one of the four lady scholars Aunt invited to Beauchamp House upon her death."

If looks could kill, the one Quill was leveling at the Duke of Maitland would have felled the fellow in a second.

"Ivy," the duke sighed. "What a prosaic name for such a lovely lady," he said as he bowed over her hand.

"Her actual name is Aphrodite," said Lady Daphne who had wandered over along with the other ladies as if the duke were a flame and they the moths. "Which is much more fitting if you ask me."

Before Ivy could respond, however, she watched as the duke got his first glimpse of Daphne. If his response to her had been that of a puppy eager for a treat, the look he gave the willowy blonde was as full of heat as anything she'd ever seen before. And if she didn't miss her guess, Daphne was not exactly giving him the cold shoulder.

Rolling her eyes, Serena made the introductions of the three ladies, and though the duke was polite to all of them, there was a little something more in his bow over Daphne's hand. As if he were making an offering to the goddess she was named for.

Ivy, on the other hand, was not as impressed with him as Daphne seemed to be. He was handsome, she supposed. If one were attracted to blond giants with aquiline features. She found she much preferred a certain marquess with blue eyes that could burn cold or hot as his mood changed, with a tendency toward seriousness. A humorous man like the duke would wear on her nerves after a bit, she suspected.

Just then the dinner bell rang and Quill took her arm, despite the fact that the order of precedence indicated he should be taking in Lady Serena—Daphne, of course, was on the arm of the duke.

"It's a good thing he fixed his eye on Daphne," Quill said in an undertone, "else I'd have been forced to call out my own cousin."

The rumble of his voice was enough to raise the hairs on the back of Ivy's neck in response. "I'm not so sure Daphne is such a good idea, either," she answered as he reached for her chair.

"I don't really care just now," Quill said ruthlessly. "So long he keeps his paws off you."

The look he gave was one that sent a thrill through her, and Ivy was forced to steel herself against the magnetic pull he exerted on her.

This was certainly not the sort of thing her mother would approve of for the dining table. Or at all. Ever.

Before she could reprimand the marquess however, he was taking his own seat beside her and chatting amiably with Serena on his left.

Chapter 18

Quill bit back a sigh as yet another peal of laughter rang out at some quip from his cousin. He was fond of Maitland—indeed counted the duke as one of his best friends in the world—but his easy way with the ladies was something he'd always envied. And while he waited for Ivy to make up her mind about his proposal, he was hardly eager to have Maitland, with his good looks and charm, lure her away. Though Ivy was showing no signs of attraction for the other man now, he hadn't known her long enough to assess whether she could be persuaded if Maitland got it in his head to woo her.

He'd simply have to warn his cousin away after dinner. That was all there was to it.

"Stop scowling," Serena said from his other side in a low voice only he could hear. "You look like you're going to leap across the table and strangle him. And while I sympathize with your fondness for Miss Wareham, I hardly think he will seduce her in front of a room full of people. Not to mention the fact that Ivy does not strike me as the sort of lady to give herself to one man in the morning and another in the evening."

Serena's words made Quill feel like an ass. It hadn't occurred to him how unfair to Ivy his jealousy was until she
put it that way.

Taking a healthy drink of wine, he turned to her with a
rueful smile. "I suppose I am being a boor, but I was hoping
for a swift decision from her. And didn't count on Maitland and his charms to distract her." Before she could
speak again, he raised a hand to ward off her scold. "I
know it's asinine. Believe me, you can't chastise me more
than I do myself."

Serena's gaze softened a little. "Have faith, Quill. If the
way he and Lady Daphne are looking at each other is any
indication, you have nothing to worry about. And aside
from that, Ivy keeps looking at you when you aren't watching her. I don't think you have anything to worry about
from my brother."

Frowning, Quill turned and caught Ivy watching him.
As their eyes met, her cheeks colored and she turned her
gaze back to her plate.

The reminder of what lay between them was enough to
dispel any doubts he had, and Quill vowed to do as Serena asked and have more faith. Having grown up with a
mother who often flouted her own lovers before his father's
eyes, however, it was difficult to acknowledge that not all
women were like that.

"Is the fish to your liking?" he asked, wishing for an
iota of whatever it was that made Maitland so easy at conversation. "I must admit Mrs. Mason's Trout Almondine
is one of my favorites."

"It's quite good," Ivy agreed, then proceeded to take another bite. "I was looking forward to it as soon as I smelled
it downstairs."

At that he frowned. "Why were you downstairs?"

"I went to ask about Lady Celeste's maid," Ivy said in
a confidential tone. "Because of the tisanes."

He supposed he shouldn't be surprised that she was back to looking for his aunt's murderer, Quill thought wryly. Here he'd been mooning away over her like a lovestruck schoolboy, and Ivy was thinking of solving a murder.

"And what did you learn?" he asked, intrigued despite his pique. "Anything of use?"

"Apparently she was quite secretive about what she put in them," Ivy said, pausing as the footman removed her plate. When they were back out of earshot, she continued, "And Mrs. Bacon said that she took a position with Mrs. Northman, Squire Northman's wife. Do you know them?"

At the mention of Mrs. Northman, Quill felt a pang of panic. Not only did he know Squire and Mrs. Northman, several years ago when he'd been young and foolish he'd engaged in an illicit liaison with the bored wife of the local landowner.

Aloud, however, Quill did not betray that he was more than distantly acquainted with the Northmans. "I believe I have met them when they were here to dine a few times."

The mention of his former lover so soon after his own unwarranted jealousy of his cousin could not be a coincidence. At least, not insofar as the Almighty was concerned. And Ivy's next words only confirmed it. "I believe I will pay a call on Mrs. Northman tomorrow," she said firmly. "I will ask about the tisanes and see if she will allow me to speak with Elsie. Surely there can be nothing objectionable about that."

Quill could think of a dozen things to object to in the notion of Ivy paying a call at the home of a man whom he'd cuckolded, but he could hardly say so aloud.

He was saved from reply by Serena however, and almost laughed aloud at her words.

"Are you speaking of the Northmans? For I received an invitation this afternoon asking all of us to dine in their home tomorrow evening. Mrs. Northman accounts herself to be a leader of local society—though to be honest, I think she will give herself more airs now that our aunt is no longer here to outrank her."

"You and I outrank this lady," said Daphne bluntly as the whole table turned their attention to Serena. "So, she has no reason for smugness, I think."

Despite his dyspepsia at the idea of sitting at the Northman dinner table, Quill couldn't help but grin at Maitland's wide-eyed astonishment at Lady Daphne's words. That young lady's plain speaking took a bit of getting used to, even if she was beautiful in her way. He himself was partial to redheads, but he could see that Daphne's willowy blonde looks were handsome enough.

Still, if Maitland meant to fix the attentions of someone like Lady Daphne, the sooner he became accustomed to her blunt talk the better. Otherwise he would live in a perpetual state of open-mouthed shock. Though come to think of it, paired with Maitland's own charm, Lady Daphne's talk might not seem so impolite.

"That is perhaps true, Daphne," said Serena with a speaking look, "but it is not the thing for you to say it aloud."

"But you are the one who mentioned that this Mrs. Northman puts on airs," Daphne protested with a frown. "I don't see what is so wrong about my own words. We do outrank her. Why is the truth so often the very thing it is impolite to say?"

Quill waited for Serena to explain, but she was forestalled by her brother who said gently, "Perhaps because the truth is so often that which hurts most, Lady Daphne."

Daphne frowned as if thinking over the suggestion. "I suppose that might be true," she said thoughtfully. "I certainly do not like being told I've made a mistake in an equation, no matter how true it might be. Is that what you mean?"

"Something like that," Maitland agreed with a nod. "Though in this case, I believe it's because to say you outrank someone is considered impolite."

Daphne sighed. "I will never understand what is and is not considered to be polite. Why can I not simply ask where Ivy and Quill sheltered from this storm this afternoon without being shushed by Sophia? And why is it impolite of me to point out that the mud on their boots was dry when they returned? It was the truth. And I fail to see how mud can be polite or impolite. Mud simply is."

A silence fell upon the table as the duke eyed Quill with a gleam of speculation in his eyes. So much for giving Ivy a couple of days to sort out her feelings on the matter, he thought while exchanging a chagrined look with her.

"It most certainly is," Maitland agreed with Daphne.

"Why don't we allow the gentlemen to their port, ladies?" Serena said, rising, though some of them hadn't yet finished dessert.

Wordlessly, the other ladies followed, and though Quill wished to reassure Ivy, he let her go with them.

Once they were out of the room, he moved to sit beside Maitland who was grinning like an idiot.

"Don't say anything," he warned the other man with a shake of his head. "For you of all people have no room to cast aspersions."

Picking up the port Greaves had just poured for him, the duke raised it in a toast. "To my dear cousin, who despite being the most disagreeable fellow imaginable still manages to charm the ladies."

"It's only one lady in particular I'm concerned with at the moment, Maitland," Quill said with a scowl. "And I'll thank you to stay away from her while you're here. I'm having enough difficulty convincing her to set aside her freedom and marry me without having to compete with your damned Viking charm."

But his cousin only laughed. "I wouldn't dream of it, old fellow. I'm just shocked to see you caught in the parson's mousetrap by dint of something as innocuous as a rainstorm. At the very least I hope you were able to kiss the chit during this tryst."

Quill's silence told what had happened in the little cottage more loudly than his words might have done.

Maitland whistled. "So, it's that way, is it? I'm surprised, I must admit. I always thought you were the more controlled of us two. I certainly never expected a pretty redhead to tempt you into giving up your freedom. Though she does possess the most spectacular pair of ti—"

His voice broke off as Quill's hand gripped him by the neck. "Mind yourself. That's my future wife you're speaking of."

When his cousin nodded, grin still intact, Quill removed his hand.

"My apologies," said Maitland with a huff of laughter as he straightened his cravat. "Won't happen again, I assure you. I was trying to assess your degree of affection for the girl. I think your grip on my throat speaks volumes."

"And I suppose you couldn't just ask like a normal person?" Quill groused. He didn't like losing control and he'd done so quite thoroughly twice already today. This was getting to become a habit.

"Where's the fun in that?" Maitland laughed, running a hand over top of his blond hair. "At the very least I know the truth now rather than the polite fiction I suspect you'd have given me if I asked. You like to play these things close to the vest."

"Because they're nobody's business but my own," Quill said heatedly. "You always were too damned nosy by half."

"Not nosy, cuz," said the duke. "Concerned. If I thought you'd been nabbed by a fortune hunter whom you held in contempt, then I'd see to it that she was paid well and sent on her way."

At the idea of Ivy as a fortune hunter, Quill laughed. Hard. She might be many things, but he rather thought that if she could be locked away in Aunt Celeste's library for the rest of her years, she would be happier than a young Maitland in the dancer filled green room of the Royal Opera House. If she could come to care one tenth as much for him as she did for one of her Greek fragments, he'd count himself a lucky man.

"I can see then," Maitland said with a grin, "that my fears are misplaced. You can't blame me though. These four chits with their bluestocking tendencies who were chosen by who knows what means by Aunt Celeste could all murder us in our beds tonight. From what Serena has told me, you know only what they've told you."

"And what the notes from Celeste's investigation revealed," Quill said firmly. "She was no fool, Aunt Celeste. Whatever her reasons for choosing these four, she made sure she wasn't bringing anyone likely to steal all her artifacts and burn the house down."

"Perhaps not, but I'll keep an eye out on them just the same," Maitland said with a grin. "The lovely Lady Daphne in particular."

"I'd watch myself if I were you," Quill said with a warning note. "Lady Daphne is lovely, but she could cut a man down with a word without a flinch."

"Oh, I certainly hope so," Maitland said wolfishly. "I like a challenge."

"So do I," Quill answered, "but I like my ballocks right where they are, thanks."

But his cousin waved away the warning. "You just mind yourself and your little redhead. Leave the sharp tongued Lady Daphne to me."

"With pleasure," Quill said raising his glass.

Chapter 19

"What a handsome man the duke is, don't you think?" Daphne asked the other ladies after they had retired to the drawing room.

Lady Serena had gone up to check on Jeremy before bed, though Ivy was quite sure Daphne would have said the same whether their chaperone was with them or not.

"You'd best watch yourself, Daphne," Gemma said with a hiss. "He's far too charming by half. I don't trust him one bit."

"What has trust to do with anything?" Daphne asked, puzzled. "I'm not looking to marry him, after all."

Despite herself, Ivy was once again shocked by the ease with which Daphne spoke about men. Now that she'd actually experienced what being with a man that way entailed, she couldn't imagine doing it with someone for whom she felt nothing. Though she didn't think she could call what she felt for Quill love, she certainly held him in some affection. And though her first instinct had been to ask for more time when he said they should marry, she was beginning to see that refusing to marry him might prove as difficult as marrying him would. And what if there *was* a child? She was just as unhappy at the thought of it being born out of wedlock as he was. No matter how she might believe in the institution itself, it was far more beneficial for men than it was for women.

"Don't fret, dear," said Sophia, putting a comforting arm around her shoulders. "It will work out. I promise."

"No thanks to Daphne," said Gemma with a frown at the blonde. "I thought we'd agreed not to divulge what we knew about happened with Ivy and Lord Kerr this morning."

Daphne frowned. "I don't see what the big secret is. I daresay the servants are all chattering about it as we speak."

"That's not the point," Sophia said with a sigh. "Now not only we know, but Lady Serena and her brother the duke know too."

But Ivy had a good idea that Lady Serena had known before Daphne's outburst, at least that was what she'd guessed on seeing the chaperone's lack of surprise at Daphne's words. She wondered if Quill had spoken to her or if she'd guessed on her own. It would be just like Quill to confess to her, she thought with a grimace. Despite his promise to give her time he would have felt the mark on his honor keenly. It was an insult to Lady Serena for him to have seduced Ivy, no matter how much Ivy might be loath to admit that's what it had been, and he would wish to unburden himself on her.

"And what has that to say in the matter?" Daphne asked.

"It means that Ivy will have to marry the marquess whether she wishes to or not." Sophia said.

"I don't see why," Daphne argued.

Ivy sighed. Sometimes conversing with Daphne was like beating one's head against a wall only to have the wall change direction and hit you on the back of the head instead.

"That's because they're either already married or they've

got no reputation to preserve to begin with," Gemma said patiently. "One indiscretion can spell ruin for someone like Ivy."

"Oh," Daphne looked genuinely troubled by the news. Just when Ivy was ready to dismiss her as completely devoid of fellow-feeling, the mathematician surprised her with a burst of compassion. "I am sorry, Ivy."

"I don't necessarily think that Daphne's pronouncement means that I shall be forced to marry the marquess," Ivy said trying to put the best face on things. "After all, his lordship and I can refute her claim. And it's not as if anyone found us in the cottage together."

She looked at Sophia and Gemma to gauge their reaction to her words, but the pained smiles that greeted her told more than outright denials would have.

"I'm sure any number of young ladies would be thrilled to receive an offer from the marquess," Sophia said brightly. "He's a feast for the eyes, make no mistake. Have you see the legs on that man? He does justice to a pair of breeches, doesn't he?"

"Indeed he does," said Gemma fanning herself at her sister's words. "And he's quite handsome in a dark, brooding way. I can quite see him as the hero of a gothic novel, all glowering scowls and feats of derring-do to rescue his lady."

Ivy sighed, and dropped onto the nearest settee. "You can stop trying to put the best face on it," she said glumly. "I quite agree that he is handsome. And that he is doubtlessly a prize on the marriage mart. It's just that I wasn't thinking to marry him myself."

Sophia poured her a cup of tea from the tray that one of the maids had brought in discreetly while they talked, and handed it to her, taking the seat beside her.

"I daresay there is a great deal of scholarly work you'd

thought to accomplish before doing anything as rash as marrying?" she asked quietly.

"Unless they are of a like mind, I've been told by another lady mathematician," Daphne offered as she settled into a nearby chair, "that husbands can be quite the impediment to scholarly pursuits."

"But that needn't be the case," Gemma offered kindly. "What of Madame d'Arblay? Her husband was quite pleased with her writing and was devoted until her death. Much more so than the lady's own father had been during her childhood." The famous novelist, known as Frances Burney to her readers had made a love match.

"That is quite true," Sophia agreed with a nod, her brown curls bobbing with her vehemence. "She did not write *Camilla* until after her marriage, and I quite enjoyed it. More than *Evelina* even. Though I still have a soft spot for Lord Ormond. So mysterious and handsome."

"Has Lord Kerr voiced any objections to your translation work?" Daphne asked, her pretty brow furrowed. "Because if he has not, then you do not know if he will do so at all. It makes little sense to bemoan something that has yet to occur, doesn't it?"

"That's the first sensible thing you've said this evening, Daphne," said Gemma with approval. "In fact, we do not know what his lordship's attitude will be toward your scholarly pursuits, Ivy. So perhaps you should put the question to him. It cannot hurt, can it?"

"Oh dear," said a deep voice as the door to the drawing room opened to reveal the Duke of Maitland and Lord Kerr. "It sounds as if they are plotting, Kerr," said the duke, raising his quizzing glass to survey each of the four ladies—lingering perhaps a shade longer on Daphne than was strictly necessary. "You must divulge all, ladies, lest you get yourselves into some scrape or other."

His pronouncement was met with four scowls from the ladies, causing his face to fall as quickly as his quizzing glass did, bouncing on its string at his side.

"What's amiss?" he asked quickly, looking to Ivy's skeptical eye like a puppy that has been chastised.

Quill exchanged an amused glance with Ivy before saying, "Perhaps that sort of thing might charm the ladies in London drawing rooms, cuz, but I think you may have insulted this lot, who were, as you well know, chosen by our aunt based upon their artistic and scholarly abilities. As such they are likely smarter than you and I put together on our best day with a fifty-yard head start."

At Quill's words, Sophia threw Ivy a speaking look. Perhaps they were right about his respect for her mind, she thought with tentative hope. At the very least he was not dismissive of her like some men were.

"I mean no offense, ladies," said the duke, eyes widened with realization. "Just being a great clumsy oaf as usual."

"I'm sure your teasing was innocent, your grace," Ivy said with a reassuring smile. "We can be a little . . ."

"Overly sensitive," Sophia finished for her as she moved to pour for the newcomers. "Force of habit really. And we've grown a bit too full of our own importance," she added with a glance at Daphne, who shrugged at her words.

"I took no offense, Duke," she said easily. "Though I do admit your words caught me by surprise. We were plotting you see . . . about—"

"Nothing at all," Gemma broke in, moving to grasp Daphne by the shoulder. "We must keep those details to ourselves, Daphne. Do you not remember?"

Ivy gave a sigh of relief, grateful that Gemma had broken

into Daphne's confession. She had no wish to have what should be a private conversation between only herself and Quill with the entire drawing room.

"Did you have good weather for your travels, your grace?" she asked hoping to change the subject.

And thankfully the duke took the hint and began to regale them with an amusing story about how his phaeton had nearly collided with a farm cart on the road near Bath. And before long Daphne and the duke lapsed into a good-natured argument on the odds this year for the Royal Ascot, and the Hastings sisters were deep in conversation about some news they'd had in a letter from home that day.

When Quill took the seat beside Ivy, she felt her heart beat faster, try as she might to calm the traitorous organ.

"If nothing else it has been an eventful day," he said quietly, so close that she could see the ring of dark blue circling the lighter blue of his iris and the light tips of gold on his brown lashes. Not to mention the warmth of his thigh innocently pressed against her own.

"If nothing else," she said a little breathlessly.

"I thought I should tell you," he continued, his gaze intent on hers, "that I spoke to Lady Serena about what happened between us today."

Ivy took a beat to decide how she felt about the news. On the one hand he'd agreed to give her a couple of days to make a decision about his offer. But on the other, as a man of honor he would not wish to keep her chaperone in the dark about what he saw as a transgression against propriety on his part.

"And what was her response?" Ivy asked carefully. "Since she did not rouse me from my afternoon sleep to cart us both to the nearest minister, I would hazard a guess that she is letting us make our own decision on the matter?"

He looked down at where her hands clasped together, her knuckles white with the effort to keep them calm. This was a man who looked closely at the world around him, she thought. Who looked before he leapt. That he had so forgot himself earlier in the day was either a sign of how much he'd wanted her, or an indication that like anyone else he could behave impulsively from time to time.

"She is convinced that the best course would be for us to marry by special license," he said with a slight shrug. "But she has agreed to let us do so at our own pace. I did tell her that you are free to decline my proposal of course."

"And did she agree to keep this news from my family?" she asked, not allowing her apprehension to enter her voice. "Until we are ready to tell them, that is?"

"As I said, she will let us go at our own pace," Quill repeated. Covering her clasped hands with his own, he spoke in a reassuring voice. "It need not be a hardship," he said softly. "We rub along well enough together, I think. And I certainly appreciate that clever mind of yours. Though I cannot claim to be much of a scholar myself."

"How many languages do you speak?" she asked, suddenly, desperately needing to know the answer. She wasn't sure why, but it was the sort of thing a lady like herself should know about the man who wished to marry her. At least, that's what she thought in this moment.

Rather than annoyance, she saw him break into a grin. "I'm not a scholar," he admitted with a shrug, "but languages were something I excelled in at both Eton and Oxford. You have to know some ancient Greek and Latin in order to even be admitted to Oxford, you know."

Ivy waved her hand in the air dismissively. "It's easily enough for a peer to use his influence to get past that requirement for his son."

"Ah," he said chidingly, "but you didn't know my father.

He was the least likely man ever to use his influence in such a cause."

She wanted to ask about his father, but decided that was a discussion that would keep for another day.

"So," she continued, "you have some Greek and Latin. And I daresay French, as well, yes?"

He nodded, and Ivy was aware of the fact that his gaze had dropped to her mouth. Really, it was most unfair of him to look at her like that in a room full of other people.

"And German," he said with the air of a boy trying to please a harsh schoolmaster. "And Spanish and some Portuguese."

At her questioning look, he shrugged. "I was in the diplomatic corps during the war. My father did use his influence there—but it was for his own reasons. Didn't want the heir to be placed in mortal danger, after all."

Surprised despite herself, Ivy felt her mouth gape for a second before she quickly snapped it shut.

"Do not look so surprised, my dear," he said with a grin. "I might be a useless aristocrat, but I'm not a complete simpleton. I can certainly carry on a concentration about which word is the best English translation for what I wish to do to your mouth just now."

"*Beso,*" she said in a whisper of Spanish.

"*Je voudrais vous embrasser profondément,*" he said in a tone so low she felt it in her bones.

"*Eu quero te beijar,*" she replied, the Portuguese words falling from her mouth before she knew what she was saying.

"Is there any tea left, or shall I ring for a new pot?" said Lady Serena in a cheerful tone as she stepped into the room.

Ivy nearly tripped in her haste to get to the tea tray—which she had little doubt had prompted the titter she heard from behind her.

"I'll do it," she said reaching for the bell pull. "I hope Jeremy was able to get to sleep peacefully?"

Though the look Serena gave her was searching, she answered easily enough. "Yes, thank goodness. He dislikes going to sleep when he knows there is amusement to be had with the adults downstairs. But I was able to bribe him with a visit to the shore tomorrow with his uncle. I hope you don't mind, Maitland."

"Not a bit," said the duke with a grin from where he stood before the fire. "Nothing I like more than a shell-seeking adventure with Jem. Will you come with us, Kerr? It seems to me we lads should stick together since we're outnumbered by ladies in this house."

Stretching out his long legs before him, Quill nodded. "Indeed. If the weather is fine."

"I hope it will be," Serena said with a worried frown. "Because I do not know what Jeremy's response will be if he is thwarted."

The way she spoke, Ivy would have assumed that Jeremy was the parent rather than the child. But she knew that Lady Serena was merely trying to make the boy happy. There was a hint of sadness in his eyes that told of some darker days when he was not such a big boy.

"I'm not afraid of his reaction," Maitland assured her. "Quill and I were boys once too, you know. And if we can't get to the shore we'll figure something out. At the very least the soldiers I've brought will prove a distraction."

"You will spoil him, Dalton," Lady Serena said with a smile as she lapsed into using his Christian name. "I vow he will be as tyrannical as you were as a boy before the summer is out."

"That's what happens when a boy knows he's a duke before he's out of short coats, Serena," Quill said with a wink at Ivy.

Sure enough, the duke gave a sound of mock outrage.

"And I suppose you wish these fine ladies to believe you were a little angel? I could tell tales about the Marquess of Kerr's childhood crimes that would fair make your hair curl, ladies."

And he proceeded to regale them with amusing stories about the cousins' childhood together.

Before long, however, Lady Serena declared it was past time they were all in their beds. And as they filed into the hall and toward the stairs, Ivy found herself walking beside Quill.

When they reached the landing, where the ladies would go left and the gentlemen right, he said in a low voice, "Sweet dreams, Aphrodite."

And wishing despite her misgivings that he could come with her to her bedchamber, she followed the other ladies down the hall into the darkness.

Chapter 20

Though Squire Northman's manor house was not even a mile away as the crow flew, the party at Beauchamp House piled into two carriages for the drive over. One carriage conveyed the Hastings sisters, Lady Daphne, and the Duke of Maitland, while the other carried Ivy, Quill, and Lady Serena.

It did not go unnoticed by Quill that his cousin kept an eagle eye on both her fellow passengers for the duration of the journey. She'd attempted to place the four unmarried ladies in one carriage together, but Quill had insisted that he and Ivy be allowed to ride together. Since the three other ladies in the carriage with Maitland served as their own chaperones, Serena had relented to Quill's demand but then spoiled things by insisting on taking her place with them.

What she expected them to get up to in a closed carriage with her watching was beyond him. He was able, when Serena managed to glance out the window at the passing scenery from time to time, to steal several glimpses of Ivy in the deep red silk she'd chosen for the evening. It was a color that might have looked a horror with her auburn hair, but instead it showed to perfection against her peaches-and-cream skin. He would bet anything that the modest jet beads she wore were warm from her skin, and he spent a good portion of the drive pleasantly imagining what she'd look like in nothing but those beads.

"Ah, that didn't take too long, did it?" Serena asked with a cheerfulness that belied the death stare she gave Quill as the carriage rocked to a stop. Clearly he'd not been as careful at concealing his thoughts as he'd hoped.

Ivy on the other hand, seemed oblivious to them both, staring with interest out the window at the torch-lit entrance to the Northman's sandstone manor house.

Far from feeling easy about the evening to come, Quill jumped down from the carriage before the footman could open the door, and set down the step. Handing first Ivy then Serena down, he squared his shoulders and prepared to make polite conversation with his former lover in the company of his almost betrothed.

While Jem had played happily at the water's edge that morning, Quill had discussed with Maitland the possible complications tonight's supper might cause him when it came to winning Ivy over to his way of thinking when it came to marriage.

"If given a choice," Maitland had said from his seat in the sand beside his cousin, both of them barefoot despite the chill in the air, "I'd make some excuse to keep from walking into that chamber of horrors. But you have no choice. It's the damnedest thing. I don't know how you get yourself into these coils."

Quill had already explained the necessity for he and Ivy to speak with the maid, Elsie, who now worked for Mrs. Northman. The fact that his cousin had come as soon as Quill had sent for him was just one of the things he appreciated about Dalton. He might be the proverbial bull in a china shop at times, but he was a good man. And he'd loved Aunt Celeste as much as Quill had. Like Quill, Dalton and Serena hadn't had the happiest of childhoods, so they too had sought refuge in the home of their favorite aunt whenever it was possible.

But just now, he was of little help at all.

"It's not as if my younger self could guess that one day I'd have to face Cassandra across the table from Ivy," Quill said, thrusting a hand through his already windblown hair. "If I'd had that sort of prescience, I'd have left Cassandra alone in the first place."

"She is a sweet handful, though," Maitland conceded with a shrug. "I wouldn't have turned her down if she'd cast out lures to me, that's for sure."

Quill sighed. "If only I knew that she would behave herself," he said. "It's not knowing that troubles me. I know she won't be so bold that Northman will figure it out. She has no wish to give herself trouble. But if she suspects anything between Ivy and me, she might drop a word in her ear just to make things difficult for me."

"It would all be much better if you'd not ended things badly," Maitland said.

"Thank you, Duke," Quill said dryly. "That never would have occurred to me."

"Don't take out your anger on me, man," his cousin protested. "I'm just here to offer my support."

Now, some hours later at the Northman manor house, Quill couldn't miss the wink his cousin directed at him as the guests were ushered into the main entry hall.

"I am so pleased you were all able to come," said Cassandra Northman from beside her thin, taciturn husband, who nodded at the newcomers but said little. "And you too, your grace. When Lady Serena wrote to ask if you would be welcome too, I wrote her back at once. A duke at one's table must never be turned away."

To Quill's relief, Cassandra said nothing untoward as he moved through the receiving line, and soon he and the other dinner guests were milling about in a drawing room that was gilded within an inch of its life, waiting for the dinner bell.

He made pleasant conversation with the local curate, who was keen to know what news there was from London, and the wife of the local magistrate, who wanted to know if he would be around in the summer for the annual fete.

Soon enough they were all shuffling into the dining room, Quill with Lady Daphne on his arm since she was the next in precedence following Lady Serena, who was on her brother's arm.

Quill was not pleased to learn he was seated at Cassandra's left with Maitland on her right. But at least Ivy was out of earshot in the middle of the table, with the curate on one side and the son of a local gentry family on the other.

"You must tell me every little thing about the latest on-dits in London, my lord," said Cassandra as soon as they were seated, punctuating her words with a rap of her fan on his arm. "It's been far too long since I was there for the season, and I'm simply dying for news."

"You might do better to ask my cousin Maitland," Quill said with a nod in that gentleman's direction, earning him a reproachful look. "He is more lately from London than I am and I daresay his news is fresher."

"But is *he* fresher?" Cassandra said with a mischievous grin. "That is the question." Turning to the duke, she gave him a speculative look, as if weighing the possibilities. At this point, Quill didn't have any regrets about throwing his cousin beneath the wheels of the metaphorical carriage. He could not afford for Ivy to find any reason to reject his suit. Even if that meant Maitland had to take a sabre cut for the whole regiment.

To his relief, his cousin seemed happy enough to flirt with their pretty hostess, and he watched with amusement as they batted the conversational ball back and forth over the various courses. By the time Mrs. Northman rose to indicate that the ladies would leave the gentlemen to their port, Quill was feeling quite happy with the evening so far.

That sanguinity lasted until the men filed into the drawing room and a quick scan of the room showed that both Ivy and Cassandra were conspicuously absent.

"Where the devil are they?" he asked Maitland in an undertone.

"Hmm?" was his unhelpful monosyllable as he fixed his gaze on the spot near the tea tray where Lady Daphne appeared to be explaining the finer points of the Pythagorean theorem to a befuddled-looking local matron. A jab in the ribs was enough to break into Maitland's reverie however. "Hey! What was that for?"

"Use your brainbox for a moment and listen," Quill hissed. "Where are Ivy and Cassandra?"

But Maitland shrugged. "I was in the dining room with you. How should I know? Why don't you ask Serena? She appears to be attempting to get your attention." And sure enough, Lady Serena was leveling a speaking glance in their direction.

Hurrying to her side, Quill tried to look casual as he asked, "What's amiss, cuz?"

"I'm not quite sure," Serena said beneath the hum of conversation. "Ivy and Mrs. Northman left the room not long after we left you all in the dining room. I hope our hostess hasn't figured out there's something between the two of you."

"What do you mean?" Quill asked, despite the fact that he agreed with her. "What has Mrs. Northman to say to it?"

"Well," Serena said tartly, "there is that fact that she was your lover some years ago."

Despite himself, Quill gasped. "How did you know?" he asked in a low voice.

Serena rolled her eyes. "You were one and twenty and as full of your own importance as any young man I've ever known—with the notable exception of my brother. I would be very surprised if everyone in the next county didn't hear of your conquest."

Wincing, Quill recalled that her assessment of him at that time was painfully accurate. "So you think it has something to do with Cassandra wishing to scupper things between Ivy and me?"

"I cannot know," Serena said with a slight lift of her shoulders. "They didn't seem to be at daggers drawn if that helps."

It did. A very little.

"I'm going to intervene," he said firmly. "Ivy is stubborn enough without Cassandra giving her more reasons to reject my proposal."

But it was Serena's turn to gasp. "You cannot simply go blundering around the house looking for them. It's possible there is an innocent explanation for their absence."

"If that is the case," he said grimly, "then they will have no reason to be surprised at my intrusion."

Serena's expression told him they would have every reason, but Quill couldn't afford to let her scruples keep him from the truth.

As unobtrusively as possible, he slipped out of the drawing room and into the hallway. Spying a footman standing at the ready, he strode over to the man. "Do you know where I might find your mistress and Miss Wareham?" And to his shame the man didn't look surprised at all. Instead, he laid a finger alongside his nose and winked.

Good god, he thought in spite of his anxiety. *How many lovers had Cassandra had assignations with under her own husband's nose?*

Still he followed the directions the man gave him and

hurried up the stairs to the hall leading to Cassandra's bed-chamber. When he reached the door, he heard the sound of conversation within and, taking a deep breath, he gave a brisk knock and strode inside, as if he had every reason in the world to enter his hostess's bedchamber without invitation.

Instead of Ivy and Cassandra deep in conversation about *him,* however, he found Ivy with a woman he recognized as Elsie, his aunt's former personal maid.

He closed his eyes at his folly.

Of course that was why she'd come up here. His own damnable guilty conscience had made him suspect the worst, when it was all part of the plan he and Ivy had put into place before they even left Beauchamp House earlier in the evening.

"My lord?" she asked, her eyes wide as he walked over to where she and the maid were standing beside Cassandra's writing desk. "What are you doing here?"

"I thought you might be ill," he said with a slight shrug. "I noticed you were gone from the drawing room."

Her raised brow told him what she thought about this explanation. But she clearly thought they should discuss his perfidy once they were alone, because she only said, "Well, as you can see, I am quite well. . . . Go ahead and tell him what you told me, Elsie," she said with a reassuring nod.

Looking from one to the other, Elsie seemed to relax a little. "Begging your pardon, my lord, but I was just telling Miss Wareham here that the recipe for the tisane that Lady Celeste liked for the headache, it wasn't my own." The maid looked sheepish, and even colored a little at the admission. "My mam was friendly-like with the Rom hereabouts. And she was the one who suggested I go to the old woman there. She gave Mam a tonic that was helpful with me gran's rheumatism. So when her ladyship was struck down with the headache, I went over to where the camps was and I asked the old woman."

"But Elsie didn't mix the powder herself," Ivy said with a speaking look. "She got the powder from the gypsies and added water to it."

Which, Quill realized, meant that the poison was likely added before Elsie even had the powder in hand. This was a significant breakthrough, and he saw the truth of it in Ivy's eyes.

"You've been most helpful, Elsie," Ivy said to the maid, squeezing the girl's hand. "I cannot thank you enough. And remember, please don't speak to anyone about what I've asked you."

The girl nodded. "I never thought it was right the way Lady Celeste died. But if I'd known it was the tisanes, I never would have given them to her." Tears filled her eyes. "I was only trying to make her feel better. Not kill her."

"You could have had no notion that the curative was poisoned, Elsie," Quill assured her. "I saw your years of loyal service to my aunt, and am sure you meant her no harm."

She nodded miserably, then in a soft voice as if reluctant to continue, she said, "I hate to mention it, but if there was any way you could keep from telling Mrs. Northman about my dealings with the encampment? It's just that Mr. Northman doesn't hold with the Rom. 'Specially not since they been known to steal 'is sheep from time to time."

"He won't hear about it from us," Ivy said with a warm smile. "Will he, my lord?"

"Certainly not," he agreed.

Then, the conversation over, there was nothing to do but to step back out into the hallway and brace himself for a scold.

Which was not long in coming.

Ivy's eyes flashed with exasperation as, once they were out of earshot of Elsie and safely ensconced in an alcove near the second-floor landing, she turned on him. "What on earth were you thinking? You might have ruined everything!"

Chapter 21

"You are the most exasperating man," Ivy continued without allowing Quill to speak. "Elsie might very well have refused to tell us anything because of your intrusion. You do realize that, do you not?"

She had been pleasantly surprised when Mrs. Northman proved so amenable to allowing her a few minutes with Elsie on the pretext of asking for the tisane recipe. It hadn't been expected. Especially not when she saw how the other lady's gaze lingered on Quill at dinner. But not one to look a gift horse in the mouth, she'd followed her hostess upstairs and entered her bedchamber eagerly, and had been rewarded with Elsie's confession about the gypsies. If Quill's arrival had ruined that in any way, she would have been hard pressed to keep from boxing his ears.

To his credit, however, he did seem to realize the gravity of what he'd done. "I walked into the drawing room and found that both you and Mrs. Northman were nowhere to be found," he admitted, rubbing a hand over the nape of his neck. "I was concerned."

"Because you thought she'd taken me away to regale me with tales of your affair?" Ivy asked with raised brows. She'd guessed at their former relationship almost as soon as they entered the house. There was something predatory about the way the older woman watched him, and she had little trouble adding up the clues.

"It was a long time ago," Quill said, his cheeks hot with color. "Years before I even knew of your existence."

His sheepishness went a long way toward assuaging her anger. She had been racked with jealousy when she first noticed Mrs. Northman's proprietary hand on his arm. But it hadn't taken a few minutes before she recognized Quill's own discomfort with the other woman's overtures. Which had gone a long way toward making Ivy feel better about the matter.

Of course, there was still the fact that she'd had to guess at the thing rather than hear it from his own lips.

"I should have told you," he said quietly, as if reading her mind. "I didn't want to give you a disgust of me so soon into our relationship," he admitted. "Especially since you were still thinking over my proposal. And the fact that she is now Elsie's employer, and we needed her permission to question the girl, well, I thought it best to keep my own counsel."

Stepping closer, he crowded her into the little alcove until Ivy felt the wall at her back. "You forgive me, don't you?" he asked, before kissing her gently on the mouth.

It was difficult to stay angry when he was so sweetly apologetic.

Drat the man.

"I'm still thinking it over," she said with a dignified sniff. Which earned her a kiss in the soft spot beneath her left ear. A kiss that made her toes curl and caused a throb of longing deep within her.

"I'll just have to make it up to you," he said before taking her mouth again, this time all sweetness gone as he slipped his tongue inside and caressed her in a stroke of hot need. Ivy slid her arms up over his shoulders and clasped him to her, her fingers threaded through the silken hair of his nape.

If there were ever a means of building heaven on earth, she had little doubt that it would be constructed from kisses and sighs and aches the likes of which she'd never imagined were even possible between a man and a woman. The vibration of her groan as he slid his hands up to cover her breasts where they ached within the prison of her stays felt loud to her own ears. But she was too far gone to care. Especially when Quill—clever Quill—tugged down the bodice of her crimson gown and bared her nipple to the cool air. And when his hot mouth closed around it, she would have cried out with the joy of it if he hadn't placed a hand over her mouth to quiet her.

"Well, isn't this interesting."

The sound of an amused voice behind them made Ivy and Quill still at once. Ivy opened her eyes to see Quill's mouth tight with annoyance, his expression grim. Was he angry at getting caught, or at getting caught by Mrs. Northman, she wondered, her heart still pounding with un-slaked lust.

He braced himself on the wall behind her and took several deep breaths as he stared down at the floor. She wanted to push him off of her, but a glance down indicated his own excitement at their passion was plainly evident in his evening breeches.

At least she didn't have to deal with *that,* she thought wryly. How uncomfortable it must be to be a man sometimes.

Still, their interruption was still there. Which she made plain with another conversational sally. "I did wonder if there might be something between you and one of the young ladies, Quill," said the Squire's wife. "But my money was on Lady Daphne. She seems more like your type. I certainly would never have guessed this one would pique your interest. What with her carroty hair and, shall we say, *buxom* figure? I do dislike to call a spade a spade, but really my dear, if you do not push away from the table you'll be as fat as Prinny."

Ivy shoved Quill's chest so that she could get a closer look at her accuser, but he turned and spoke before she could draw breath. "Jealousy doesn't become you, Cassandra," he said coldly. "And I will thank you to keep your opinions about my betrothed to yourself. They are, like the rest of you, unwanted."

The other woman's eyes widened as his words hit their mark. But she fired back easily enough. "Not entirely unwanted," she said with a cat-in-the-cream-pot smile, "unless I miss my guess about your delightful cousin, Maitland. One can only hope all of him is built to proportion." She gave a shiver of anticipation that made Ivy's gorge rise.

"I can assure you, madam," the duke drawled as he prowled up behind her, "I would sooner bed a she-wolf than the likes of you. And I daresay the she-wolf would be more affectionate and less grasping." He surveyed her with his quizzing glass, then added, "I can assure you it is proportional, and I know how to use it. More's the pity for you."

Ivy would have laughed at Mrs. Northman's expression if the situation weren't so utterly mortifying. Not only had she been discovered in an embrace by Quill's former mistress, but now his cousin was there to see the whole contretemps. It was worse than the time her sister had callously revealed Ivy's crush on her father's prize pupil. A young man of twenty to her thirteen, and who had laughed heartily upon learning of it. At least there had been no fear of losing her reputation then. This incident had every possibility of making her a byword amongst the neighborhood as well as the *ton*.

"If you were hoping for my silence in this matter," their

hostess said in a hostile voice, "then you are sorely mistaken, Lord Kerr. It will take only one letter from me to my sister in London for the rumor of what I just saw to spread far and wide within the *ton*, not to mention what I will do to this slut's reputation here on the coast. There will be nowhere for her to go when I'm finished."

The vitriol in the matron's voice sent ice dancing down Ivy's spine. Quill, however, was having none of it. Stalking over to where Mrs. Northman stood with her hands fisted and her lip curled in anger, he bent so that his face was level with hers. "If I hear so much as a hint of scandal where Miss Wareham is concerned," he said in a silky tone that might have come from the devil himself, "then I will see to it that you are never admitted into another genteel entertainment again. Not a London drawing room. Not Almack's. Not the local assembly. Not the subscription ball in Bath. Not even the taproom at the Fox and Pheasant."

"It is never a good idea to anger my cousin, Mrs. Northman," Maitland said pleasantly from her other side. "He might not look it, but he can be quite as ruthless as one of them pagan gods in the classics Miss Wareham knows so much about. And I suppose I should mention, I'll lend my own social capital—my being a duke and all—to his campaign as well. Cousins, you see. We're loyal that way."

Without a backward glance at their hostess, Quill turned and offered his arm to Ivy. "Come, my dear. I find the company here quite beneath our notice. Much better to get back to Beauchamp House where the air is purer."

In a daze, Ivy allowed him to lead her away.

"What a coil," Quill said as they strode down the hall away from Mrs. Northman.

They'd only got as far as the first landing, with Maitland close behind, when just as they passed a large bronze statue of Pan displayed prominently on a faux

Greek column, a hidden door behind it opened abruptly, toppling both.

"Oh, I am sorry," Elsie gasped from where she stood in the doorway. "I didn't know—" Her eyes widened as she saw the fallen ornaments. "Why was that there?"

Quill, who had just missed bearing the brunt of the heavy piece, frowned. "Is it not usually kept here, Elsie?"

She shook her head. "No, my lord. It's kept just to the side." She pointed. "There. One of the housemaids must have moved it today to clean for the party tonight."

She turned to Ivy. "You weren't hurt, were you miss?"

"No, it missed me." Ivy shivered. She turned to the others. "Quill? Maitland?"

"Right as rain," Maitland said with a shake of his head. "It would take more than a chap in cloven hooves to damage this hard head."

Grateful for the duke's bit of levity, Ivy smiled. "You may go, Elsie. We'll tidy this up."

She watched the girl go, and waited as Quill and Maitland lifted the column and placed the statue back atop it.

"The carpet is depressed here where it's usually kept," Quill said as he stood up from where he'd moved to examine the floor. "Elsie was right."

"If you don't mind, I'd like to leave now," Ivy said, starting for the stairs. "I've had about all that I can endure of surprises for one night."

Wordlessly, Quill and Maitland followed.

Quill's mood on the drive back to Beauchamp House was much darker than it had been on the journey out.

The fact that Serena had separated him and Ivy into separate carriages did nothing to improve things either. Though they'd not told her about what had happened with

Cassandra, the fact that both he and Ivy, and later Maitland, had disappeared from the drawing room for an extended period of time had alerted her to the fact that something was amiss, and she'd hurried Ivy into the first carriage with the Hastings sisters, leaving Quill to ride back with Lady Daphne and Maitland, who flirted shamelessly all the way.

By the time the carriage stopped in the drive of Beauchamp House, Quill was ready to throttle anyone who so much as breathed in his direction. And his humor was not improved when he stalked into the entrance hall to find Serena waiting for him, her mouth a line of impatience.

"I would like to speak to you, please," she said without preamble as he brushed past her toward the stairs.

"In the morning," he said in a tone that brooked no objection. "I need to speak to Ivy."

Now that they were back on home territory, he didn't care who heard him.

"She's gone up to bed with a headache, Quill," Serena said hurrying after him. "I think you'd better get some rest too. You've got a long journey ahead of you tomorrow."

"Where are you going, my lord?" asked Daphne as she and Maitland followed behind them at a slower pace. "I don't suppose you'd wish to bring a few things back from London for me if that's your destination. I left some very important books, and I'd like to—"

Quill heard Maitland's low voice telling her to hush and was grateful for that at least.

When they reached the landing at the third floor, he turned to Serena and took her by the shoulders. "I know my duty. I will do it. But I beg you will leave us alone for now."

He saw a flicker of understanding in Serena's eyes as she took his meaning. And though she squared her jaw, she gave him a reluctant nod.

Not caring if Maitland or Daphne saw his intention, he

strode down the hall and without knocking opened the door to Ivy's bedchamber and walked in.

To find it empty.

A frisson of panic ran through him before he realized Ivy and her maid were likely in the dressing room.

In for a penny, in for a pound.

When he opened the door to the dressing room he found Ivy being unbuttoned from her gown by her maid.

"Get out," he said to the wide-eyed girl. Bobbing a curtsy, she was gone before Ivy could even turn to give him the full force of her scowl.

"You have no right to come into my dressing room and order my maid about," she said with a huff of anger. "You get out."

"Not until we've had a conversation," he said curtly.

When he didn't begin at once, she raised her brows in exaggerated annoyance. "Well? You're so keen to talk to me. Then talk."

He noted the shadows beneath her eyes and the traces of dried tears, and cursed himself for being a scoundrel.

In a gentler voice he said, "Come, let's go into the other room where you can be comfortable."

"I would have been a great deal more comfortable if you'd let Polly finish getting me out of this corset," she said in a harassed tone.

Wordlessly he moved behind her and began undoing the buttons that ran down her back. The action so reminiscent of their afternoon in the little cottage that he found himself swallowing back a groan of desire.

But that was what had got them in this mess in the first place. So he steeled himself against the sight of the vulnerable skin of her back and let her step out of the gown before going to work on the lacing of her corset.

With a modesty that was somewhat amusing given what they'd been to each other, she refused to turn around when the corset was unfastened and said in a cool voice, "Please hand me the robe on the hook there."

He glanced around and saw the one she meant and held it as she slipped first one, then the other arm through the sleeves and allowed the stays to drop to the floor before cinching the belt of the cotton wrap. Turning to him with a glower, she turned with hauteur and stalked out of the tiny dressing room into the bedchamber beyond.

Where the candlelight and the turned-down counterpane loomed large.

Swallowing, Quill followed her, unable to keep from noticing how her hips swung from side to side as she walked.

But if Ivy was in any mood to continue what they'd started in the alcove at the Northman house, she was giving no indication of it. In fact, if he didn't know for a fact that she was the same woman he'd held in his arms, he would never have guessed it.

Clearly he was going to have to do some persuading if he wished to gain entrance into the bed behind them.

"Well," she said with a tilt of her chin, "you have something to say, I gather. Say it then get out."

The coldness in her tone might have made him back off if he hadn't seen the pulse beating in her neck. Or the way her eyes darkened when their eyes met. She might be angry. As she had every right to be. But she wasn't completely done with him.

At least he hoped not.

"I apologize for not telling you about Cassandra before we went to her house this evening," he said firmly, deciding that straightforward explanation would be his best strategy. "I should have let you know that you might be facing some jealousy from that quarter. And for that I am deeply sorry."

But to his discomfort, her gaze only grew stonier.

"Do you think I give a damn that you bedded that horrible woman years ago when you were little more than a boy?" she asked, a flash of something he couldn't interpret in her eyes. "My own experience with you tells me that you learned how to be so seductive somewhere, my lord. No man is born knowing exactly what he's about in that arena, I think."

"What do you know about it?" he asked, surprised at her candor despite himself.

"Have you forgotten that my father lets university boys run tame in our household?" she asked, a hint of impatience in her tone. "They will kiss anything that moves at that age," she said with a shake of her head. "And a number of things that don't, I wager. Though I've never seen it, thank heavens."

"Did they kiss *you*?" he asked, annoyed at the thought of her in the arms of someone else—even if it was a passel of damned schoolboys.

"No," she said with a lift of her chin. "But that doesn't mean I am ignorant," she added, some of the bravado dissipating at the admission.

"Oh." The monosyllable was an inadequate expression of his relief, but it was all he could manage at the moment.

"My point is not that I've been kissed before," Ivy said in a softer tone. "It's that I know how little a kiss can mean. But that's clearly not the case with you and Mrs. Northman. It's not the idea of her that I mind, so much as what she meant to you. And that you failed to tell me suggests that you wished to keep that a secret."

It was something that hadn't even occurred to him, the notion that she feared he might still be holding a torch for Cassandra.

"God no," he said, truly appalled at the idea. "I hope you don't think I could ever cherish tender feelings for a woman with so little human charity that she'd say what she did to you."

The relief in her eyes was enough to make him step closer. "I did fancy myself in love with her in my salad days," he admitted with a wry smile. "But almost as soon as I declared my undying love for her she laughed so heartily as to make it impossible for me to ever fancy her again—well, not quite that, I suppose; at one and twenty I was little more than a walking cock-stand with eyes, so it was impossible not rise to the occasion."

Her eyes widened at the crudity, but she also laughed, which had been his intention.

"You're incorrigible," she said with a shake of her head.

"She's not much different now than she was then," he continued, slipping his arms around her waist and pulling her closer. "I've matured and she's remained the same. Which is sad when I think of it. But I suspect our sympathy is wasted on her. I doubt she would thank us. And I know that I can think of other things I'd much rather be doing."

Ivy didn't resist when he kissed her then, and Quill set himself to prove to her with his every touch that he meant every word he'd said about Cassandra.

If truth were told, he'd been a little repulsed by her when he first saw her tonight. Seeing her with the eyes of a man rather than a boy. And he'd known with the certainty of a man that Ivy on her worst day was worth ten of Cassandra.

"Ivy," he said, his voice husky with wanting her, "yesterday in the cottage was an impulse, a moment out of time. Will you let me make love to you now, in a proper bed, when there is the promise of marriage between us?"

She pulled back a little, her eyes searching, and Quill hoped that she could read the affection for her in his face. If not love yet—it was far too soon for such a heady emotion between them—then at the very least, there was genuine friendship there. And there were far worse foundations for marriage.

Whatever she saw in him must have given her reassurance, for she gave a little smile, her green eyes bright with emotion.

"Yes," she said on a breath. And he knew that it was more than just in response to his request just now. It was an assent to follow him into far more than one night.

Unable to contain his relief, he scooped her up into his arms with a whoop, startling a little shriek from her.

"Put me down, you silly man!" she protested. "I'm far too heavy."

But he liked the feel of her in his arms. The solid weight of her, and the warm press of her against his chest. It evoked a primitive emotion he'd never imagined himself capable of. But then, Ivy had been wringing emotions from him from the moment they met.

"You're as light as a feather," he said with a grin as he pulled her closer. "I'd be a poor sort of man if I couldn't carry my lady to bed."

"I do not doubt your ability, my lord," she said primly, "but your wisdom."

Reaching the bed, he gently placed her down on the soft mattress, enjoying the play of candlelight through the thin fabric of her robe.

"You'll forgive me, I trust," he said, shrugging out of his coats, and unwinding the cravat from around his neck, "if I disagree. I quite think this is wisest decision I've ever made."

"Then we will simply have to agree to disagree," she said watching from beneath her lashes as he tossed his cravat to the side and pulled his shirt over his head in one fluid motion and dropped it.

He couldn't help but notice the appreciation in her eyes

as she scanned his bare chest. "Will we?" he asked in a purr.

"Perhaps you're right," she amended as he put one knee on the bed, and shifted to prop himself over her.

"Of course I'm right," he said, leaning down to kiss her on the nose. "Wisest decision I ever made."

And to his surprise, he meant it.

Chapter 22

Ivy's breath caught in her throat as she saw the predatory gleam in Quill's eye as he held himself over her. She was keenly aware of the fact that beneath her robe she was wearing nothing at all. And the heat of his big body curled around her like the tentacles of a spell meant to bind her to him forever.

"Are you quite comfortable?" she asked politely, as she tried to find somewhere to look besides into his all-too-knowing gaze. For some reason the easiness of the little cottage was scarce here and she felt her inexperience in carnal matters far more keenly now than she had before.

He smiled, and she noticed a single dimple in his left cheek. It gave him an impish air, so different from the serious nobleman whom she'd first met in the taproom of the Fox and Pheasant. "I am quite comfortable," he said, raising his brows. "In fact, I would count myself quite content if I never moved from this spot. Do you think it would be feasible?"

His absurdity was the very thing to set her at ease, and relieved she considered his question. "I don't know," she said with mock seriousness. "It might be difficult to take all our meals in this position."

"Or, I could feed you," he said with assurance. "In fact, I'd insist upon it. It would be the least I could do for your allowing me to rest my . . . ah . . . self against your sweet. . . . self for the rest of our days." He punctuated his pauses with tiny thrusts that made Ivy well aware of just how much he was enjoying their current position.

"In fact," he continued, dropping his head to tug on her earlobe with his teeth, "I think I might be getting a little hungry right now."

"Oh," Ivy said, breathless at the sensation of his mouth making its way down her neck. "I'm sure I could send for something from the kitchen. It's late, but Polly would bring something if I asked." She continued to babble as he untied the knot at her waist and opened the robe to reveal her nude form. Her breasts budded in response to the chill air. Almost painful in their tautness.

"I'll just make do with what we have here," he said, closing his lips around first one, then the other peak, sucking each one into the moist heat of his mouth. The sheer carnality of it making Ivy writhe with pleasure. "So pretty." His breath on her wet skin made her shift beneath him.

While he caressed her with his mouth, his hand slipped down, down, over the slight round of her belly, pausing to tease a fingertip over the dip of her navel, and resting at the top of her pubis. The memory of his hands on her in the cottage, combined with the suckle of Quill's mouth on her breast had Ivy almost bucking beneath him, searching, aching to the feel of his touch on the sensitive skin between her legs. Where even now she could feel the damp proof of her desire.

But she needn't have worried. The hardening of his erection against her hip was enough to tell Ivy that he was just as eager as she. The hiss of his breath when he slipped first one, then another finger into the moisture told the tale far more eloquently than words.

"So wet for me," he crooned into her ear, as he teased over her hot flesh, always staying just shy of that spot where she needed him most. Making her search him out with her hips, even as he danced a finger over the sensitive bud near the top.

"Please, Quill," she murmured, aching for something more. More pressure, more heat, more . . . just more.

And when he thrust his fingers inside her she nearly came off the bed in her relief. Not knowing or caring how she looked, she followed her body's lead and lifted her hips, following his hand as it moved in and out, stroking into her just like she needed.

"That's it," he said, kissing her with open mouth, mimicking the motion of his fingers with his tongue, before shifting downward.

When he removed his hand she almost wept at the loss, and for a moment she was puzzled to see him press her knees wider with his shoulders.

"What are you . . . ?" she began, only to gape as she met his eyes. With deliberation, he leaned in and licked her. And though she was shocked, she couldn't have told him to stop if her life depended on it.

"Just relax," he said, his deep voice vibrating against her sensitive core. And she let her head fall back, and reveled in the sensation as he used lips and tongue and fingers to bring her to a writhing need that had her crying out with the ache of it. Until without warning, the thrust of his fingers coupled with the suck of his mouth sent her hurtling over, her body no longer hers to control.

She could taste herself on his mouth when he moved up to kiss her sweetly before coming into her with a strong thrust that reignited the sparks she thought had been doused.

Quill pressed his forehead against hers and watched her as he moved in her, his hot gaze igniting a fullness in her heart even as his body stoked the fire at her core. It was the most intimate moment of Ivy's life. More even that the afternoon in the cottage, when they'd both kept parts of themselves hidden from the other. From self-preservation or unconscious distrust she couldn't guess. All she knew was that this, now, was as binding as any marriage ceremony. She gave herself to him then, body and soul, and she knew with a certainty that he gave himself to her.

Clutching him to her, the strong heat of his back beneath her fingers, Ivy's body was all too soon gripping him in a heartbeat rhythm all its own, and when she felt the explosion of feeling this time, she felt him follow her, his cry only seconds after hers as he let his weight come down on her.

Ivy was still asleep when Quill slipped out of her bed the next morning.

Leaving her naked and warm, one breast exposed by the sheet tangled beneath her body, had been one of the most difficult things he'd ever done. Soon, he told himself, he wouldn't have to leave her at all. He just had to get to Oxford to speak to her father, and then to London for a special license. And there was also the matter of Aunt Celeste's killer to catch.

But first, he told himself as he washed and dressed for the day beneath the exasperated eye of his valet, they needed to find that damned gypsy woman.

He would have left Ivy to find her on her own—or at the very least with Maitland and the other ladies—but he disliked the idea of her traipsing about the countryside without him by her side. They were all but convinced that his aunt had been murdered. And once someone chose to take a life, the decision to take another was but a stone's throw away.

Though he would have preferred to make the trip to the

gypsy encampment with only Ivy, that was not to be the case. Once the others got wind that they were planning to visit a gypsy, fortune telling fever had taken hold. Over the breakfast table it was decided that the Hastings sisters, Daphne and Maitland would go along with them.

"I'm desperate to know what the future holds," Sophia said with a grin. "It's thrilling to guess what might happen."

"It's pure nonsense," Daphne asserted with a tone that brooked no argument. "I daresay this woman you're seeking employs the same sort of tricks and gimmicks as they do at a country fair. Only with more skill and more flowery language."

"I think you are far too quick to dismiss it," Ivy argued. "Who are we to say what is and is not possible? I am not ashamed to admit that there are some things in this world beyond my understanding."

"But you're both being romantic," Gemma said, her scientific nature aligning with Daphne's mathematical one. "Daphne has a point that fortune tellers are notorious for spinning tales out of nothing. You remember the one we visited in the village back home, Sophia? The one who said that we would soon go on a journey over water? As far as I know neither of us has done so. It was a fiction she told so that you would give her more coins, nothing more."

"That is patently false, Gemma," Sophia retorted. "We crossed several streams and a river on our journey here, didn't we?"

"Perhaps we should wait to see what this particular gypsy fortune teller has to tell us before we make a decision," Quill said diplomatically. "After all, this one might be the one who is entirely sincere."

"We'd best be off if we don't wish to miss the good weather," Maitland said, wisely refraining from engaging in the discussion. "After all," he said with a wink at Quill, "we don't wish to be caught in a storm like Miss Wareham and Kerr were the other day."

Quill and Ivy both sighed as a collective titter rose from the table. The rest of the residents of Beauchamp House, with the exception of Serena who was still a bit incensed about the whole thing, had been remarkably unfazed by the scandalous behavior of the linguist and the marquess. But that didn't stop them from taking every opportunity to tease them about it.

Not waiting to see if they would comment, Ivy pushed her chair back and rose. "I'll go get my wrap."

The other ladies soon followed, leaving Quill and Maitland to wander from the room in their own time.

"You look chipper this morning for a man who was caught in the parson's mousetrap last night," Maitland said with a grin as he rose from the table. "One would almost imagine you're happy about what happened."

His good mood was far likelier due to the hours he'd spent in Ivy's bed, but Quill was hardly going to tell his cousin so. "Perhaps the means was not what I would have wished for," he said with a shrug, "but I cannot say that I am entirely displeased with the outcome. Though I do not look forward to informing Ivy's father of what happened."

"You utterly outrank the man," Maitland argued. "The fact that you, a marquess, wish to marry his daughter at all should have him worshipping at your feet. It's a far better match than the daughter of a disinherited duke's son and a social nobody could have ever hoped for."

"Don't be an ass, Maitland," Quill said in exasperation. "I am well aware of the difference in our social rankings. But the fact remains that I have compromised the man's daughter not once but twice—the second time publicly in the house of my one-time mistress. It is hardly the most auspicious of occasions upon which to ask for the hand of the woman I . . . hold in esteem."

If Maitland noticed the pause—where Quill had just stopped himself from saying he loved Ivy—he didn't mention it. The slip was likely the result of lack of sleep, Quill assured himself. After all, though he was fond of Ivy and resigned to marrying her, he couldn't possibly have fallen in love with her. For one thing, it hadn't been long enough; and for another, he wasn't even sure he believed in the sentiment. Much like the power of the gypsy woman to tell the future, love was a thing he'd believe when he saw it. And it was unlikely he'd see either anytime soon, if ever.

"You're far too nice about these things," Maitland said as the two men strode into the entrance hall to call for their greatcoats. "In the good old days you'd have thrown the fellow's daughter over the pommel of your saddle and taken her over his protests. And marriage wouldn't have even been a part of the equation."

"So you think I should just dispense with visiting the man altogether and simply send him the sheet's with Ivy's virgin blood, then?" Quill asked dryly in a voice low enough to thwart eavesdroppers. "I look forward to watching you deal with your own in-laws when the day comes. I suspect you will have a rude awakening."

"The thing of it is," Maitland said with a laugh, "you care too much what others think. I get the sense that you consider the responses of those around you before you make the least little step. I've learned to live my life without giving a damn. And I've managed well enough so far."

"Yes," Quill argued, "but you've had no one to answer to but your mother since you were in short coats. Having a father with a sharp tongue and a cane at the ready will make a man learn to think before he acts."

"From what I've heard, my father was just as headstrong as I am," the duke said cheerfully. "So it's doubtful he'd have been the steadying influence you think. Like Lady Daphne and Miss Hastings on the subject of fortune tellers, however, I suspect we will never reconcile our opinions on the matter, so let us dispense with this talk of fathers and discipline."

"With pleasure," Quill said, taking his hat from Greaves. "Though I will add that I plan on striking out for Oxford this evening and I would ask that you keep a watchful eye over Miss Wareham. She has proved to be level-headed thus far, but the quest for Lady Celeste's poisoner may prod her into acting rashly in my absence."

"You think there's danger afoot, then?" Maitland asked, frowning. "I thought poisoners were generally too timid to strike out physically."

"I suspect that's the case," Quill agreed, grateful that he could speak openly about Celeste's murder with at least one member of his family, since he'd yet to inform Serena about the real cause of their aunt's demise. "But I cannot think that the questions we've been asking will go unnoticed. And if I'm gone, that will leave Ivy alone."

Maitland had only the chance to nod before they were joined by the ladies filing down the stairs, having added hats and coats for the cross-country walk.

Chapter 23

"I missed you this morning," Ivy said in a low voice as she and Quill walked behind the others along the path leading to the field where Elsie had claimed to find the gypsy fortune teller. "Though I suppose it would not have done for Polly to find you in my bed."

It had come as a shock to her how painful his absence had been to her. Whether it was because of the vulnerability she felt after giving herself to him so fully, or simply because she was beginning to want him with her whatever the circumstances, she didn't know. The stark reality had been that she woke alone in her bed, and hadn't liked it one bit.

"Not that we haven't created enough scandal in the household to last a year's time," Quill said with a grin, "but, yes I did not risk having your maid find me. It may take only a day or two for the news from the Northman's dinner party to travel to the staff at Beauchamp House, but by that time, I hope to have settled things with your father and have a special license in hand."

"So you will travel to Oxford?" she asked, her stomach twisting at the notion of how her father would response to Quill's arrival. Alton Wareham might have been born as the son of the Duke of Ware, but he had little respect for the aristocracy, an institution he declared an affront to the common people. He didn't use his courtesy title, and he would greet the news that Ivy was to marry a marquess as nothing short of a disaster.

His response would be more cheerful if she announced she were to marry a bootblack.

"Is that strictly necessary?" she asked Quill, not quite knowing how to bring up the subject of her father's feelings about the peerage. "After all, isn't it customary to use the special license, *then* announce the marriage to the family?"

Quill frowned. "I'm not sure it's wise to use the word 'customary' when it comes to situations like ours. I rather think it changes from circumstance to circumstance." He searched her face. "Is there some reason why you would rather I not speak with your father? I must admit it is not something I am looking forward to, but I assumed that was part of my penance."

"Penance?" Ivy asked frowning.

"For ruining you," he said simply.

Of course he thought in those terms, Ivy fumed.

"I am not a side of beef or a keg of small beer to be ruined," she said through clenched teeth. "And I will thank you for not speaking of me as if I am."

A flicker of impatience crossed his handsome face. "I do not think of you like that," he said. "But it is how the rest of the world will speak of it. Especially if they learn about what happened in Northman's hall last night. I understand your dislike of the way the world discusses such things, but it is pointless to argue about wording when we must focus on practicalities."

"My opinion on the subject," Ivy said coldly, "is not pointless. Words like 'ruined,' and 'compromised' reinforce the idea that ladies are commodities, and I ask that you do not use them around me. Or at all, if we are being frank. It only perpetuates these archaic notions, and the sooner men in power—men like you, as a peer of the realm—begin changing how you speak of it, the sooner such things will cease to matter."

"But they do matter, Ivy," he argued. "I understand why you object to the terms, but you would sooner force the moon to go round the sun than convince a father that his daughter's innocence is worth nothing. It's why there are dowries and laws of succession for God's sake."

Understanding dawned in Ivy. "So it's because you think my father will offer a dowry that you wish to see him?" she asked, aghast.

"Don't be absurd," Quill said dismissively. "I don't need your father's money. But if you wish to have a widow's portion or provisions for our children, it would do some good for us to sit down and make some decisions. Not that I don't mean to speak to my man of business about that regardless. But it would be good for you to have a man there to look out for your interests besides me."

"Well, excuse me for forgetting who I'm dealing with," Ivy snapped. "I forgot to whom I was speaking. Of course you have no need of my father's money. But he will likely accept whatever bride price you choose to pay him. He might reject the notion of the peerage in theory but he is not above taking their money. Even when it means giving it to the man who 'ruined' his daughter."

"Ivy," Quill said, thrusting a hand through his hair, "be reasonable. If you do not wish me to meet with your father before the marriage, then I will not do so. But I don't understand why you are so angry about this. So far as I can tell, my sin is that I used a word you do not like—which you just used by the way—and I dared suggest that your father might ask for a settlement on hearing of our impending marriage. Is that the whole of it?"

"That was *sarcasm* you silly man," she hissed. "And stop making me sound like the one at fault here."

He shrugged as if to say "but you are," and Ivy wanted to shriek. Why were men so obtuse?

"I'm going to go up ahead and speak with the other ladies," she said curtly. "We will finish discussing this later."

Not caring what his response to that would be, she hurried up to join the others, leaving Quill to stare after her.

"That looked unpleasant," said Maitland, who had lingered so that Quill could catch up with him. "In your lady's black books already?"

"Nothing so dire," Quill responded thoughtfully. *I hope,* he added silently to himself. He wasn't quite sure where Ivy's ire had sprung from, but he had little doubt it stemmed from her feelings about her father. As a man whose relationship with his own father had been strained at best, he could relate. But he'd been unable to even mention it thanks to her tirade about commodities, and kegs of beer, and all that rot.

"Maitland," he asked now, watching as the four women up ahead leaned their heads together and spoke in low voices—doubtless talking about the perfidy of men and plotting for ways to have him roasted on a spit before nightfall, "have you ever considered that by calling a lady 'ruined' when she's been . . ." He searched for a word that conveyed the meaning of ruined but could come up with nothing that worked so well as it did.

"Breached?" his cousin asked, eyebrows raised. "Sullied? Tupped? Prematurely drunk?"

"Compromised," Quill said tightly. He should have known better than to ask Maitland's opinion. He lacked the gravitas necessary for such a conversation. Though to be fair, he suspected most men would make the same sorts of quips. Men simply didn't take the matter as seriously as women did. But he pressed on because he had to talk to someone about it. "Did you ever consider that by using those terms, it unfairly places ladies in the same light as beef and corn and other commodities?"

"I'm not sure how unfair it is," Maitland said with a shrug, "but if you ask any man who's been forced to pay through the nose for the honor of marrying the lady he's . . . compromised, then I suspect he'd say it's accurate enough." He glanced at his cousin with a frown. "Why, has Miss Wareham been smarting over the fact that she's no longer . . . ah . . . as she once was?"

"She just flew into a rage because I mentioned my intention of speaking to her father before I get the special license," Quill said pettishly. "As if the man didn't have the right to at least hear it from my own mouth that I took her innocence. Not in so many words of course. I don't have a death wish. But you would have thought I told her I was going to bring the bloody sheets as you said earlier. She was livid at the idea there was anything to tell beyond that we're marrying. As if a father hasn't got a right to know."

"Not to mention the effect it might have on her sisters' chances," Maitland said practically. "Though that's something her mama is more likely to cut up rough about."

"Right," Quill said, feeling a much-needed sense of vindication. Perhaps Maitland wasn't the wrong man to speak to about this after all. "I thought it was perfectly natural that I would explain to Mr. Wareham what I intended to do right by her despite the fact that we'd anticipated the vows, and instead I was met with fury and recriminations. Then when I brought up the dowry. Well, you can guess how well *that* was received."

"I am sorry old chap," Maitland said, clapping him on the back. "I thought Miss Wareham was a sensible creature, but you can never tell with bluestockings. They get their backs up about the queerest things. Lady Daphne ripped up at me last night because I confused Pythagoras and that other maths chappie. You know the one, the Greek one who's not Pythagoras?"

"Euclid?" Quill asked, amused despite himself.

"That's the one." Maitland beamed. "You would have thought I'd said up was down, day was night, and the moon was made of Christmas pudding to see Lady Daphne's reaction. I thought she'd never speak to me again."

"But she did?" Quill guessed.

"Of course," Maitland said with a shrug, and a gesture from his head to his toes, as if to say, "Who could resist this?"

What must it be like to live such a charmed life, Quill thought wryly. If he didn't realize just how seriously his cousin took his ducal responsibilities despite his savoir-faire, he'd be green with envy. Though there was the fact that he and not Maitland had won Ivy. Despite their spat, he was as infatuated with her as ever. And despite the ease with which they'd got along so far, it was not unexpected that they'd disagree about something. Couples bickered. It was the way they solved their disagreements that mattered.

They'd reached the edge of a clearing by now, and beyond the four ladies who walked ahead of them he could see a colorful gypsy caravan in a little copse of trees.

So much for a gypsy encampment.

This appeared to be a gypsy camper.

Singular.

The ladies waited for them near a horse chestnut tree that was sporting a few bursts of green in honor of the chilly spring.

"It's much smaller than I expected," Sophia said with a pout as Quill and Maitland reached them. "I was hoping for a carnival at the very least."

"Or some handsome gypsy men," Lady Daphne said with a frown. "Since the fortune teller will be useless for anything practical."

"I wish to get the recipe she used in Lady Celeste's tisanes," Ivy reminded her with a roll of her eyes, which to Quill's relief, she shared with him. Like a joke that only they shared.

"I know," Daphne said with a wave of her hand. "But that seems just as foolish as seeking your fortune."

"You would not say so, I think, Lady Daphne," Quill said, happy when Ivy slipped her arm through his, "if you suffered from the same headaches my aunt did. And indeed that Miss Wareham does."

They had agreed upon the fiction that Ivy needed the recipe for her own personal use. Since she'd known the other ladies for a couple of days, they could hardly dispute the matter.

"Poor Ivy," said Gemma with a sympathetic smile. "I know how horrid they can be. I suffer from them myself at times. So I'm just as eager for the recipe. Even if I do agree with Daphne about the fortune telling."

"Well none of you will make me ashamed to ask her for my fortune," Sophia said with a dignified sniff. "For I wish to know what's to come even if the rest of you don't."

"And I'll join you, Miss Hastings," said Maitland with a grin as he took her arm.

Quill couldn't help but note that Lady Daphne's eyes narrowed at the way his cousin was making so free with Sophia's arm. If they weren't careful, Maitland would have the two ladies fighting over him. Though if he didn't mistake his guess, Miss Hastings was only being friendly. She had a romantic nature, but there seemed to be nothing beyond friendship in her manner with the duke.

They approached the caravan and soon saw that an old

woman sat in a little chair just outside the red-and-green-and-yellow-painted house on wheels, laddered steps leading into the interior just behind her.

"What brings you to Madame Albinia?" she asked, rising with some difficulty as they approached. "A fortune for the ladies? A tonic for the gentlemen?"

As they got closer, Quill saw that she was older than he'd first thought. Her wizened face had seen many years in the sun, and her fingers were twisted with arthritis. But her black eyes were bright enough, and if he didn't miss his guess she'd not failed to notice that Sophia at least was eager to have her fortune told.

"We were told by the maid at one of the manor houses nearby that you have a tonic for the headache," Ivy said with a smile as she stepped closer to the woman. "I was wondering if I might speak to you about what goes into it?"

"That is valuable knowledge, lady," said the old woman with a wave of her hand. "Some pay me well to give them the secrets of my years of potion-making and physicking."

Wordlessly, Quill flipped a half crown in the woman's direction, which she caught with an agility that belied her age. "The ladies would like to have their fortunes told as well," he said with a nod that indicated the coin included that as well.

After biting the coin to ensure its value, the woman nodded. "Fortunes first, then tonic."

Resuming her seat by the fire, she had the young ladies approach her one by one—even Daphne, who despite her earlier derision appeared to be just as eager as Sophia had been—and told them things that Quill suspected were calculated to be both probable and vague. Daphne would soon search for a very valuable thing, but to find it she would risk her greatest love. Sophia would meet a handsome stranger who would make her choose between love and happiness. And Gemma would go on a great quest where she would best a strong man.

Each of the ladies heard her fortune with what looked to Quill like genuine excitement. And there was something otherworldly about the way the old woman held each girl's hand in hers and closed her eyes as if summoning some invisible spirits to her side, who then whispered each fortune in her ear.

When Gemma stepped back and Ivy stepped forward, however, the woman raised her hand and stood.

"You wished for the tonic, yes?" she said with a nod, as if answering her own question. "You will come into the vardo." As if the matter were settled, she turned and began to make her way slowly up the steps leading into the colorful wagon.

"No," Quill said, staying Ivy with a hand on her arm. They had no notion of who had poisoned his aunt yet. For all they knew the tonic had been poisoned when the old woman had given it to Elsie for her mistress. "She can bring it out here."

But Ivy waved away his concern. "You're right here. It's not as if she's taking me across the sea. And if it will make you easier, I promise not to ingest anything while I'm inside."

She made sense, but he still felt a pang of uneasiness at the idea.

"Do you come, lady?" the old woman asked from the doorway of the caravan where she stood waiting.

Ivy squeezed his hand then stepped forward to carefully climb the laddered stairs.

Chapter 24

The inside of the caravan, or vardo as the old woman had called it, was just as colorful as the outside, with gilded scrollwork and decoration on every surface. There was a neatly made bed on a platform at the back and shelves on either of the long walls that Ivy could see were stacked with all sorts of things, including what looked like herbs and various powders.

She expected the old woman to take out a bottle of the tonic before giving her the same sort of vague fortune as she'd given the others. But instead, almost as soon as she stepped inside, Madame Albinia took her hand and scowled down at it.

"Is there something amiss?" Ivy asked after a few minutes passed during which Madame Albinia muttered words in what Ivy guessed was the Romani language.

As if she were being brought out of trance, the old woman looked up, blinking, her eyes still lit from within. Finally, shaking like a dog after being caught in the rain, she said in a fervent voice, "You are in great danger, lady. Great danger. You must leave this place at once. Take your man and go. Do not come back."

Perhaps because she'd asked about the tonic, and Ivy

expected the old woman might wish to rattle her, Ivy had prepared herself for something dire. Or at the very least, something mysterious. But something about the old woman's pronouncement chilled her to the bone.

"What do you mean?" she asked dumbly, staring down at her palm as if it would tell her what the gypsy woman was talking about.

"From the moment you speak," Madame Albinia said with a frown, "I see the light around you. But many people, they have the light. But I bring you here, into the *vardo* to see for sure. And for the tonic." As if reminded of the request for the tisane ingredients, the woman began to gather items from the various bottles and jars on the shelving.

When she'd finished gathering the ingredients, she named them off as she added them into a jar. "Lemongrass, feverfew, chamomile, and mint."

Momentarily distracted from the dire fortune the woman had given her, Ivy asked, "That's it?"

Despite her seriousness, the old woman grinned. "Did you expect magic beans? The Rom have the gift, but we use the fruits of the earth too. There is nothing otherworldly about the tonic. Only knowing what herbs to put together."

Ivy smiled ruefully. "I suppose I was expecting some sort of special quality that would explain its effectiveness."

"And its poisonous effect, as well, lady?" Madame Albinia asked with a keen look. At Ivy's shocked sound, she gave a slight smile. "I hear things. And when Albinia's tonic is used as poison, it angers her. This one, the one you seek, they are not what you think."

"What do you mean?" Ivy asked, desperate to know anything that might help them find Lady Celeste's killer.

"I do not know exactly," she said, "but the reasons for killing the Lady Celeste, they are from long ago. And they know you seek them. It is why you are in danger. If you wish to remain safe, you should go with your man away from here."

Ivy's gaze sharpened. "Who are *they*?"

But the seer only shook her head and repeated, "You should go."

Before Ivy could repeat her entreaty, they were interrupted by Quill, who stepped up onto the ladder and peered inside.

"Almost finished in here?" Quill asked with a cheerfulness that didn't meet his eyes. Clearly he'd sensed something was amiss.

As if she'd expected him, Madame Albinia nodded. Turning to Ivy she said aloud, "Remember what I say. Or there will be great heartache."

With a speaking look, she handed the jar of tonic ingredients to Ivy and waved her away, as if she no longer had the energy to talk to them.

Quill's mouth was tight as he listened to the fortune teller, but he said nothing until they were out of the *vardo*. "What did she mean 'heartache'?" he asked with a scowl.

But Ivy wasn't sure she wished to share what Madame Albinia had told her yet. At least not until she'd had a few minutes alone to think about it. As if she feared speaking the words aloud would give them power. Seeking to reassure him, however, she said, "Of course it was nonsense. All danger and long journeys, just like she gave the others."

"Then why did you look so stricken when I came in?" he asked with suspicion, clearly sensing that she was prevaricating. "Your face is ghostly white."

But she waved that away. "Oh, I felt a little faint. It was quite warm in there."

She could tell he didn't want to let it go, but was saved from further discussion by their arrival at the horse chestnut tree where the others had gathered.

"Did you get your tonic ingredients?" Lady Daphne asked with a raised brow. "I was afraid for a moment that she'd cast some sort of spell over you and we'd need to rescue you. Lord Kerr was happy enough to go in after you, however, so you were saved from a stampede."

"What do you know of stampedes?" asked Maitland with a snort. "And what *is* a stampede if it comes to that? Something with a lot of people, I can guess, but what?"

Daphne rolled her eyes as the rest of the party laughed.

"I did get them, as it happens," Ivy said once they'd settled. She held up the jar. "Would you believe it's nothing more than common herbs we could have gathered ourselves?"

"I am shocked," Gemma said with mock surprise. "Shocked I tell you. That a gypsy woman would pass off a healing potion as something magical when it is in fact ancient and easily known. Why, next you'll tell us that our fortunes were untrue."

"Come over here by me, Gemma," said Daphne with approval. "We who hold logic and science in high regard should stick together."

"Oh, don't be smug, ladies," Sophia said slipping her arm through Ivy's. "Just because Ivy and I are more interested in art and language than in your boring old numbers and rocks doesn't mean that we are simpletons. It takes a great deal of skill to look at a painting and know if it is any good, just as I imagine it takes skill for Ivy to examine a few lines of Greek and determine if they came from a famous poet or a simple fishmonger."

"It is doubtful that a fishmonger would've been able to write," Ivy said with an apologetic smile, "but I think the spirit of your argument holds true."

The chatter of her friends did much to dispel the aura of ill portent that had seemed to follow her out of the little

caravan. And as they walked back toward the path to Beauchamp House she let their wordplay punctuated by the
occasional quip from the duke distract her from what Madame Albinia had told her about Lady Celeste's murder,
as well as the warning that she herself was in danger.

Soon, however, she fell back and before long—just as
they had done on the way to the clearing—she found herself walking alone with Quill, some distance behind the
others.

"What did she really tell you, Ivy?" he asked, his blue
eyes shadowed with worry. "Because I don't believe it was
just the same sort of claptrap she told the others. Was it
something to do with the person who killed Aunt Celeste?"

"Perhaps it wasn't strictly as innocuous as I told the
others it was," Ivy said reluctantly. "But I was hoping to
think it over for a bit."

"So that you could twist it into something innocuous?"
he asked, with brows drawn.

"Not in so many words." She bristled. "But more that I
wished to think about it. To make sense of it. Because it
might not be as dark as what I interpreted it to be."

"You'd best just say before you truly worry me," he said
gently. "Because at this point I'm suspecting the worst.
And I don't even truly believe in such things."

"She said that I was in—"

And almost as soon as the words left Ivy's mouth she
heard a loud report from the trees on either side of the path,
and she felt a sharp pain in her upper arm just before Quill
threw her to the ground.

All of Quill's senses were on alert as he crashed to the
ground, shielding Ivy with his body. He scanned the trees
on either side of the path, trying to determine where the
shot had come from. The windy day made it impossible to
tell which of the moving branches was from human motion

and which from the breeze. Up ahead he could hear the whimpers of the other ladies, and Maitland's order for them to stay down.

Beneath him, Ivy was breathing heavily, but she kept silent, either too shocked to talk or sensing that he needed quiet to tell where the bastard was.

When several minutes passed without another shot, Quill eased off of her. "I think it's safe now," he said, still scanning the area to ensure that he hadn't been premature in his assessment. "Are you all right?"

"I think so," she said, her face pale, but standing easily enough when he gave her a hand up. Wordlessly, he brushed the leaves and twigs from the skirt of her gown, using the contact to reassure himself that she was, indeed unharmed. "Please tell me that was just a hunter making a wild shot."

He wished that he had the words to erase the stricken look in her green eyes, but Quill didn't think lying would make things any easier for her. "I'm afraid that's unlikely," he said, pulling her to him in a quick hug. "This is not precisely an area known for good hunting."

"Were either of you hit?" Maitland demanded as he and the other three ladies backtracked toward them.

"No," Quill said, glancing up at them. "You?"

"No," Maitland said, his usual lighthearted expression replaced with grim anger. "Not for lack of trying. Who the hell would be out shooting on a commonly used footpath?" His question didn't need an answer. They all knew that no one with any sense would.

"We need to get back to the house at once," Quill said, reaching for Ivy's arm. But her cry of pain made him stop. "Did you hurt yourself in the fall?" he asked, moving to get a look at her upper arm, which she was probing it with her fingers.

"I don't know," she said frowning. "I did feel something,

but it happened so quickly I'm unsure of whether it happened before or after I fell."

Her hand came away covered in blood, and Quill uttered a low curse. "You're hit, damn it."

And even as he spoke, she swayed on her feet, whether from blood loss or pain he could not tell. In one swift move she was in his arms. "We have to get her to the house at once."

"Here," Maitland said, pressing his handkerchief against the wound, which was bleeding slowly but steadily now. "I'll run ahead and send for the doctor. Do you want me to send the carriage?"

"It will take too long," Quill said, his mind entirely focused on the task at hand. "We've only half a mile or so to go."

With a nod, Maitland headed in a jog toward Beauchamp House.

"She said I was in danger," Ivy said, resting her head against his shoulder as Quill carried her past familiar landmarks but seeing none of them.

"Who said, Ivy?" Sophia asked, from where she hurried along beside them, flanked by Daphne and Gemma.

"Madame Albinia," Ivy said in a weak voice. "Told me I was in danger. They know I'm looking for them."

"Whom are you looking for?" Daphne asked, her voice puzzled. "I think her mind is disordered. She's not making any sense."

But Quill knew precisely whom Ivy was looking for.

A murderer who would not hesitate to kill again.

He should never have let her go into that gypsy caravan alone. He'd suspected the old woman was up to something, but if he'd guessed she would've put Ivy in real danger, he would never have allowed the visit at all. Hell, from the start he should have told her *he* would search for

Celeste's killer. He'd been blinded by his attraction to her. His sense of fairness had told him she deserved to be in on the hunt since Celeste had asked her personally to see to it in her letter. But fairness be damned, he fumed. He had gone against his instincts as a gentleman and look where it had got them.

"It hurts, Quill," she said, moving her head restlessly against him. "So much."

That the stubborn woman he'd argued with that morning was admitting as much was an indication of just how much the wound must be paining her.

"I know, darling," he said softly, all but running now, grateful that the path was so deeply ingrained in him that he could have walked it blindfolded. "We'll be at the house in a few minutes and we'll give you something for the pain."

"Should have listened to her," she muttered, her breath soft against his throat. "Told me they're after me, but I didn't believe her. Thought it was gypsy piffle."

"I'll keep you safe, Aphrodite," he said in a low voice. He hadn't managed to today, but that was because his guard was down. But he'd be damned if he'd let the blackguard who killed his aunt harm Ivy again. If that meant finding him and beating him within an inch of his life, then so much the better.

She laughed in a soft whimper against him. "Only one who calls me that," she said in a wavering voice that ended in a moan of pain.

"Because you are a goddess," he said gently. "My love."

He didn't care if the others heard him. And if they did they gave no indication as they trudged on behind him.

Finally, he saw the roof of the house come into view and, buoyed by the sight, he increased his pace. And when Maitland came hurrying toward them, directing a pair of footmen with a litter, he shook his head. "I've made it this far with her," he said in an impatient tone. "I'll get her into the house."

"Dr. Vance has been sent for and should be here soon," Maitland said, walking at a fast clip beside him. "Serena has the maids bringing hot water to her bedchamber, and her maid is ready to help as needed."

"Thank you," he said to his cousin, knowing he could have asked for no better man to assist him in this situation.

Soon they were bounding up the stairs and into the house. Moving past gawking servants who seemed to overrun the hallway, he took Ivy up the main staircase and finally into her bedchamber.

"Here, Quill," Serena said, waiting at the bedside. "Put her down here."

His arms and back were aching like mad, but he didn't feel them until after he'd gently deposited Ivy onto the bed. If it weren't for Maitland following close behind him, he'd have sunk to the floor.

"Come on, old chap," his cousin said in a soothing voice. "She's safe now. Let's get you a chair."

"I'm not leaving her," Quill said in a harsh voice, though he was too weak to break way from the other man's steadying arm.

"Just come into the dressing room for a moment while they undress her," Maitland said as he led him to the doorway leading into the small room. "We all know you intend to marry her, but one mustn't flout convention before the servants. Shameful lack of imagination they've got."

Maitland prattled on in similar fashion as he shut the door behind them and—from where Quill didn't stop to wonder—produced a decanter and two glasses and proceeded to pour.

"I find there's nothing like a jot of brandy to ease the nerves in a situation like this," he said, handing Quill a generous helping. "Drink it up like a good lad."

Doing as he was told, Quill swallowed the fiery liquid and found himself reviving a little, though his legs chose that moment to let him know they needed a rest. Dropping into a chair that was far too small for a man of his size, he brushed a hand over his forehead, the enormity of what had happened suddenly threatening to crush him.

"Someone tried to kill her, Dalton," he said, reverting to his cousin's given name, as he'd called him when they were boys. Closing his eyes against the memory of the shot and his immediate instinct to get Ivy down as quickly as possible, he said in a hoarse voice, "What if I'd lost her?"

Unbidden, the memory of the near miss on that momentous journey back from the village rose in his mind. And what of the bronze statue that had almost hit her at the Northman dinner party?

He'd marked them down as accidents, but now he wasn't so sure. Had someone been trying to kill her all this time? The very idea chilled him to the bone.

Sighing, the duke crouched before him. "But you didn't lose her. She's well. In no small part because you had her out of harm's way before another shot could hit her."

"Wasn't fast enough," Quill said, shaking his head. "She's hurt because of me."

"She's hurt because some idiot with a pistol decided to take aim at her," Maitland said firmly. "If you weren't there she would very likely be dead now. Instead she's got a flesh wound that will likely hurt like the devil for a week or two and then will be forgotten. That's because of you."

Quill tried to get his mind around the idea that he'd saved her, but he could only think of how his decision to let her investigate had nearly got her killed.

"I'm going to find him, Dalton," he said grimly. "And he will pay for what he did this day. And what he did to Aunt Celeste."

"And I'll be by your side when you do it," Maitland

agreed with a nod. "I'll even help you bury the damned body. But right now, your lady needs you to keep a level head. And to keep from getting yourself killed."

Brushing his hand over his face, he knew his cousin was right. He drained his glass and set it down on a nearby shelf.

"Do you think they're finished yet?" he asked, staring at the door as if trying to detect what was happening on the other side through sheer force of will.

"There's one way to find out," said Maitland, rising to his feet and draining his own glass.

Quill stood too and opened the dressing room door.

Chapter 25

Ivy hissed as Serena and Polly tried to ease off her pelisse.

"I am sorry, miss," the maid said in a stricken tone, "but the ball pushed the cloth into the wound. I'll fetch a scissors to cut around it."

Soon, after some further moments of pain, Ivy was dressed in a clean shift, with the bedclothes pulled up over her bosom for propriety's sake, as Dr. Vance inspected her upper arm. "The good news, Miss Wareham," he said as he gestured for Serena to place the lamp he'd used to better see the wound on a nearby table, "is that the ball went straight through. So, while I know it hurts quite badly, at least there is no need for me to dig around in your arm to retrieve it."

At that description, Ivy felt the room spin a little.

"Unfortunately," Dr. Vance continued as he opened the black bag he'd carried into the room with him, "there is the matter of the fabric in the wound. I'm afraid removing it will be quite painful. So, be a good girl and drink this laudanum and you won't feel it a bit."

But Ivy shook her head, though the motion made her feel a little ill. "No laudanum," she protested. "It makes me violently ill."

"But my dear girl," the doctor chided, "the pain will feel a great deal worse, I can assure you. Come now, be sensible."

"If she says she doesn't want laudanum, doctor"— Quill's voice broke in—"then she shan't have it." The relief Ivy felt was so great, she sank back against the pillows with the force of it. Her agitation gone now that she knew Quill was there to fight for her.

"Lord Kerr," said Dr. Vance, his usually pleasant face pinched with annoyance, "I will thank you to let me know what's best for my patient."

"I will instead let Miss Wareham be the one to know what's best for her, sir," Quill said firmly. "She is surely the one who knows how laudanum has affected her in the past. Why can't she get roaring drunk instead? I daresay it may make her feel ill too, but its aftereffects will be of a much shorter duration."

The doctor's expression said he thought this was a foolish notion. Yet, he was a man who knew which side his bread was buttered on.

"Very well, my lord," he said with a supercilious sniff. "If that is how you wish to handle the matter, I shall leave you to it. I will be downstairs enjoying a cup of tea. When Miss Wareham is, as you so eloquently put it, 'roaring drunk,' send for me and I will clean the wound."

"He is a good physician," Serena said from where she sat on the other side of the bed, "but Dr. Vance can be a bit of an old woman at times."

"Thank you," Ivy said, reaching for Quill's hand with her uninjured one. "I would probably have allowed him to sway me if you hadn't intervened."

"I doubt Serena would have let him dose you against your will," Quill assured her, kissing her forehead gently.

"I'd have tried," Serena said wryly, "but I suspect the

good doctor is not very fond of having his wishes contra-vened by ladies."

"Well, we've routed him regardless," Quill said in a tone that sounded falsely cheerful, but Ivy was too dis-tracted by the throbbing in her arm to make mention of it. "Maitland, bring the brandy if you please."

And as if Quill had conjured him from the air, the Duke of Maitland appeared bedside, holding a decanter of am-ber liquid up high. "At your service, your grace," he said, making an exaggerated leg to his cousin before handing him the liquor and a glass.

Seating himself beside her, Quill poured a generous glass of brandy and put it to Ivy's lips. "Sip it so that you don't choke," he told her in a gentle tone. "There's no rush."

The brandy burned at first, but the trail of warmth as it slid down into her felt comforting, and soon Ivy was feel-ing much more the thing. "This is really quite pleasant, isn't it?" she asked after she'd finished the first glass. She wasn't generally one for strong spirits, but if this was how they made her feel, perhaps she should start drinking them more often.

"I think she's well on her way," Serena said from what to Ivy seemed like very far away, though she was sure Ser-ena was standing only a little behind Quill.

"One more glass I think," Quill said, giving Ivy another sip. But when Ivy felt herself hiccup, he pulled the glass away. "Or perhaps she's had enough now."

"I'll go get Vance," Maitland said.

When did he get here? Ivy wondered, her fuzzy brain trying to make sense of the scene.

"He accompanied us upstairs when I carried you inside," Quill said patiently, as he patted her uninjured hand. *Oh, that's right,* she remembered as if through a fog, *I'm injured.*

"Someone shot me," she said, her voice sounding slurred to her own ears.

"They did, indeed," Quill said, and she could tell that he was angry. Was he angry at *her*? She must have said the words aloud for he assured her, "No, sweet, I'm angry at whoever shot you. But you rest now. And concentrate on healing. I'll keep you safe from danger."

Danger. Danger. There was something in the back of Ivy's mind trying to catch her attention. But the fog was so thick now, she couldn't quite get to it. *Danger.* She could hear an old woman saying the word. And other things too. Things she needed to tell Quill. But just as soon as the thought occurred to her, it was gone again.

"Ah, I see she's all but insensible," Dr. Vance said from where he appeared behind Quill. "I hope this works as you think it will, Kerr, else Miss Wareham will be in a great deal of pain."

Ivy heard the doctor as if he were speaking from a very long way away. Then she heard Quill respond, but couldn't make out the words. Just the familiar deep rumble of his voice.

I'll just close my eyes for a minute, she thought, . . . *and take a little nap . . .*

And then she knew no more.

Though Dr. Vance strongly suggested that Quill leave the room while he extracted the bits of cloth from Ivy's wound, Quill had answered in no uncertain terms that either he remained at her side, or it was the good doctor who could leave.

Perhaps knowing when he had been bested, the physician muttered something about high-handed aristocrats, but did not further object.

Holding the hand of her uninjured arm tightly, lest she awaken and need him, Quill took up the position on the other side of the bed from the physican, and watched with grim anger as the doctor used a pair of tweezers to pluck bit after tiny bit of cloth from the oozing wound in Ivy's upper arm. Though she flinched, and groaned in pain from time to time, she did not awaken fully, and by the time the doctor was finished, she was snoring softly.

"I know you will not believe it, as worried as you are, my lord," Dr. Vance said as he sprinkled basilicum powder over the wound before pressing a clean bandage over it, "but this is not, as these things go, all that bad. Your lady was incredibly lucky it only struck her arm. Do you know who was out shooting today? Has anyone come forward?"

In one thing, the doctor was correct, Quill thought, staring down at Ivy's sleeping form: he didn't wish to hear how much worse her wound could have been. The fact that she'd been injured at all was something he would rue to the end of his days.

"It was no accident," he told the other man with a scowl. "You know as well as I do that the hunting in this part of the county is all but nonexistent. And no one with any sense would practice his aim so close to the footpath."

"But that's impossible," Dr. Vance said, his mouth opening and closing like a trout on a line. "Who would wish to harm Miss Wareham for God's sake?"

Caution kept Quill from revealing too much of his suspicions about who had reason to wish Ivy dead. He might wish to, but now was not the time. Instead he shrugged. "I have no idea. For a sweeter, more innocent lady you're not likely to meet."

The doctor's jaw clenched. "You don't suppose whoever it was that poisoned your aunt . . ."

Not wanting to give the other man a hint either way, Quill shrugged. "I have no idea. But if I find out who harmed her, he will rue the day he decided to go after the woman I love."

Swallowing in the face of the marquess's vehemence, the doctor set about putting his instruments back into his black bag. Placing a small vial on the table, he said, "I'll leave the laudanum just in case she has more pain that the brandy can manage." Turning to Serena, who just returned from emptying the basin of dirty water, he said, "Keep her wound dry and clean. And make sure to use plenty of powder on it. If she begins to turn feverish, send for me at once. Make her comfortable, and don't let her out of bed for several days at least. And give her beef broth to replenish the blood she lost."

Despite his anger with the man, Quill said a grudging thanks as the doctor opened the door to leave. Turning, his eyes shadowed, Vance said, "I am sorry, my lord. If I could go back . . ." He left the unsaid words hang in the air for a moment before stepping out and shutting the door behind him.

Quill could feel Serena's gaze on him like a tangible thing from where she stood behind him.

"Why didn't you tell me that aunt was poisoned?" she demanded quietly. "Or that you and Ivy were trying to determine who did it?"

He did her the courtesy of not denying that he and Ivy had been looking into the matter.

"Do you recall the letter Aunt left for Ivy," he said tightly, "the one I presume you left for her in her bedchamber that first night?"

"Yes," Serena said, her brows drawn. "I remember it."

"Aunt told her she suspected someone was trying to kill her. And as it happens, she was being poisoned," he said, feeling exhausted all of a sudden. The events of the day, the long journey back from the scene of Ivy's shooting, were finally taking their toll now that Ivy was resting comfortably.

But Serena had just learned now why it had even happened. And she wanted answers. "Why would she tell a stranger and not one of us?" she demanded, the hurt in her voice evident even through Quill's fatigue. "She'd never even met Ivy. And why Ivy of all the ladies?"

"I don't know," Quill said wearily. "Perhaps Aunt didn't trust us to look at the thing with the necessary lack of emotion?" Though even as he said it, he knew it wasn't fair to Ivy. She'd been affected greatly at the knowledge her benefactress had been murdered. She just hadn't had decades of memories to go along with it. "Who knows why she did it, Serena?" he asked with a sigh. "The simple fact is that she did do it, and because Ivy didn't quite feel she should go about investigating it alone, she told me. And here we are."

"All this time," Serena said with a shake of her head. "I thought the two of you were conducting a love affair. But you were merely conspiring to find who killed Aunt. And now you've compromised her, so you'll have to marry her."

That started a huff of laughter from him. "Oh, the affair is quite real," he admitted with a weary grin. "But, yes, what initially had us putting our heads together was an attempt to discover who poisoned Aunt Celeste."

"Ivy might have been killed," Serena said, her voice tight with emotion. "*You* might have been killed."

He could see that she was just as upset by the news as he'd feared she would be. But to her credit, her back was straight, and his cousin seemed ready to do battle.

The fact that he might have lost Ivy to a murderer today was something he wasn't ready to think about just yet. But something he could do was reassure his cousin. "We are well. All of us. And of all people, Aunt Celeste wouldn't have wanted us to hide ourselves away in fear. And I will do what it takes to protect Ivy and the rest of this family."

Serena shook her head. "Stubborn man," she said softly.

"When will you learn that we can take care of ourselves?"
Her eyes softened. "But we do appreciate some assistance
from time to time."

She reached out a hand to touch his arm. "I am glad
you're both alive. See that you remain that way."

Giving her a crooked smile, he said, "I plan on it."

She was silent for a moment as she looked at the sleeping Ivy.

Quill had leaned his head back against the headboard
when Serena's peeved voice broke through his exhaustion.
"You told Dalton, didn't you? That's why he suddenly appeared out of nowhere."

At his nod, she muttered a word he'd not heard her use
since they'd first learned it as children from one of the
grooms.

"I'm going to rip him to shreds," she said, striding
across the room to the door, the purpose in her gait spell-
ing imminent doom for her brother.

"Don't kill him," Quill called after her.

"I haven't yet," was her tart reply. "Though lord knows
he's given me reason enough over the years."

Quill heard the door close behind her with a snap, and
giving in to the demands of his body, he closed his eyes
and slept.

Chapter 26

Ivy awoke the next morning in pain. Both in her head, which informed her in no uncertain terms that it was not fond of strong drink, and her arm, which was throbbing in concert with her head.

She thought at first that she must have slept on it wrong, but that was before she felt a heavy masculine arm draped over her middle and the events of yesterday came rushing back to her. The morning light made her close her eyes again at once, but when she raised her lids more slowly, she saw Quill lying on his stomach beside her, his handsome face looking younger somehow in sleep.

His morning beard shadowed his jawline and, as if approaching a wild thing, she reached out tentatively to brush her fingers over the prickly stubble. She gasped when, without opening his eyes, he brought up his large hand to cover hers. Bringing her palm to his mouth, he kissed it.

Then, as if he too had just remembered why he was there, his eyes flew open and he scrambled into a sitting position.

"How are you?" he asked, his brow furrowed. His hair was sticking up at odd angles, but to Ivy's mind he was looking far more handsome than he had any right to at this hour of the morning. She certainly suspected she paled in comparison. "Is your arm paining you? Were you able to sleep?"

He stood and hurried over to the other side of the bed to pour her a glass of water. "I'll ring for some tea, shall I?" He rang the bell pull, then sat down on the edge of the bed and made as if to hold the glass to her mouth.

"Stop," Ivy said, pushing his hand away. "I can hold it myself, Quill. I'm not incapacitated." She tried to sit up and, despite her impatience, was grateful when he helped her by adjusting the pillows. After taking a long sip of the water, which felt like heaven on her parched tongue, she handed the glass back to him.

"Why are you here at this hour anyway?" she asked, as she watched him put the water back on the table. "Where is my maid?"

He blew out a breath and ran a hand through his hair, only making it worse. "I stayed in here with you last night because I wasn't convinced that a footman outside the door would be enough to keep out whoever took a shot at you yesterday."

"And Lady Serena allowed this?" She was rather shocked since the chaperone had seemed earlier to not want to add further flames to the fire of gossip surrounding her relationship with Quill.

"I gave her no choice in the matter," Quill said with the air of a man used to getting what he wants. "Someone tried to kill you yesterday, Ivy. I'm damned if I'll let him make another attempt while I'm here to prevent it. Serena knows better than to cross me when I'm protecting what's mine."

That declaration should have set her back up, but Ivy was strangely reluctant to call his words into question when he was so intent upon keeping her safe.

"And Polly?" she asked, referring to the absent maid.

"I told her to let you sleep as long as you needed to," he

said. "I'll ring for her if you'd like to have her take care of you while I dress."

Since she'd very much like to relieve herself, she nodded. "I wonder if any of my gowns will work with my bandage," she said thoughtfully as he slipped on his waistcoat and picked up his coat from where it lay draped over a chair.

"You won't need to worry about that for a couple of days at least," he said pulling his cuff from the sleeve.

"With the exception of a headache from the brandy I drank," Ivy said reasonably, "I am quite well enough to go downstairs."

His expression turned mulish. "No you are not," he said firmly. "It's very likely that your wound will cause a fever, and you must rest as much as possible to reserve your strength."

"But that's nonsense," Ivy argued. "I see no reason on earth why I should remain cooped up in this bedchamber when I can be looking over Lady Celeste's collection of relics and artifacts. Or looking over some of her translations. I've been so intent upon finding out who killed her that I've not spent even an entire hour in the library. Surely that is unobjectionable. It's not as if I'll be out combing the countryside in search of a killer."

"It's only nonsense if you discount the importance of your health," he said, not looking appeased by her explanation. "You might be carrying my heir, I'll remind you."

If anything could have been more calculated to set her back up, Ivy could not have imagined it.

"Ah," she said with a scowl. "I see now why you are suddenly so interested in my health. I might have known it was only because you see me as a brood mare."

"Don't be absurd," he retorted mildly. "Of course I see you as much more than that, which you should know by now. I only meant to remind you that if you will not rest for your own sake you might do so for the sake of the child." He leaned forward and kissed her, taking care to avoid touching her injured arm.

"The child we aren't even sure exists," Ivy said, exasperated. Though his reassurance made her feel a bit more sanguine about his admonition for her to rest, it didn't dismiss the fact that she'd be stuck alone all day.

Standing upright, he gave a put-upon sigh. "If you must go to the library, then I suppose you must. Have one of the footmen there to fetch things for you, though. I don't want you to make your arm worse with overuse."

"Where will you be?" she asked. Somehow she'd hoped that he would come with her to look over the collection. Though he'd never expressed a particular interest in translation, she'd perhaps foolishly expected him to be there when she first looked at his aunt's books. Or perhaps that was just a wish on her part to read some of the more salacious bits of poetry to him. She couldn't be sure.

His face hardened. "I'm going to see the magistrate, who in this case is Squire Northman, about the attempt to kill you yesterday. I hold out little hope that he'll be able to do anything to find them, but I wish to follow proper procedure in case I do find the miscreant." He didn't say what he'd do if he found them, but it was implied that he wanted it on the record that he'd reported the crime before he meted out his own brand of punishment for the attempt on her life.

At the mention of Northman, Ivy blanched. "Do you really wish to risk seeing Mrs. Northman again so soon?"

But if the idea bothered him, Quill didn't let on. "I'm not ashamed of you, Ivy," he said with a quizzical look. "If anything, the fault lies with Cassandra for being so histrionic about it. And since we are betrothed now, I don't think it's an issue. I doubt I'll see her today anyway. It's far too early in the day for her to have risen. She keeps London hours even in the country."

Ivy wasn't quite sure his lack of worry was warranted, but she supposed it was too late to worry about reputations—hers or his—at this point. And his dismissal of Mrs. Northman went a long way toward quieting any fears she might have had that he nursed a lingering affection for the lady.

"Shall I fetch you something from the village while I'm out?" he asked her, moving back so that Polly, who had just entered with a bowl of hot water, could place it on the side table.

"No, nothing," she said with a smile at his sweet offer. "Just be careful yourself. You seem convinced that yesterday's shooter was after me, but it's entirely possible that you were the target. You were standing right next to me, after all."

But he waved away the suggestion. "I wasn't the one who'd just been warned by a gypsy fortune teller that I was in danger."

When she opened her mouth to counter his argument, he shook his head. "But nonetheless, I will take care. At this point, I suppose we cannot afford to discount any theory about the shooter."

And with a wave, he stepped out of the room, leaving Ivy to Polly's tender care.

After ensuring that Maitland would keep close watch over Ivy in his absence, Quill set out on horseback for Squire Northman's house. But when he arrived, he saw Dr. Vance's familiar carriage waiting at the door. A pang of foreboding ran through him.

"Is someone in the house ill?" he asked the groom who stood waiting to take the horse's reins.

The young man winced. "One of the maids, my lord" He looked around as if to see who was watching them. "Took her own life, like."

With a curse, Quill sprinted up the stairs of the portico and when the door opened, he didn't wait for a greeting from the butler. "It was the maid Elsie, wasn't it?" he asked the man, who looked aghast at Quill's lack of decorum.

"I'm sure if you will wait in the drawing room, my lord, Mr. Northman will explain in due time what has happened," Watson said in a dignified huff.

But his lack of reply to the question told Quill all he needed to know. Brushing past the indignant servant, he hurried through what looked to be the servants' hall and followed the sound of weeping and murmured whispers to a small group of servants standing near an open door.

"My lord," the butler called out from behind him. "I'm sure if you will just come with me Mr. Northman will be happy to—"

"It's all right, Watson," said Northman himself, as he stepped out from the door where the crowd was gathered. "I'll speak to his lordship here."

Quill glanced back at the butler, who looked perturbed at the breach of protocol, but was silent.

Northman, who looked grim, gestured for Quill to come forward. "You lot should go down to the kitchens and have some tea. I'll let you know of any news as soon as I'm able."

Watson came forward and ushered the servants, a couple of footmen and three weeping maids, back toward the other end of the hall.

"I don't suppose you know why my wife's maid, whom you and Miss Wareham questioned only days ago," Northman said with a scowl to Quill as they stepped into the grim little bedchamber where Elsie had drawn her last breath, "would wish to take her own life?"

Quill was silent for a moment as he looked to where Dr. Vance stood over the body of Elsie, which was lying stiff on the floor. It was obvious from the posture of the corpse that her death had not been a peaceful one. Her face was contorted in a rictus of agony, and her hands were tightly fisted against her chest. He wondered suddenly if this is what it had been like for Celeste and was assailed by a renewed sense of determination to find out who had done this to her. To them both. For he was sure now that whoever had killed his aunt had also killed her maid.

The doctor, who had been making notes in a small bound book, turned and met Quill's eyes. It was clear that the other man had come to the same conclusion.

To Northman, Quill said, "I have a suspicion that the same person who killed my aunt might have killed Elsie."

If the magistrate was shocked by the news, he didn't show it. Instead he scowled. "What makes you think that Lady Celeste was deliberately murdered? I thought we'd decided that she likely died of a wasting disease, Vance."

That he and Vance had discussed the possibility that Celeste's death may not have been from natural causes was evident from Norman's words, and Quill would have demanded an explanation, but Vance spoke up, cutting him off. "I told you at the time, Northman, that I could not be sure without sending the body to London for autopsy. And that was not what the family wished. Now, thanks to some pointed questions from his lordship and Miss Wareham, I have decided that it is likely that Lady Celeste was poisoned by the tonic Elsie was giving her for her headaches."

The squire looked grim. "Has my wife been in danger this whole time?" he demanded with icy calm.

Vance had the good grace to look abashed. "I would never have allowed her to come here if I'd suspected the maid at the time of Lady Celeste's death," he said defensively. "It was not until Lord Kerr began asking questions that it occurred to me that the tisanes were the likely source of the poison."

That didn't seem to reassure Northman much, but he did not belabor the point. "So, Elsie has also been murdered? What about this indicates that she didn't simply take her own poison in a fit of conscience?" He gestured to the overturned teacup on the floor beside the body, the dregs of the last sip clinging to the bowl of the floral-patterned porcelain.

"Aside from the fact that there are far less agonizing ways to die," Quill said, stooping to pick up the cup and sniff it. As he'd suspected, there was no strange odor. No indication that it was been laced with anything other than tea. "There is the fact that the amount of poison needed to kill her so quickly would be all but impossible to drink in such a concentrated source as a single cup of tea."

"Would it not depend upon the poison?" Northman demanded. "Surely they all cannot taste foul."

"I suspect in Lady Celeste's case," Dr. Vance said, taking the cup from Quill and sniffing it with diffidence, "that the culprit was aconite. Since the visit Lord Kerr and Miss Wareham paid me earlier in the week, I have done some research into substances that might cause symptoms that mimic those of a wasting disease or cankers of the bowel, and aconite seems to be the most likely source. And it could easily be masked in a brewed tonic of the sort Lady Celeste was in the habit of taking."

"But if there was no sign of aconite in Elsie's tea," Northman said, his mouth tight, "then how the hell did she ingest it?"

Quill stooped and pulled a small box—the sort that was often used by confectioners to preserve sweetmeats and other sweet delicacies—out from beneath the bed, where it lay on its side. The lid was off, and Quill looked inside before showing it to the other two men. At the bottom there was both greasy residue and some crumbs.

"Did Elsie receive any gifts in the past several days?" he asked Northman. "Anything unexpected or perhaps a surprise to mark her birthday or some other special day?"

Northman pokered up. "I am not in the habit of keeping track of the personal lives of my household staff, Lord Kerr. I couldn't even tell you when the damned woman's birthday was, much less whether she received any gifts on the occasion."

"Then we should question your housekeeper," Quill said, not bothering to ask whether it would do any good to speak to Northman's wife. Cassandra was also not the sort to show an interest in the lives of her servants. Even one so personal as her own maid. "I suspect the poison was delivered over the course of a few days, which would be easy enough to do if it were used as an ingredient in a pastry or sweetmeat."

Vance nodded his agreement. "Aconite might have been unpalatable in a single cup of tea, but spreading it out over several pieces of candy or biscuits would make it less noxious."

Cursing, Northman shook his head. "I would have liked to know there was a madman poisoning people in my district before he struck in my own household, Vance."

"And shooting," Quill said, not wishing to lose sight of his original reason for seeking the magistrate out. "Yesterday someone made an attempt on Miss Ivy Wareham's life as we walked back to Beauchamp House from the gypsy fortune teller's caravan."

Looking as if he wished himself anywhere but the Sussex coast at that very moment, Northman cursed again. "I guess you'd better come up to my study so that I can take down the details and have my investigator look into it."

Turning to Vance, he said, "I'd like for you to testify at the inquest, doctor, so please ensure that your report is as thorough as necessary."

The physician shot a look of sheer loathing at the magistrate's back as Northman turned and dismissed him. Quill filed that away for future reflection, and with a look of commiseration with the doctor, turned and followed Northman from the room.

Chapter 27

A bit of toast and tea in her room was all Ivy could stomach thanks to yesterday's pain-relieving dose of brandy, so she arrived in Lady Celeste's magnificent library before any of the other ladies.

Once again she was hit with the wish that she'd been able to meet the woman with the diverse scholarly knowledge who assembled such a collection. Not to mention the artistic sensibility that had directed Lady Celeste to design the room itself, with its gorgeous inlaid ceiling and rich mahogany and gilt-edged shelving. The visual effect was breathtaking, and Ivy was certain that it had been her benefactress's intent to overwhelm each visitor who stepped into what had clearly been a labor of love for the lady.

But with the thought of Lady Celeste's life came the thought of her premature death. And even as she took in the details of the room that had been Celeste's personal domain, Ivy wondered for the first time if there weren't some clue to the identity of who had killed her hidden here. The thought was overwhelming given that the collection, according to Greaves, contained some seven thousand volumes. If Celeste had thought to secrete some message in one of the books, it would take more than Ivy working with her uninjured arm to find it in enough time to catch the killer before he struck again.

With a sigh, she stepped over to the shelves behind the massive desk Celeste had used for her own personal studies. If Ivy were going to hide something, it would definitely be near where she spent the most time. And the books on these shelves, if the wear on their spines was any indication, were amongst Lady Celeste's favorites. Unlike the rest of the shelves, these few behind the desk seemed to be arranged in some order that only their owner had understood. Multi-volume novels were sandwiched between mathematical treatises and philosophical works.

For instance, she thought with a smile for the happy disorder of it, here were two volumes of Samuel Pepys diaries beside the third volume of Madame d'Arblay's *Cecilia*. Whether Lady Celeste had simply shelved them as she finished or she kept them there to reread favorite passages, Ivy had no idea. It was one of those circumstances of day-to-day life that was lost along with Celeste. And like so many details of that lady's thoughts, the reason for it was impossible to learn now that she was gone.

If only Lady Celeste had, like Pepys, kept a record of her . . . Ivy stopped, her hand reaching out toward the shelf in question, arrested by her train of thought.

What were the chances that a woman who so valued philosophy and scholarship and the life of the mind would not have kept some sort of record of her studies or, if not her scholarly pursuits, then at the very least of her thoughts? It was hardly uncommon for a lady to keep a journal, but for a woman of Lady Celeste's proclivities to *not* do so would be positively unheard of. Especially if she knew, as her letter had indicated, that she was not long for this world.

Thus it was that when Sophia, followed close behind by Daphne and Gemma, wandered into the room after breakfast, it was to find Ivy balanced on the rolling ladder along the shelves on the wall behind the big desk using her good hand to remove a single volume at a time to see if there was anything behind it.

"What on earth are you doing out of bed?" Sophia asked aghast, hurrying to stand gaping up at where Ivy seemed to hang upon the library wall. "You were shot yesterday, Ivy. You should be resting."

"Or at the very least refraining from climbing ladders when you've only one hand to save yourself with," Gemma said from beside her sister. "You might have waited until someone else was in the room before you decided to tempt fate and gravity by taking your life into your own hands."

"Fate and gravity have nothing to do with one another," Daphne said staring up at Ivy with interest. "One is an abstract concept that relies upon supernatural beliefs to sustain it that cannot be proved or disproved, while the other is a natural law that can easily be proved by dropping any common object from a height equal to or greater than the length of said object. I doubt it is possible to tempt either because they do not possess human feelings."

"Yes, thank you, Daphne," Sophia said with a small sigh. "I believe that was one of those 'figures of speech' we were discussing yesterday. I doubt Gemma meant literally that fate and gravity would be wracked with the desire to make Ivy fall from this ladder."

Ivy could see from her elevated height that Daphne wished to argue the point, so she spoke up. "I am looking for Lady Celeste's private diaries, and since you have come in at just the moment when I was considering the folly of my decision to climb this ladder, I will thankfully accept your help in descending."

With Gemma holding her waist and Sophia holding the ladder, Ivy carefully made her way, step by step, down from her perch.

Daphne spoke up almost as soon as her feet were on the floor again. "I believe I saw some journals in Lady Celeste's bedchamber last evening when we were playing hide-and-seek with Jeremy."

"Why were you in that part of the house?" Sophia asked, her pretty face scrunched up in puzzlement.

"Why were you playing hide-and-seek on the night I was shot?" Ivy asked, cutting to what, for her, was the more pertinent question.

Gemma smiled sheepishly. "Jem overheard his mother and Lord Kerr speaking about what happened and he was frightened that whoever shot at you might try to get into the house. So the duke thought a game of hide-and-seek might prove a useful distraction."

On hearing that young Jeremy had been frightened, Ivy felt a pang of distress for the boy. From what she'd heard, he'd already had what wasn't a particularly uneventful childhood, so hearing that someone living in the same house had been shot must have been upsetting.

Gemma, however, was distracted by something else. "Speaking of the duke," she said, her eyes narrowed on Daphne, "both you and he were missing for quite a long time while the rest of us played. You didn't see him somewhere near Lady Celeste's diaries, did you?"

To Ivy's astonishment, Daphne blushed. Something Ivy hadn't been sure was possible.

"I may have run into him in the vicinity," she said, looking just past them into the room beyond, her usual habit of not making eye contact seeming more intentional than usual, though Ivy knew that was absurd. "We hid together for a while before realizing that no one would be coming to find us there."

"I'll bet you 'hid,'" Gemma said with a smirk. "I suspect you two have been doing quite a bit of 'hiding' over the last day or so."

Daphne frowned. "Of course we haven't. At least, only while we were playing hide-and-seek. It would be odd to hide during the normal course of a day."

Ivy shared an amused look with the Hastings sisters. "I think what she meant, Daphne," she said with a grin, "was that you and the duke have been spending some time together. Alone time."

The cloud lifted and Daphne nodded. "Oh, yes. We have. He is quite good at kissing. Though I haven't been able to convince him to take me as a lover. He is convinced that it would not be proper. And no amount of convincing on my part will sway him on the matter. It is really quite frustrating."

Ivy, Sophia, and Gemma all stared at her.

An uncomfortable silence descended upon them.

"I've shocked you," Daphne said with what sounded to Ivy like disappointment. "I don't know why I cannot seem to tell what will and will not shock my acquaintances. I do not wish to distress you all. Certainly not while Ivy is still recovering from a gunshot wound."

Her innate sense of fondness for the other girl made Ivy push past her surprise at her declaration about the Duke of Maitland, and she moved to touch Daphne on the arm. She'd sensed from their first meeting that anything else would prove uncomfortable for her. "We are surprised, dear, by your plain speaking, but not distressed. Pray do not become distressed yourself. It's just that we are not used to hearing such things, and well, as perhaps your mother has told you, it's not quite appropriate to speak of such things in public."

"But you're my friends," Daphne said, looking even more puzzled. "We are not in the middle of a ballroom. I know well enough not to speak of such things in drawing rooms, or in mixed company, or at the mantua-makers." The way she listed off the locales where she knew not to speak told Ivy that these had been where she'd done so in her mother's presence.

"She's right," Gemma said with a rueful smile. "We are her friends, and we are alone in here. So she's technically correct."

Before Daphne could tell them that technically was the only way to be correct—something she'd done on a previous occasion when Gemma used the term—Ivy spoke to the issue at the heart of their discomfort. "Daphne, I realize that it is frustrating for you to be rejected by the duke, but he is quite correct that it would be quite improper for him to ahh . . ." She searched for a word that was explicit enough for Daphne to understand, but not so graphic as to offend the other two ladies.

"Engage in sexual congress with me?" Daphne supplied, not betraying with so much as a blush that the term embarrassed her. Ivy wondered what must it be like to be so comfortable with speaking about such things. It had to be difficult, of course, since her plain speaking often landed Daphne in trouble, but on the other hand it would be such a relief not to be constantly afraid of saying the wrong thing.

"Yes, that," Ivy agreed with an apologetic smile to Sophia and Gemma. "Lord Kerr and I were only found kissing at the Northman's house and we are now betrothed because of it. If you wish to, ah, do *that* with the duke, then he would of course, need to marry you."

"First of all," Daphne said patiently, "the duke and I would not engage in sexual congress anywhere where we might be seen by anyone. That would be quite odd." Before Ivy could respond to that, she went on. "And secondly, why is it that men are allowed to do it without marrying their partners but ladies are required to? It is highly illogical that ladies cannot f—"

Sophia placed a finger to Daphne's lips to stop her words. "We understand, dear. It does seem wretchedly unfair that ladies are required to marry the men they do *that* with. But nevertheless, it is the way of our world. And as your mother has explained to you I feel sure, those who do it without benefit of marriage risk any number of problems. Bearing a child out of wedlock, for instance, or being ostracized from society. Poor Ivy will be the subject of a great deal of talk, I suspect, thanks to her interlude with Lord Kerr in the Northman hallway."

"In point of fact," Daphne argued, "my mother died when I was only a small child, so I was left to learn about such things from books. There is a quite interesting pamphlet called *Aristotle's Masterpiece* that contains all sorts of ridiculous notions—that a child conceived out of wedlock, for instance, will be born covered all over with hair. Truly ridiculous stuff—especially when one considers how many children of the aristocracy are born on the wrong side of the blanket. I believe that—"

"Oh, I am sorry, Daphne," Ivy said, latching onto the news about the other lady's mother, hoping to divert her before one or all of them broke down in tears of exasperation. "It must have been quite difficult to lose your mother at such a young age." It also went a long way, in Ivy's opinion, toward explaining why Daphne was so ungoverned in her conversation.

But much as she would like to discuss the matter more, it was the death of Lady Celeste that was foremost on her mind at the moment.

"Perhaps we can continue this discussion later?" she asked hopefully. "After we've gone to find Lady Celeste's journals? For I truly fear that if we do not find out who killed her, someone else will die very soon."

She'd known her interruption would perhaps upset

Daphne, at the very least, but all three of the other ladies gasped. And Ivy realized what she'd just done. In her effort to soothe Daphne she'd let the truth slip out.

"Lady Celeste was murdered?" Sophia demanded, her eyes pinning Ivy to where she stood.

"How long have you known?" Gemma asked with a stricken expression.

"So that's why you were shot," Daphne said as if something had finally clicked into place.

Ivy's mind raced, searching for some way of explaining things that wouldn't make them more annoyed than they already were.

But she was saved from reply by Quill, followed by Maitland, striding into the room.

"Elsie is dead," Quill said without preamble. "Poisoned, and likely by the same thing that killed Celeste."

When Quill arrived back at Beauchamp House, he was displeased to find that instead of keeping by Ivy's side in the library as per his request, Maitland was instead seated in a chair outside the door of that room.

"Why the devil aren't you watching over Ivy as I requested?" he demanded of his cousin, who stood as soon as he saw Quill approach.

Northman had listened with mounting frustration as Quill told him about the letter from Lady Celeste that had prompted his and Ivy's investigation into her murder, their suspicion that the medicinal tisanes had been the means by which the poison was administered, and their visit to the gypsy woman the day before. When he got to the point at which Ivy was shot at, the magistrate had cursed.

"I hope you're happy now, Lord Kerr," Northman had spat out. "Not only should you have reported this business about your aunt as soon as the letter surfaced, but you've very nearly got your lady killed because of your damned aristocratic notion that you can handle all of this on your own."

Quill had forborne from pointing out to Northman that while he was a magistrate, it wasn't as if he had a stable of men at the ready to seek out criminals as was the case with Bow Street. This was a relatively rural locale and as such had been run by the landowners and aristocrats who lived there for centuries. And he was quite able to take care of himself and those whom he cared about. Ivy included. Instead, he had accepted the admonishment without replying and took his leave. Promising without really meaning it, that he would let the other man know of any further developments.

He had felt the need to report Ivy's shooting, of course, because it was the right thing to do. But now that another life had been taken, Quill knew that there was no time to wait for the wheels of local justice to find the killer. He would simply have to do that himself. And if Northman disliked it, he'd simply have to live with his anger.

Now, however he was back at Beauchamp House facing Maitland, who contrary to Quill's request had seen fit to sit outside the library rather than at Ivy's side. "Well? Why aren't you bloody well in there?"

Maitland's jaw clenched and his cheekbones reddened. "The other ladies are in the library with Miss Wareham. And if there were anything untoward happening I would have heard them cry out."

That his cousin would not meet his eye made Quill's brow furrow with suspicion. "What aren't you telling me?" he demanded. "Are you hiding out here?"

When Maitland's face only turned redder, Quill knew he had his answer. Diverted momentarily from the murders, he tilted his head. "What happened? I thought you were smitten with Lady Daphne?" It wasn't like his cousin to leave off pursuing a woman so soon after catching her scent. "Has she given you the heave-ho already?" It was rare that the duke, with his golden good looks and sunny personality, was rebuffed, but it did happen on occasion. And Quill knew that when it did, Maitland wasn't happy about it.

"If you must know," the duke said with a dignified sniff, "it is I who have chosen to back away from Lady Daphne. For the time being at any rate."

This was novel. "I know she can be outspoken, but surely that's nothing you can't handle. After all, it's not as if you don't put your own foot in your mouth from time to time."

Maitland glanced to either side, as if ensuring that they would not be overheard, then in a low voice hissed, "She wants me to sleep with her, Quill!"

In spite of his cousin's very serious distress, Quill couldn't help himself. He laughed.

"It's not funny," the duke said, reaching up to grip his blond locks in frustration. "I am not in the business of debauching innocents. I am a gentleman. If she were a widow, or a bored wife, perhaps, but I won't touch an unmarried lady without some kind of understanding between us and you damned well know it. Not only is it beyond the pale, it goes against my code as a gentleman."

"And what was her response to this?" Quill asked, his interest piqued by this unusual turn of events. He'd known Lady Daphne marched to her own drum, but this was a surprise even for her.

"When I said that she'd have to marry me first, she told me I was being foolish," Maitland said, his eyes wide with outrage. "I'm a duke of the realm, by god, and she behaved as if a proposal from me was utterly unnecessary!"

That his cousin had, in fact, asked the chit to marry him told Quill just how far gone he was over her. To his knowledge, Maitland had never before asked a lady to marry him. And since he knew well enough how sharp the pain of rejection could be, he bit back his amusement and clapped the other man on the shoulder. "Perhaps she'll come around," he said, despite the fact that he suspected Lady Daphne could be quite as stubborn as Maitland when she felt like it.

"Well, she'll have to if she wants me to give her the benefit of my legendary lovemaking skills," Maitland said, in a not-altogether-joking mode. He'd always been a bit full of himself when it came to that, Quill thought with a roll of his eyes. "I won't settle for anything less than marriage, and she'll simply have to capitulate or miss out."

It would have been quite satisfying for Quill to point out to his cousin, who had only recently been taunting him over his own fall into the parson's mousetrap, that he himself was about to dive in headfirst. However, there were other more pressing matters to attend to.

"Much as I would love to continue this discussion of your 'legendary lovemaking skills,'" Quill said dryly, "there is the matter of a murderer on the loose that needs my attention right now. And if you are too frightened to go into the library with me to discuss the goings-on at the Northman house with Ivy and the other ladies, then I suggest you make yourself scarce."

But despite his earlier refusal to enter the library, the duke had never been one to back down from a challenge from his cousin, so he indicated to Quill that he should proceed. Opening the door, the marquess stepped inside to find the four ladies clustered together behind Aunt Celeste's enormous desk.

"Elsie is dead," he said knowing that the other three ladies were not even aware that Celeste had been murdered but deciding it was high time they all spoke openly about the entire matter. "Poisoned, and likely by the same thing that killed Celeste."

To his surprise, however, neither the Hastings sisters nor Lady Daphne seemed particularly shocked by the news that their benefactress had been murdered.

"I told them about Lady Celeste," Ivy said in response to his questioning look. "I thought it was time to enlist the aid of three of the most intelligent ladies of my acquaintance in our search. Besides, who is to say that this person will not make an attempt on their lives next."

"Not if I have anything to say about it," Maitland said hotly as he shut the library door behind him. "It's time we put this monster out of commission once and for all."

"I agree, cousin," said Quill with equal ferocity. "And since all the ladies are now aware of the situation, perhaps we should discuss our next move in this deadly game."

"First tell us about Elsie," Ivy said moving to take a seat at one of the large library tables, and waiting for the others to follow suit.

Once he had taken a chair beside her, Quill explained what had happened to Elsie, including the details of the poisoned confectionary and his discussion with Northman. "Though I know the magistrate would like us to sit back and let the authorities find out who is doing this," he said in conclusion, "the fact that he is brazen enough to kill beneath Northman's own roof, in addition to the fact that he took a shot at you, Ivy, while we were all there to see it, tells me that the killer is desperate now. And I, for one, am not willing to just sit by and let him try to kill you again."

Ivy gave a shiver and, not caring about the impropriety of the gesture, he covered her free hand with his own.

"Something occurred to me while you were gone this morning," Ivy said into the silence that followed. Quickly she outlined how she'd come to think about the possibility that Celeste kept a journal. "And since Daphne recalled seeing some journals in Lady Celeste's bedchamber last night, we were about to make our way up there."

Feeling like a fool, Quill shook his head. "Of course, she kept journals. Don't you remember that she was always scribbling away in them when we were children, Maitland?"

"Yes," his cousin said, his voice rising with excitement. "I don't know why I didn't think of them either. I suppose that after a certain time she never let us see her with them, and I simply forgot altogether."

"Then let's go upstairs and get them," Ivy said in a firm voice. "Because Lady Celeste deserves to have justice."

Chapter 28

Though it felt a bit ridiculous for them all to go upstairs to Lady Celeste's bedchamber at once, that is what they did. Ivy and Quill led the way with the others following close behind. When they arrived in the darkened chamber, however, all eyes turned to Daphne, who said, "They were stacked on the little shelf behind the writing desk, there."

Sophia and Gemma went to open the curtains to let in the daylight, and Ivy took a moment to look around the room where Lady Celeste had lived for most of her adult life. It was decorated in the colors of the sea—light greens and blues with a burst of white here and there in the trimmings of the bedclothes and on the valances over the windows, which looked out, as it happened, on the sun-dappled waters of the channel. There was a hint of rosewater and lavender in the air, almost as if Celeste had only just walked through the room, leaving her scent behind.

Crossing to the writing desk, where Quill had taken a seat and was scanning the low shelves that ran along the wall behind, Ivy picked up the lamp he'd just lit and held it so that he might see the rows of books better. "Here," he said tersely. "There must be decades worth of diaries here. This may take longer than we'd hoped." He began pulling out the volumes in stacks of three and piling them onto the surface of the desk.

"There are six of us," Ivy said with a practical air. "Perhaps we can each take a decade to look over."

"We should go back to the library where we can take notes," Gemma said, grabbing a handful of volumes and not waiting to see if the others would follow.

It was a good idea, so Ivy tried to gather up a few of the diaries into the crook of her good arm, but ended up dropping one.

"I'll carry yours," Quill said, edging her out of the way as Sophia, Daphne, and Maitland picked up the rest of the books and filed out leaving Ivy and Quill alone.

"I hope she knows we are trying," Ivy said in the suddenly quiet room. "That we appreciate what she did for us and will try to avenge her."

Slipping an arm around her shoulders, Quill said against her hair, "I think if Celeste is watching us now at all, she's having a very hearty laugh at how quickly her favorite nephews have succumbed to two of her chosen bluestockings."

At his words, Ivy looked up at him with wide eyes. "Did Maitland tell you about Daphne then?"

"More like whined," Quill said with a laugh. "I was not very sympathetic, I'm afraid. It is far too amusing to see the tables turned on him for a change."

"I must admit to feeling some sympathy for the poor man," Ivy said with a shake of her head. "I think anyone would be flummoxed by such a direct request from a lady as beautiful as Daphne. We did try to explain to her that it's not quite proper to tell a gentleman in those terms what she wants from him. Though I do see your point about the whole marriage bit. If it's good for the goose, why wouldn't it be good for the gander?"

Well, it will be a while before Aunt Celeste sees any

resolution on that front, I fear," Ivy said wryly. Then turning serious, she added, "But I do hope we will succeed in finding her poisoner. I do dislike the idea of her spirit being restless because this thing is unresolved. I certainly know I will not be able to rest easy until he's caught."

"Then I suppose we should join the others and see if we can find some clue in the journals," Quill said, snuffing out the lamp, then gathering the remaining journals in his arms and following Ivy from the room.

When they reached the library, they found that Serena had joined them and had taken a stack of journals to go through as well.

"I believe you have the earliest years there," Gemma said, looking up from where she'd opened the first of a stack of six books. "Just call out if you find something that might be useful." She gestured to a slate and a bit of chalk. "I'll make notations as we go. Even if you're unsure, tell us. It will be better to have too much than too little information."

Resuming the chairs they'd vacated earlier, Ivy and Quill sat side by side and began to go through their diaries.

The room was silent for a long while as everyone scanned the diaries.

As they went through the journals, Daphne, who had been reading the past ten years of entries, had mentioned when Lady Celeste began to search for the four ladies she would leave her estate to. Quill hadn't considered that the decision to leave Beauchamp House to a quartet of women outside the family was anything but caprice. But the passages Daphne had shared revealed that, far from whimsy, Celeste's decision had rested on a genuine wish to see that her collection was put in the hands of scholars—lady scholars like her—who would put it to best use.

Only about a quarter hour had passed before Daphne issued a most un-Daphne-like noise.

Frowning, Ivy looked up and saw that everyone else was also staring at the blonde, too, "What is it? Did you find something troubling?"

When the mathematician looked up, Ivy was startled to see tears in her eyes. "My goodness," she said, moving to sit beside her. She exchanged a wide-eyed look with Sophia who seemed just as puzzled as Ivy. "You must tell us, my dear. If it can help us find the killer, no matter how awful, we need to know it."

Accepting the handkerchief that Maitland had wordlessly handed her, Daphne blew her nose loudly and said, "It's not so much a clue as it is just something that . . ." She seemed at a loss for words. "Well, I suppose it moved me. That's all."

"Are you going to keep it to yourself then, dear?" Serena asked with a raised brow when Daphne didn't elaborate.

"What?" Daphne looked up as if she'd just noticed they were all there.

She was behaving very oddly, Ivy thought, surveying her friend. Perhaps her interactions with the duke had set her off-balance. Interesting.

"Oh." Shaking herself a little, as if emerging from a trance, Daphne blinked. "It was just this passage in one of the later journals. From about three years ago, I think. She talks about her reasons for choosing us, and why she wished to ensure that female scholars benefitted from the collections she'd amassed over the years. It just struck me a little, I suppose. That she felt so strongly about it. That she chose you all. And me."

Picking up the journal she'd been reading, Daphne opened it and began to read aloud:

I know my family will think me mad for it, but I am determined that my life's work will not go to waste. That the books and artifacts and art I so painstakingly

purchased, piece by piece, in an effort to expand my
own knowledge of the world, will serve to further the
education of women with the good sense and intelligence to put their minds to good use. I am confident
that the young ladies I have my eye on will only be a
credit to their sex and their chosen disciplines. It is my
hope that once they realize how important this is to me
that my nephews and niece will understand and let my
heirs do what they were put on earth to do without
causing them grief for it.

Perhaps because the way in which my own pursuit
of scholarship was discouraged by my parents, I know
all too well how difficult the way can be for those of
us who were gifted with intellectual ability, but had the
misfortune to be born women. One day I hope that it
will be possible for anyone with the requisite talent—
be they rich or poor, male or female, aristocrat or
serf—to pursue her true calling. But until that day, I
will do my part to open the door for these four, whom
I hope will prove themselves worthy of my gift.

The silence in the library was so thick you might have
heard a feather fall. And Ivy found that her own eyes
were damp. "Oh, I wish I could have met her just once,"
she said, feeling the loss of their benefactor more keenly
than ever. "If only to thank her for choosing me. Though I
cannot imagine what set me apart from the countless other
lady scholars out there."

"Me too," said Sophia, also a little misty.

"I want to find whoever killed her," Daphne said, her
earlier sentiment gone now, leaving in its place a grim determination. "Not only did he rob us of the chance to meet
Lady Celeste, but he also took her from the place she loved
best in the world. Against her will." Her fists clenched.

"I dislike it above all things when a woman is forced to do something against her will."

Ivy got the feeling that there was something more than just mourning the loss of Lady Celeste behind Daphne's declaration, but she decided to speak with her about it later.

She was about to suggest that they get back to work, when Gemma spoke up. "Why didn't she send for us? When she knew she was dying, I mean?" The younger Hastings sister, who was generally the least likely of the quartet to take something to heart, seemed to be particularly upset at their benefactor's decision. "I know it can't have been pleasant," she went on, "but we would not have cared about that. So long as we'd been able to meet her. To thank her."

Serena, who had been silent up to now, cleared her throat. "I think I might be able to shed some light on that," she said sadly. "I think it's easy not to guess, when all you've known of her has been her hopes and dreams set forth in these journals. Or the individual messages she left for each of you upon your arrival here. But I knew Aunt Celeste, as did Maitland and Kerr, from the time I was little. And despite her intelligence, and zeal for reform, she was, in point of fact, a bit shy."

"You aren't telling us that she didn't call us to her because she was afraid of meeting us, surely?" Sophia looked skeptical in the extreme. "Because I won't believe that the same woman who defied her family and left her entire estate to four strangers was too timid to actually see them at least once."

But Serena shook her head. "No, not in so many words. It was more that meeting people—even those she knew she would enjoy getting to know—was hard for her. After a dinner party once, she took to her bed for a week. 'Refilling the well' she called it. And as much as she would have loved meeting you, I think in those last few weeks she was using every bit of strength she had to fight off her illness. And then, by the time she knew it was hopeless, it was too late."

"It did take a lot out of her," Quill confirmed, his eyes reflecting his own sorrow at the loss of his aunt. "Meeting people. She could be as animated and witty as can be, but she didn't have an endless supply of energy. And I can well imagine her thinking she had all the time in the world to meet you only to find out she was wrong."

"I want to know who it was," Gemma said fiercely. "I want to know who killed this remarkable woman."

Ivy agreed. "I think we all wish to find out who did this. So, let's dive back into the journals and find something. There has to be some clue here that will tell us something useful."

With murmured assent, they all got back to perusing their portions of the journals.

She was nearing the end of the volume from the summer after Celeste's debut when Ivy reached a notation that had her heart quickening with excitement. Celeste had fallen in love with a man named Ian. And when Ivy moved on to the next journal, she found another mention of Celeste's passion for Ian, followed by a lament about the unfairness of the parents who wouldn't let them be together. But it was the description of their thwarted elopement along with vague but unmistakable descriptions of what had occurred between them on their single night together that had Ivy convinced that she'd discovered something that could be the clue they were looking for.

She read the tear-stained words of the page Celeste had written some three months after the elopement:

My dearest love has been sent away, but God has given me something to remember him by. If only I can manage to convince Mama and Papa to let me keep the child. Surely even they cannot be so cruel as to wrest a babe from its mother's arms—especially when it is entirely their doing that its father is rotting away in some country parsonage in Yorkshire.

Then, ten months later, again in tear-stained script, she'd written:

It is done. They have taken the only real things I've ever loved from me. I only hope that my dear little girl will have a happier life than the one I've been given. I will never forgive Father for his perfidy. He might have agreed to give me Beauchamp House outright as a peace offering, but there will never be peace between us again. And I will never be happy again.

Ivy brushed away her own tears at the thought of what Celeste had endured at such a young age. That she'd been separated from the man she loved—a clergyman it sounded like, so likely not smart enough for the Duke and Duchess of Beauchamp to allow to court their daughter—was one thing, but to also have the child born of that love torn from her very arms? Well, Ivy would not have blamed Lady Celeste a bit if she'd become a bitter, cold, unfeeling woman after that. And yet, from all appearances, she'd gone on to make a name for herself in scholarly circles and to amass one of the most impressive collections of books and artifacts in Europe, let alone England.

"Lady Celeste had a child," she said aloud, eliciting gasps and shocked sounds from her fellow readers. "A girl who was cruelly taken from her when it was but a month old."

"Oh, poor Celeste," Serena said, her lovely features contorted with sadness. "I knew our grandparents were cruel, but I had no notion they'd do such a thing."

"What makes you think they were responsible?" Maitland asked his sister. "I'm not disagreeing about their character, mind you, I just wish to know what makes you think it was they who did this."

"I always had the sense from Aunt Celeste," Serena explained with a sad smile, "that she'd once had a great love but for some reason they'd been separated. She never came right out and said so. But she told me when I was foolish enough to elope with Fanning that I must follow my heart. That she'd tried to do so herself but had been cruelly thwarted. Of course, it turns out that eloping with Fanning was far from the great love story I'd wished it to be, but that's neither here nor there."

"You never told us this," Quill said, looking hurt that his cousin hadn't taken him or her own brother into her confidence.

"I forgot about it after Fanning," Serena admitted with a sigh. She'd confided in the four bluestockings about the horrors of her marriage, so it wasn't surprising to Ivy to learn that her attention had been focused solely on her own safety and that of her child during that period. That Quill's cousin had managed to regain a sense of her own self-worth and power after the way she'd been treated was a testament to Serena's strength. And it was something Ivy admired about her wholeheartedly.

"He had a way of demanding all my attention," Lady Serena continued. "Then when Jeremy was born, and Fanning died, Celeste was adamant that I should come to her. And she said something the first time she held Jeremy that should have told me, but again I was awash with my own thoughts. She said that it had been over twenty years since she'd held a baby. I thought she meant any child at all, but of course she meant her own."

"But who was the father?" Quill demanded. "I always thought Celeste never married because she preferred going

her own way. I dislike the thought of her alone and lonely
for all those years."

Ivy pointed them to the mention of the vicarage in Yorkshire. "It seems to me that if the daughter of a duke were
to fall in love with a clergyman—perhaps one who wasn't
from a particularly prosperous family—that would be
something her noble parents would make every attempt to
nip in the bud."

"Only they were too late to stop an elopement," Maitland said quietly. "But if they were away long enough to
consummate the thing, why in God's name didn't grandfather allow them to marry? If I were Celeste and this vicar
fellow, I'd have calculated that being away for an entire
night together would seal the deal, so to speak. Instead
grandfather had the vicar sent away and forced Celeste to
give up her child?"

"We knew he was a cold, unfeeling man," Quill said
with a shake of his head. "You only have to look at the fact
that of their six children, not one visited unless he or she
was summoned. And not even then in the case of your
father, Maitland and Serena. My own mama would only
ever say that they were not very kind people, and leave it
at that. I suppose we were lucky that they both died before we were of an age to interest them."

"But what happened to the child?" Sophia reminded
them. "What did Celeste's parents do with it?"

Ivy scanned the pages before her. "It doesn't look as if
she knows," she said after a few moments of reading. "She
asked, 'begged' was her word, to have the baby returned
to her, but her parents refused."

"Poor Celeste," Serena said, closing her eyes in distress.
"I don't think I'll ever be able to forgive my grandparents."

Sophia interrupted. "We must find this vicar. What if
he blamed Lady Celeste for his banishment and decided
to kill her for it?"

"But why do so over twenty years later?" Gemma asked, puzzled. "It's hardly what one would expect from a vicar in any case."

"Which is why we need to learn who he was and find his location," Ivy said with a nod. "What if he only found out where she was recently?"

"I think I know someone who might be able to tell us," Serena said suddenly, her eyes bright with excitement. "Because I think Ivy is correct that he only found Aunt Celeste a short while ago."

"What do you mean?" Daphne asked, frowning.

"Our local vicar has only been in the village for a little over a year," Serena said. "He's around the same age as Aunt Celeste, and more importantly, his Christian name is Ian."

"I do wish you'd let us come too," Serena protested as Quill lifted Ivy into his curricle. He was momentarily diverted from his cousin's words by the feel of Ivy's curves against him. *Soon,* he told himself. *Soon we'll be able to hide away from the rest of the world and not worry about murder and such.* Ivy's sharp intake of breath and the darkening of her green eyes told him she was thinking along similar lines.

She, however, seemed better at holding a conversation at the moment.

"It would look odd for all seven of us to appear on his doorstep," Ivy said as she settled herself onto the carriage seat. "And we don't wish to frighten him away if he is indeed the man we're seeking."

"God knows there are plenty of vicars named Ian," Maitland said wryly. "We are likely jumping to conclusions over this odd coincidence."

"We'll learn something soon enough," Quill said, taking his seat beside Ivy and grasping the reins in one hand. "Finish looking through the journals for some further mention of the child. It's possible that the father sought her out at some point and perhaps can shed some light on who would wish to kill Celeste."

With a wave, he set the horses into motion and they were off.

"The girl would be thirty-two years old by now," Ivy said over the sound of the horses' hooves on the road. "Lady Celeste must have found it impossible not to mark her birth date every year. I wonder if she ever saw her."

"We don't know that my grandfather even let her know where the child was placed," Quill said, unable to imagine the pain his aunt must have suffered over this whole affair. "Knowing how he wished to punish her, I cannot imagine he would."

"But once she was on her own," Ivy said, her voice echoing his own sorrow, "surely she tried to find her. Or at least had someone search for her."

"I don't know," Quill said. "The others read those later diaries, but no one made mention of any kind of search. Nothing beyond her quest to find the four of you."

He felt a little ashamed for so misconstruing his aunt's motives when he'd first learned of her decision to leave Beauchamp House to the bluestockings. Like the rest of the family, he realized, he'd not really taken his aunt seriously as a scholar. But the insight into her character he'd gained from the journals reminded him that she was, once upon a time, a young woman with hopes and dreams and that even into her later years she wanted to make her mark on the world.

The fact that one of her choices had turned out to be Ivy, well, that was more than serendipity. There was no way Celeste could have known that he would find one of her beneficiaries irresistible, of course, but he liked to think that she would have found their mutual attraction pleasing.

"A penny for them," Ivy said into the silence. "Though I can guess you're thinking, as I am, about Celeste and her heartache."

"Indeed," Quill responded. "I can't help but imagine what I'd have done in Ian's position. I simply cannot fathom letting the father of the woman I loved keep her from me. It's impossible for me to think that if your father told me to leave you be, that I'd listen. Nothing would keep me from your side, Ivy."

Ivy slipped her hand into his free one. "I feel the same," she said. "But you must consider that Ian was likely a younger son who relied upon the patronage of men like your grandfather for his living. Perhaps we shouldn't judge him too harshly. You are a marquess with wealth and property. Would you be able to stand it if your decision to defy my father meant living in reduced circumstances in a hovel, with no prospect of any means for keeping your wife and child fed and sheltered? You've always known you would inherit the marquisate, have you not? You don't know what it is to live from one week to the next not knowing where your next meal would come from."

He knew she was speaking from experience, and felt a pang of dismay at the thought of her in such circumstances. "Your father was cut off from his family for marrying your mother, was he not?"

"Yes," she said with a nod. "And when I was small I do remember there were days when Mama wept over our lack of funds. But soon after, Papa was able to secure a position as outside tutor to several tradesmen's sons who needed the help to gain entry into university. And one job begat another and he was able to earn a decent living. But for a time there, when he was unable to secure work at the

University, and had no way of doing so, we were in difficulties. It is no easy thing to defy your family. Especially
when one's father makes sure that none of your erstwhile
mentors will give you a reference. When you're cut off
from the world you once knew. And anyone who says it is
easy hasn't really had to face the consequences up close."

"Perhaps I spoke too soon," Quill agreed, trying to see
Ian's defection in a different light. "But I still do not understand how he could have left his child. At least he could
see that Celeste would be cared for by her family. But once
the child was given away, there's no telling what happened
to her. What sort of family took her in."

"But who is to say your grandfather even let him know
there was a child?" Ivy argued. "Celeste certainly was
unable to speak to him after their ill-fated elopement. I
daresay young Ian was trundled off to Yorkshire within
hours of their being found on the road and never saw or
heard from Celeste again."

"Until recently," Quill said thoughtfully. "If this Ian is
indeed the same one from Celeste's letters."

They'd reached the drive leading to the little church
where Quill remembered many a Sunday service in the
front pew with Aunt Celeste. He tried to imagine what sort
of man was the pastor now. If he was indeed Celeste's Ian,
what a shock it must have been on that first Sunday when
she arrived at the door. Had he remembered her at once?
Had she remembered him? It was impossible to imagine
being able to simply greet the love of one's life as if nothing had ever passed between them.

"Oh look," Ivy said as they neared the vicarage. "There
is Mrs. Vance. I suppose she's come to visit the vicar, too."

And sure enough as he pulled the curricle to a stop,
Quill saw that there was a gig with a piebald horse tied up
to a nearby tree just to the side of the house. Mrs. Vance,
her face composed, stood in the doorway of the vicarage.

"I'm afraid if you've come to see Reverend Devereaux," she said with a brief smile, "he's away at the moment. He just left to go to a deathbed. My husband sent me to fetch him."

Ivy's disappointment was evident in her voice as she said, "Oh how sad. We were hoping to speak with him. I suppose you don't know when he'll be back?"

"I'm afraid not," Mrs. Vance said with a shake of her head. "I don't know how much experience you have with sickbeds, but sometimes these things take days. I don't anticipate that the vicar will stay there for that long, of course, but it could be tomorrow before he's able to see you. I presume you're here to request the banns to be read?"

Quill nearly rolled his eyes at her ill-concealed attempt to get some gossip from them. But Ivy spoke before he could. "News does travel fast in this village, doesn't it? I see you've been speaking with Mrs. Northman."

But the censure in Ivy's tone didn't cow the inquisitive matron. "I hope you won't think too poorly of me, Miss Wareham. I only knew Dr. Vance for a matter of days before I decided he was the one for me, so I'm hardly one to cast aspersions," she said with a smug smile that seemed more proud than abashed. And I do love a love story, so do let me know your plans."

There was something about the woman's smile that made Quill feel a bit of sympathy for the good doctor. And he didn't like the comparison she drew between herself and Ivy. Both couples might have made hasty betrothals, but he had a feeling that Mrs. Vance had been the one doing the chasing in her relationship.

"Oh, you'll be the first to know," Ivy assured her with a sunny smile that was, if Quill guessed aright, just as sincere as Mrs. Vance's.

"I suppose we'll be off, then," he said, eager to get away

from the doctor's wife before she attempted to wheedle more information from them. "Have a pleasant afternoon, Mrs. Vance."

And before she could reply, he'd given the horses a little flick of the reins and they were on their way back the way they'd come.

"You didn't need to flee her," Ivy said once they were out of earshot. "She's simply a childless matron with nothing to occupy herself with but other people's news. Quite sad really."

"Sad for those who fall prey to her tattling tongue, you mean," Quill said sourly. "I daresay she had the whole of the tale of our run-in at Northman's the other evening before we'd even arrived back home. That sort has ears everywhere. She's likely known Aunt Celeste was murdered from the day she died."

"You're probably not far off there," Ivy said with raised brows. "She did seem a bit gleeful when she asked about the banns. As if she knew good and well that we'd have to be married by special license."

"I suppose we should be glad, then," he said, "that she didn't cut us. Though I can't imagine she'd ever turn her back on a marquess. No matter how scandalous his behavior."

"You've a high opinion of yourself, don't you?" Ivy asked with a grin.

"It is more that I have a low opinion of others, my dear," Quill said with a shrug. "It takes a great deal of scandal to put off a true social climber. And I fear Mrs. Vance, for all that she's a country doctor's wife, would dearly love to be more than that."

"I suppose we're going to have to wait to meet with Reverend Devereaux now," Ivy said, changing the subject. "I confess I'm disappointed. I thought we might be able to solve at least part of the mystery this afternoon."

"It will keep for another day," Quill said, patting her on the hand. "Perhaps the others will have learned something else from the journals by the time we return."

"I hope so," Ivy said with a little sigh. "Because I begin to fear we'll never find out who killed Celeste."

Chapter 29

They'd only gone a mile or so when Ivy realized that Quill wasn't following the way back to Beauchamp House.

"Where are we going?" she asked. "I thought we were going to see what the others might have learned."

"I apologize," he said, looking pensive. "I should have said something, but it only occurred to me while we were talking that I saw something in my portion of Celeste's journals that I may have misread."

He turned down a lane that seemed to lead toward the seafront.

"Well, I'm listening," Ivy said, impatient for some explanation. "I do admit if we're going to the shore, I'm excited by the prospect. I've wanted to go since we arrived but haven't yet found the time. What with getting compromised, and shot and so forth."

Quill laughed. "If you'd only said something I'd have been happy to take you. Dalton and I took Jeremy the morning after we arrived."

"So, what did you remember?"

"Celeste made mention of a visit to St. Clement's, which I read before your revelation that she'd had a lover," he

said, directing the horses to a clearing near the portion of
the Beauchamp House property that led to the chalk cliffs
overhanging the sea.

"A church?" Ivy asked. "Could it have been one of Ian's
parishes perhaps?"

"Not knowing the context, of course," he said, "I
thought as you did, that it was just a visit to a local church—
for it appeared that her visits were made from Beauchamp
House, not on some journey to another county. But, the
entries seemed rather . . . floridly described. Ecstatic."

Ivy looked puzzled. "What, you mean as if she were
having some sort of religious experience? Like a saint?"

"Aunt Celeste wasn't particularly devout," Quill said
dryly. "So, when I recalled the other St. Clement's in this
area it made a bit more sense."

"What did?" Ivy made an impatient noise. "Really,
Quill, you are being quite vague about this."

"St. Clement's is also the name of a series of caves
along the coast here," he said patiently. "One of which is
just here on the stretch of land that's part of the Beauchamp property."

It took Ivy a moment to process what he was saying.
Religious experience, cave, Beauchamp House.

"Oh!" she said softly when she realized what he was
implying.

"Yes," he replied. "Oh."

"She met her lover there," Ivy said, realizing that she
too had read references to the cave in her sections of the
journals. "I thought she was simply having qualms of conscience about her defiance of her father. That she was
simply going to church frequently. Though I admit to not
knowing if there was a St. Clement's church in the area."

"There have always been rumors that one of the caves
had a tunnel leading up to Beauchamp House," Quill said

before jumping down from the curricle. Jogging over to the other side, he reached up for Ivy and held her close for a moment before setting her down on her feet.

"Do you think they're true?" she asked, a little breathlessly, wishing they could just leave off their investigation for the afternoon and be together. It felt a very long time since he'd kissed her properly.

"I think we're going to go find out," he said, slipping his arm through hers after he'd secured the horses on a nearby tree. "There are stairs over here leading down to the beach. And if I remember correctly, the cave is only a few feet away."

"You must admit," Ivy said as they walked along the path leading to the stone stairs, which she could see from this vantage point, "it must have been dreadfully romantic for her to meet him here. Their own little place along the shore. Far from the prying eyes of the village—and her disapproving parents. I cannot help but sympathize with Celeste. What an awful heartbreak for her to endure at so young an age. It's no wonder she never married."

"I had always wondered why she remained unwed," Quill admitted as they reached the top of the stone steps. "Though I suppose I believed my mother when she said that Celeste was far too demanding to ever think of marrying. She was quite envious of her I think. All that freedom to do whatever she liked. Mama didn't have an easy time of it with my father. I believe my grandfather Maitland chose him for her because they were cut from the same cloth."

"Do you remember him? Your father I mean?" Ivy asked, curious about the late marquess. Quill seemed to be close to his mother, but he hardly ever mentioned his father.

"Only a few times when I was small," Quill said, keeping

a tight grip on her hand as he let her precede him down the cliffside. "He wasn't very interested in me, to be honest. I was a child and therefore beneath his notice. He called me into his study a couple of times to make sure I was able to recite my letters and numbers and that sort of thing. But he died before I was old enough to go to school, so I don't recall much more than that."

Ivy, who was quite close with her own father, felt a pang of sympathy for him. She had a hard time imagining what her life would have been like if she'd had the same sort of parents as Lady Celeste, or a father like Quill's. Despite their restricted means and the house full of sisters, she realized she'd been rather luckier than she'd previously thought.

"And yet," Ivy said squeezing his hand, "you've turned into a decent man. I suppose your mother is to congratulate for that?"

"She and Celeste." Quill smiled. "I actually spent more of my formative years here than at Kerr Castle. Which is why I was so dead set against you and your fellow bluestockings inheriting it. I see the error of my ways now, of course."

They'd reached the bottom of the cliff, and Ivy leapt from the last step onto the rocky ground. The sun had come out and dappled the sea as it lapped peacefully against the shore. She could smell salt on the air, and a brisk wind threatened to take her hat from her head.

Sucking in a deep breath of the fresh air, she smiled at Quill. "I should hope so," she said, slipping her arm through his as he followed her down. "At the very least I think you should know we're not the social-climbing upstarts you once thought us."

"Well," he said with a lopsided grin, "perhaps the other three aren't . . ."

"Beast," she said with mock anger. "You know you love me."

Her words hung between them for a moment, like a feather caught up in the breeze.

She saw his eyes darken, and he slipped a hand up to tuck an errant curl behind her ear. "I do indeed," he said, leaning in to kiss her. "More than I ever thought possible."

Ivy felt her heart speed up as Quill's words sank in. He loved her.

She slipped her uninjured arm up around his neck and gave herself over to the desire she'd been holding back all day. Opening her mouth under his, she welcomed the invasion of his tongue as he pulled her closer, let her feel the hard press of him against her aching body.

His kiss was everything she'd never thought she'd needed. At twenty-three, she'd long ago begun to suspect she'd never find her other half, that she'd be doomed to the same kind of solitude that Lady Celeste had endured. But she knew now that Quill was the one she'd been searching for.

"My sweet love," he whispered against her, his breath hot against her ear, making Ivy shiver. "I would desperately love to follow this to its natural conclusion, but I'm afraid we are not alone."

And turning, Ivy saw that there was indeed a party of fishermen farther down the shore.

"Drat," she said in a low voice.

"My thoughts exactly," he said with a wry grin. "But I suppose that will keep us on point. It's not as if we're here for our own amusement, after all."

At the mention of their true reason for being on the shore, Ivy felt a pang of conscience. "You are right, of course. Let's see this cave and mayhap we can find some other clue to Ian's identity."

With a regretful sigh, Quill led her to where an indentation in the cliffside was almost hidden by the rocks on

the near side of it. If Ivy hadn't been searching for it spe-
cifically, she'd never have guessed the mouth was there.

"I remember coming here as a boy," Quill said as they
neared the entrance, which was just high enough for Ivy
to step inside, while Quill was forced to duck his head.
His voice echoed off the walls of the cave's interior,
which opened up into a higher, more spacious area than
Ivy would have imagined from the outside.

"I wish I'd known to bring a lamp, or a candle or something," Quill said. "The back is quite dark, isn't it?"

"What's this here?" Ivy asked, as she stepped over to
where she'd seen something that looked far more square
than one would expect of a natural formation. Sure enough,
as she stooped she saw it was a wooden box. "Look, it's a
casket of some sort." Opening it, she found a candle and a
few small sticks.

"They're lucifer matches," Quill said, taking one from
her and striking it against a bit of rock lying beside them.
To her surprise, a flame lit the air, and Quill used it to
ignite the wick of the tallow candle. "Whoever has been
using the cave recently must have left these for conve-
nience's sake."

"It's certainly convenient for us," Ivy said with a smile.
There was an unmistakable sense of excitement running
through her. Not just because she was here with Quill,
alone, but because of the cave itself. It was hard not to feel
the sense that this place had been the den of smugglers
and lovers and any number of adventurers who had found
refuge in the snug rock room.

"I wonder if we can find the door leading up to Beauchamp House," Quill said as he moved farther into the
darkness.

"I thought you said that was just a legend," Ivy said,
following along behind him. "You sound as if you believe it."

"There were definitely smugglers here during the war," he said, raising the candle to throw the light farther back. "I remember Maitland and I found a couple of brandy bottles down here once. And if Celeste was meeting Ian here, then it would be easier to do so if there was a way for her to get here without being seen."

"It makes sense," Ivy agreed, her eyes darting around them as they moved farther from the cave's entrance and the natural light it let in.

"Maybe you should wait here while I go up ahead," Quill said when she stumbled on a rock behind him. "You're so damned ready for anything that comes your way, I forget you're still recovering from your wound."

Ivy wanted to protest that she could handle herself, but she was indeed feeling rather tired. And perhaps just a bit lightheaded from the closeness of the cave. "I dislike admitting as much," she said wryly, "but I do think I'll go back closer to the entrance. I have never been particularly fond of tight spaces, and the farther we get from the entrance, the more constricted I feel."

"My brave girl," Quill said kissing her on the forehead. "Why didn't you say so as soon as we stepped inside? I'd not have made you come this far. Come, let's go back the way we came and I'll get you back to the house."

But Ivy wasn't willing to let her weakness stop them from finding a possible way into Beauchamp House through the cave. "No! You must go ahead. I'll wait just outside for you to return. It's a lovely day out and I could use a bit of sun on my face and fresh air."

"Are you sure?" he asked, his eyes worried in the candlelight.

"Yes," she said, giving him a little shove. "Now go. I'll be waiting for you. And maybe I'll be able to find something else hidden away near the entrance. Maybe some artifact from Celeste and Ian's time here."

He nodded. "All right. But call out if you need me. With this echo I'll hear you at once."

With a peck on his cheek, she sent him off and turned back toward where the sunlight shone into the cave. Picking her way carefully over the stone floor, she was soon stepping out into the open air, unable to hold in the deep breath of relief at no longer being trapped in the enclosed space.

"Well look what we have here," said a cool voice from the large rocks on the side of the entrance.

Ivy looked up, startled to find she wasn't alone. "Mrs. Vance?" she asked, surprised to find the doctor's wife here. "How odd to see you here."

"Not particularly," the woman said, sliding off the rock where she'd been seated. "There's a tunnel from the vicarage that leads into the cave. I could hear his lordship's deep voice booming against the cave walls. He's got quite a deep one, hasn't he? Not at all like poor Vance's nasal twang."

A hint of unease ran through Ivy. There was something . . . off . . . about the way the doctor's wife was speaking to her. A lack of emotion that gave her a sense of foreboding. "Why were you in the cellar at the vicarage?" she asked, recalling that the vicar himself had been called away. And how did she know that there was a tunnel there? Something was not right here.

"That's where I had to put the vicar, of course," Mrs. Vance said patiently. "I could hardly lock him up in the front room where anyone could see. My father and I have a great deal to catch up on, don't you know? Which we'll have to do in a bit of a rush thanks to you."

"Mrs. Vance," Ivy said, trying to keep her voice steady as she spoke. "What have you done?"

"Surely you've guessed by now, Miss Wareham," the other woman said with a small smile.

And before Ivy could cry out, Mrs. Vance struck out with her hand, which Ivy registered with horror, was clutching a large stone.

Then the world went dark.

Chapter 30

Quill had gone several hundred feet farther into the cave when the glint of metal in the candlelight alerted him to the hinges of a cleverly crafted door built into the cave wall. He considered going back to tell Ivy, but remembering how much being in the interior of the formation had upset her, he decided to ensure that the passageway did indeed go to Beauchamp House before retracing his steps back to the entrance.

Fortunately, there were sconces built into either side of the tunnel walls and he lit them as he went, ensuring that his journey back to Ivy would be less daunting than the one in. He'd never been particularly afraid of the dark, but there was something eerie about wandering deserted passageways that had likely been used by smugglers for hundreds of years. He knew there was a tendency amongst some to think of the men who evaded the excise tax as heroes, but he was not one of them. There had been too many stories of men who crossed them being struck down, of homes set ablaze, for Quill to ever mistake them for anything but the criminals they were.

When he finally reached a set of stairs leading upward, he held his breath a little with hope, and the sight of a wooden door had his heartbeat quickening. When he pushed against it, and saw that he was in the wine cellar of Beauchamp House, his sigh of relief was genuine.

Hurrying up into the kitchens, he ignored the odd looks from the kitchen maids, and made his way to the library where he found Maitland, Sophia, Gemma, and Daphne poring over the diaries, just as they'd been when he left.

"What did you learn from Reverend Devereaux?" the duke asked, putting a finger in the book he was reading. "And where is Miss Wareham?"

Quickly, Quill related what had happened when they arrived at the vicarage, and how he and Ivy had discovered what they suspected had been Celeste and Ian's trysting place. "I'd like you to come back with me through the tunnel," he told his cousin. "Just in case you see some clue I might have missed. And I daresay Ivy, Miss Wareham that is, is growing impatient."

Looking more than eager to leave the journals behind, Maitland stood. "I remember searching for the smugglers' tunnels when we were boys," he said ruefully. "I suppose we weren't very good detectives if we couldn't find them given how many hours we spent looking."

"I think that was likely because Greaves kept the wine cellar locked," Quill said with a quirk of his lips. "He knew better than to leave it open with curious boys running about."

"What about us?" Sophia demanded as the two men began to walk toward the door. "We would like to see the tunnel too. I've spent the past four hours reading these journals, and aside from a few mentions of Lady Celeste's investigations of us four, they have been sadly mundane. I need some fresh air."

Daphne and Gemma echoed her frustration.

"And I am quite good with noticing details," Daphne added hopefully.

"And as a fossil hunter," Gemma said with a chiding tone, "I really should be allowed to examine the cave. There may be some important findings there."

Quill exchanged a look with Maitland, who opened his hands in a speaking gesture.

"Fine," Quill said with a sigh. "But you must all do precisely as I say. This is serious business, not a day adventure. And I would not like it if one of you was to be hurt while I'm in charge of you."

One of the ladies gave a whoop of triumph, and they all three hurried from the room to fetch their hats and coats.

"You're a more patient man than I," Maitland said, clapping Quill on the shoulder. "They'll likely take a half hour at least to decide which hats to wear."

"Lady Daphne will not, I daresay," Quill said with a wink. "She seems quite sensible except for her unaccountable wish to bed you."

Before Maitland could respond to that, they heard the noise of approaching footsteps and turned to see Serena hurrying toward them.

"Dr. Vance's wife has disappeared," she said without preamble. "I've just had a visit from one of his servants asking if we'd seen her. And now the doctor himself is in the drawing room."

"Ivy and I just saw her at the vicarage," Quill said with a frown. "She had gone to fetch the vicar to a sick bed. On Dr. Vance's orders, no less. Why is he not there himself?"

Something about the situation made him uneasy. And without waiting to hear Serena's response, he hurried away from them toward the drawing room.

When he entered, he found the doctor there, pacing back and forth, as if under the weight of some great worry. Upon seeing Quill he stopped and said, "She has lied to me, my lord. And now she's gone."

The unease in Quill's gut turned into full-blown panic. "What do you mean, man?"

"I was searching for a pen knife in her sitting room this afternoon," Dr. Vance said. "And I found a bottle of aconite powder hidden in one of her desk drawers. As well as a journal containing all sorts of details about Lady Celeste—her interests, her direction, and any number of personal details about her life. There was also a description of Reverend Deveraux and the name of his wife, his children. And each church where he'd been posted over his career."

"Why was she keeping a journal about Aunt Celeste?" Maitland asked. "And what the devil is aconite powder?"

"The journal entries were dated two years before I ever met her," Dr. Vance said, his mouth tight. "I think she may have married me to get close to them."

"And aconite poisoning shares many of the same symptoms with the illness that killed Celeste," Quill stated. "You weren't called out to a sickbed today were you?"

"No," the doctor said, looking puzzled. "Why?"

"The last I saw your wife," Quill said curtly, "she was at the vicarage, saying she'd just come on your orders to send him to a deathbed in the village."

Turning to his cousin, he said, "Maitland, you should go with Dr. Vance to see if she's still there."

"Where are you going?" his cousin asked, even as Quill walked away

"To get Ivy," Quill said over his shoulder, beginning to run toward the wine cellar.

Because his gut was churning now with very real fear. Fear that Mrs. Vance might get to Ivy before he did.

And that lady was a stone cold killer.

Ivy came to back to consciousness with the feeling that the earth was shifting under her. She would have moved, but she found her limbs uncooperative and her head aching as if it had come into contact with something quite heavy. A grunt of exertion made her open her heavy eyelids, and she saw Mrs. Vance's face contort as she tried to move something heavy.

That something heavy was Ivy.

She tried to feel beneath her with her hands, but found to her dismay that they were tied together. And her gunshot wound hurt like the very devil. It felt on fire. And if she wasn't mistaken, it was bleeding again.

And though there were lit candles along the walls, she saw that they were in a dark tunnel. The memory of the cave, of Quill, came rushing back. Could they be in the same tunnel he'd told her about? The one leading up to Beauchamp House?

Deciding that her best chance at freedom lay in feigning unconsciousness, she closed her eyes again, and soon felt the cart, or whatever device Mrs. Vance had used to move her, come to a stop. A hinge squeaked loudly, and soon she was being trundled forward again, over a threshold of some sort and through a doorway so narrow she could feel the scrape of it against her shoulders.

"There," said the doctor's wife with a sigh of relief, letting the cart drop down onto the floor.

Ivy was unable to keep from crying out at the sudden movement.

"So," said Mrs. Vance with mock cheerfulness. "Someone is awake. Look, Father, I've brought you a visitor."

Not bothering to continue pretending to sleep, Ivy opened her eyes and looked around. They were in a damp-smelling chamber with no windows. A quick scan of the room revealed a man she presumed was the Reverend Ian Devereaux judging by his collar.

The vicar, who was tied to a chair with a handkerchief

stuffed into his mouth, only moaned in response to his long-lost daughter's taunt.

"You haven't met yet, I don't think," Mrs. Vance continued, "but this is Miss Ivy Wareham. She's been making things difficult for me, these past few days. Putting her nose into things that don't concern her."

"I should think the deliberate murder of two women and an attempt upon my own life is just cause for concern," Ivy said, her voice scratchy from her dry throat.

"None of it concerned you." Mrs. Vance was pacing now, with a frenetic energy that told she was feeling threatened by the presence of someone who talked back. Ivy considered her options and decided that it might be best to placate the woman rather than challenge her. A calm Mrs. Vance was less likely to kill her prisoners, she thought.

"You are right, I suppose," Ivy said, trying to infuse her voice with apology. "I was simply concerned about Lady Celeste's untimely death. I should have left it alone and applied my interest to my studies."

"Yes, you should have," Mrs. Vance said smugly. "Now look at where you are. You might have simply gone about your business, and married that handsome marquess of yours, but instead you're here. And I'm afraid I'm going to have to kill you along with my father, here. Because I can hardly let you live now that you know I'm the one who killed Celeste and that fool Elsie."

Ivy blinked at hearing the confirmation so clearly from the murderess's lips. "You cannot know how much I wish I'd kept to my own affairs," she said with feigned regret. She might not be in this predicament if she'd not decided to listen to Lady Celeste's letter, but she could not in good conscience have ignored her benefactress's request that she find her killer. She could only imagine what that lady's

response would have been to the knowledge it was her
own daughter who had poisoned her to death. Poor Lady
Celeste.

"But why did you do it?" Ivy asked, truly wanting to
know what had prompted this woman, who seemed to have
a comfortable life as the wife of a prosperous country
doctor, to kill her birth parents. "They certainly did not
give you up because they wished to, Marianne." She used
the woman's Christian name in an attempt to build a bond
between them. Anything that might make her see Ivy as
less of an enemy and more like a friend.

A flicker of unease passed through Mrs. Vance's eyes.
"What do you mean they didn't wish to? They did it,
didn't they? This hypocrite has spent his life preaching
godliness to people while he himself is a fornicator who
didn't even deign to marry my mother when she fell pregnant. I hardly think running away from responsibility is
the action of a man doing his Christian duty." She shook
her head in disgust. "And Lady Celeste, a wealthy duke's
daughter, who was so ashamed of me that she didn't
even deign to place me with a family befitting my rank
as her daughter—she doesn't deserve my sympathy. If
anything I hold her more accountable than this miscreant." She gestured toward where the vicar was looking
at her through eyes that were at once horrified and mourn-
ful. "At least he didn't give me up after carrying me for
months inside his body. It takes a very despicable sort of
woman to give away her child."

"But Lady Celeste wanted to keep you," Ivy insisted,
though she knew there was little chance Marianne Vance
would believe her. She was far too accustomed to the nar-
rative of her abandonment that she'd built up in her head. "It
was her parents, the Duke and Duchess of Maitland who
insisted that you be given to the couple who raised you.
And it was they who sent your father away to Yorkshire to

a church on the Earl of Moreland's estate. They were power-ful enough to have him banished from this part of the country. And they did."

"How do you know any of this?" Marianne spat out. "You never even met the exalted Lady Celeste. And yet, you and those other three ungrateful bluestockings came here to take possession of her house. Her home. The place I should have, would have, inherited if I had been given my birthright."

Ignoring the jibe against her and the other bluestock-ings, Ivy said, "Because I've read her journals from that time. She was devastated by what her parents did. And she even went so far as to search for you for several years. But the duke and duchess were quite good about erasing all traces of you. It was as if you'd never existed." She had no proof that Lady Celeste had, in fact, looked for her child, but Ivy had a feeling that the woman she'd come to know through her journals would not have sat idly by while her child was raised by strangers.

"Yes," Mrs. Vance said with contempt, "that's because the couple they gave me to were rotten to the core. They were cold and unfeeling. And they forced me to work like a dog on their farm from the time I could walk until they had the good grace to die when I was seventeen. The only good thing they did was leave that despicable farm to me so that I could sell it the first chance I got and use the money to set myself up in Bath. Which is where I lived for nearly a decade before I met the good Dr. Vance."

Curious in spite of herself, Ivy asked, "How did you know that he worked in the same village Lady Celeste lived in?" Shifting her weight to ease the discomfort of her arm, she felt the bonds around her hands were looser than she'd thought before. Maybe she could get them off herself?

Not daring to show what she'd discovered, she turned

her attention on Marianne Vance and listened to her answer while she pulled against the rope behind her back.

"I didn't, not at first," Marianne said with a laugh. "I had found several letters from the old Duke of Maitland in my father's papers, and he had mentioned Celeste and the vicar, here. It was really just a matter of serendipity that Dr. Vance mentioned the grand lady in his county—Lady Celeste Beauchamp. And I knew I had to get there. Vance was already taken with me, so it was just a matter of making myself pleasing to him before he was falling all over himself to marry me. That the recently widowed Reverend Devereaux had only just moved into the area was a happy coincidence I discovered when Dr. Vance brought me to my new home."

"But why did you decide to kill Celeste?" Ivy asked, aghast at the cold calculation that had led Marianne to marry a man she didn't love for the sole purpose of getting close to the mother who abandoned her. "If you had only told her who you were she would have welcomed you with open arms. She loved you. She looked for you for years."

"Not. Hard. Enough," Marianne said coldly. "And why should I introduce myself to the woman who let me be taken from her when I was a defenseless babe? That sort of person doesn't deserve sympathy, certainly not mine. By the time I met her, I was already planning her downfall. The couple who raised me died of a stomach complaint, or so the doctor believed, shortly after Serena's husband died in hunting accident. So I already knew how much easier it was to put a dose of aconite into an herbal tisane, when compared with engineering lying in wait with a gun—though both have their uses. And when my dear husband mentioned that Lady Celeste suffered from dreadful headaches, it was only a matter of suggesting to her that she try the tisane recipe that I'd used for my own dear mother to set things in motion. I made sure to tell her that Elsie should get the ingredients from the gypsy woman, of course. After, I'd given the maid herself my own little powder to add to the mix, telling her that Dr. Vance had given it to me expressly for Lady Celeste's use. Vance is too much of a snob to speak to the likes of Elsie, so I knew he'd never find out, and I knew that adding the gypsy woman to the mix would throw suspicion her way before it ever came back to me." She smirked. "And I was right of course."

"But how did you know Lady Celeste would even drink the tonic?" Ivy wanted to know. She kept her gaze focused on Marianne while she tried to work her hands against the ropes. She'd crush her own fingers if it meant getting out of this cellar with her life intact.

"I didn't," the doctor's wife said with a shrug. "But fortunately for me, her headaches got worse. And by that point she was willing to try anything that promised to give her relief. If she'd continued being recalcitrant, of course, I'd have had Elsie give her something to make them worse. I know any number of herbs and powders could have done the trick."

"But why kill Elsie?" Ivy asked, wondering what could possibly have got the maid killed. As far as she knew there was no reason for Mrs. Vance to wish her dead.

"Because once Lady Celeste died and you began asking your questions," Marianne said grimly, "she figured out that I'd been the one to help Lady Celeste along the road to her demise. After you and Lord Kerr visited her on the night of the dinner party, she sought me out to let me know what she suspected. And demanded that I pay her to keep quiet. I couldn't have that, could I? So I sent her some pastries I'd laced with rat poison—far more efficient than the slow death I'd devised for Lady Celeste. Fortunately, I knew Elsie had a sweet tooth. The sugar disguised the taste of the poison quite nicely. At least I suspect it did since she was found dead the next morning."

The dispassionate tone Marianne Vance used to relate the details of her crimes was more chilling to Ivy than outright glee would have been. There was something amiss with the other woman. Some lack of feeling for her fellow human beings that made her lack the capacity for empathy. A woman like this would not feel even a flinch of conscience at taking a life. And she certainly would not be talked out of her plans.

Still, Ivy knew she had to keep her boasting about her own cleverness if she was to survive this. Quill had surely got back to the cave entrance by now and discovered she was missing. Hopefully he would recall how odd Mrs. Vance's behavior had been at the vicarage and go back there for answers.

She was making some headway with the ropes, and had managed to get one hand out almost to the palm. But she was beginning to lose hope.

"And what of the gypsy fortune teller?" she asked aloud. "Surely you didn't pay her to tell me I was in danger."

Marianne laughed. "No, not at all. She was just being her own foolish, gypsy self. And I'd never even spoken to her, so I knew if she mentioned anyone it would be Elsie. It was good of you to tell the servants at Beauchamp House that you all were going to visit her caravan that day, though. My dear friend, the kitchen maid, was able to get word to me as soon as you set out, so I was able to hide along the path."

"You're the one who shot me?" Ivy demanded. She's thought perhaps Marianne had hired someone—a local man, or a lover—to shoot at her. The news that she'd done the deed herself was startling somehow.

"Do not sound so surprised, Miss Bluestocking," said the doctor's wife with a laugh. "For someone who is a champion of the female sex, you sound quite skeptical that a lady would be a good enough shot to wound you. I learned to shoot on the farm. Got quite good at it, though it was never my favorite sport. Too bloody for my taste. I much prefer the safe distance poison provides. Not to mention that it makes the victim suffer for quite a bit longer."

As she at last managed to get one hand free, then the other, of her bonds, Ivy couldn't help but say to her would-be killer, "And yet you missed, if you wished your shot to take my life." She was careful not to let her triumph at freeing her hands show in her face. It would do little good to alert Marianne to the fact that she'd worked her way loose before she had a chance to do anything with her newfound freedom.

Marianne's eyes narrowed. "Your damned marquess was in the way," she spat out. "Or I'd have hit your chest, which is what I was aiming for. And I'll soon finish what I started." She lifted her arm and Ivy saw, to her horror, that her captor held a pistol in her hand.

Mrs. Vance scowled at her over the gun, taking aim. Ivy prepared herself to leap to her feet, which Marianne had left untied in her haste to get Ivy into the cellar.

But they were both startled by a loud banging on the front door of the vicarage.

Taking advantage of Marianne's diversion, Ivy made her move.

Chapter 31

There was no sign of Ivy when Quill made it back through the tunnel and out to where the cave opened onto the rocky shore. Calling out to her in the hope that she had just decided to walk a bit along the waterfront, he almost tripped when his booted foot became entangled in something.

His heart leapt into his throat when he saw it was Ivy's hat—a straw and ribbon confection that framed the heart-shaped face he'd come to love so well. He stooped to pick it up and was shocked to see a smudge of crimson just where the crown of her head would be. He broke into a run and was up the cliffside stairs in a trice. His horses were just where he'd tied them up what seemed like days ago, and in minutes he was driving like a madman along the road to the vicarage.

He had no doubt now who had injured Ivy and who had taken her away.

It was Dr. Vance's wife, who had so cheerfully lied to them earlier when they inquired about the Reverend Deveraux's whereabouts. Who had been so welcoming that day in the doctor's offices, and who had mourned the loss of Aunt Celeste.

He did not allow himself to wonder what sort of woman could do those things. Because she now had Ivy. Smart, sensible, sensual Ivy. Who had stolen his heart that first day in the Fox and Pheasant with her wry humor and her love for books.

There was no question he would get to her in time.

To imagine anything else was to give up.

Torquil Beauchamp, Marquess of Kerr, never surrendered.

And he was damned if he'd let Marianne Vance be the one to make him start now.

He had too much he needed to say to Ivy.

With a curse, he cried out for the horses to speed up.

As luck would have it, he reached the vicarage before Maitland and Dr. Vance did.

The exterior of the little house looked as benign as ever. With its picturesque climbing roses budding in anticipation of spring and its cheerful green door, it looked like what it was—the home of a widower of middle years who served the community and lived alone.

There was no sign that Ivy or anyone else had been here since they'd come hours earlier to pay a call on the vicar. Mrs. Vance's horse and cart, however, were still where they'd been tied up earlier. If she'd used the cart to move Ivy, she'd done a remarkable job of placing it exactly where it had been before.

He leapt down from the curricle, tossed the reins over a post, and hammered on the vicarage door.

"Mrs. Vance!" he shouted. "Mrs. Vance, I've come for Miss Wareham. I know you have her. Let me in."

Whether from the force of his pounding or the fact that it wasn't locked, the door swung inward, just as he heard Maitland and Dr. Vance approach in the doctor's open barouche.

Cautiously, he stepped into the dark interior and heard someone shouting from the back of the house. Caring only that Ivy might need him, he all but sprinted to the kitchen and followed the high-pitched cries to an open door at the top of a staircase leading down into darkness.

Following the steps, he was almost to the bottom when he heard a cry of triumph.

Please God, let that be Ivy.

The light became brighter as he made his way down, and when he reached the damp room he saw at once that Ivy was standing over Mrs. Vance, a dueling pistol leveled at her with a hand that was steady as a summer rain.

"You won't do it," Mrs. Vance sneered. "You don't have the bottle. I doubt you've ever held a pistol in your whole sheltered existence. You're just like she was. A pampered, ungrateful dabbler. You think you're so brave for studying things that no one but your kind care about. While girls like me were working just to stay clothed and fed, you were weeping over life's unfairness. You don't know the first thing about unfairness. Unfair is when your aristocratic parents give you up so that you have no chance of gaining your birthright. Unfair is when your mother gives away her priceless collection and her home to a quartet of spinsters with no claims on her."

Neither of them noticed where Quill stood silently, his heart in his throat as he watched Ivy glaring at her erstwhile captor.

"Try me," she said to the woman on the floor. "You've killed who knows how many people now. And you intended to kill both your father and me just now. If you make a sudden move, make no mistake, Marianne, I will shoot you. I might not have practiced as you did, but we're quite close now. I should be able to hit you somewhere."

Without turning around, she said to Quill, "Darling,

would you please get the rope from the cart there and tie her up. Then you'd best see to the vicar."

He shouldn't have been surprised she'd known he was there, Quill realized with a grin, but he was. Clearly he needed to learn that Ivy was up to any rig. Even capturing murderers.

"With pleasure, my dear," he said as he stepped farther into the room and retrieved the rope that had been used earlier to subdue Ivy.

When Mrs. Vance was trussed up like a Christmas goose, Ivy lowered the pistol with a sigh and would have collapsed if Quill hadn't been there to catch her. Taking the gun and placing it on a high shelf where it would do no harm, he carried Ivy to a nearby chair.

The sound of boots alerted them that Maitland and Dr. Vance had arrived on the scene.

"Good god!" Dr. Vance cried out. "It's true, Marianne You tried to kill Miss Wareham and Reverend Devereaux. And *did* kill Lady Celeste and her former maid, Elsie."

"See to Devereaux, Duke," Quill told his cousin, who had looked to him for guidance on what to do. "He may need Dr. Vance's attention."

With a nod, Maitland crossed over to where the vicar was tied up.

Quill turned his attention back to Ivy. He crouched before her, and when their eyes met, she launched herself into his arms, throwing them both to the cellar floor.

"I was so afraid," she whispered against his neck, the solid weight of her in his arms a relief after the terror he'd felt when he found her hat. "She would have killed us both. Even you, if you'd come a few minutes earlier. I was only able to overtake her thanks to your pounding on the door. Oh, Quill. I thought I'd never see you again."

He didn't even know what he said to her, crooning reassurances and words of love and devotion that bubbled up out of him like a newly discovered sweet water well finally set free from where it was hidden underground. And he let her cry. Which he knew even the strongest of ladies—and men—needed to do sometimes. Especially when they'd endured the sort of hell Ivy had.

"I love you, Quill," she said, moving her head back so that she could look him in the eye. "I love you so much. And I was so afraid I'd never see you to tell you how much."

"I love you too," he said kissing her eyelids, then her cheeks, then her nose, then, finally, her lips.

They were kisses of love, but also promises.

That no matter what else happened, he loved her. And she loved him. And they would be together.

"When I realized she had you, Ivy," he said against her cheek, "I thought all was lost. But I should have known better. My sweet, brave, bluestocking. You are made of sterner stuff than that. And I should have trusted you to save yourself."

He felt her thumb softly stroke beneath first one, then the other, of his eyes, gliding in the moisture there. "My sweet marquess," she said with a smile in her voice. "You *do* love me." There was affection in her voice, but also wonder. As if she couldn't quite believe it.

"More than life itself," he said solemnly. "Which is why we will leave for London tonight so we can be married by special license at once."

"What about asking my father for permission?" she teased, a little breathlessly.

"All respect for your father, my dear," he said pulling her closer, "but he will just have to wait."

And there, on the floor of the vicarage cellar, he kissed her properly.

Until, that is, the sound of a throat clearing broke the spell.

"I do not like to interrupt," Maitland said, clearly lying. As Quill well knew, his cousin *loved* to interrupt. "But we're taking the vicar and Mrs. Vance upstairs now. And I thought perhaps you'd like to, I don't know, take yourselves back to Beauchamp House so that you can continue this"—he made a gesture in the air with his hand—"there."

Sighing, Quill knew that any continuation would have to wait until the other bluestockings and Serena were informed about what had happened here.

Pushing up to her feet, Ivy offered him a hand, which he took with a smile.

"We'll be gone by the time you get back," he informed his cousin, who rather than looking surprised simply nodded. "See that all of this is taken care of."

"Northman will wish to question you both," Maitland said as they started up the cellar stairs.

"Northman can bloody well wait until we get back," Quill called back over his shoulder.

He and Ivy had important business to attend to.

Chapter 32

Some few weeks later, having been assured by a beaming Greaves that the residents of Beauchamp House were assembled in the library, Ivy and Quill stood in the doorway of the now-familiar chamber and saw, to their surprise, the Duke of Maitland lecturing the others.

"I think it's highly likely that my man will find evidence of more crimes when he visits Marianne Vance's childhood home next week," he said with a flourish. "I've been reading Bentham on the criminal mind, and it seems to me that—" Seeing Ivy and Quill in the doorway, he broke off with a wide grin.

"I see you've taken up a new hobby since our departure," Quill said as the assembled household gathered around the newlyweds to welcome them.

Grinning, Maitland shrugged. "Beauchamp House is full of books, would be a shame not to take advantage of it."

"Don't be modest, brother," Serena said with a roll of her eyes. "You'd think he was on the verge of becoming a Bow Street Runner with the amount of attention he's devoted to explaining what made Marianne snap."

"I suspect we've all found our own ways of dealing with what happened," Ivy said quietly as she accepted a hug from her erstwhile chaperone. "Perhaps Maitland's is just different from ours."

"Always so wise, Ivy," said Serena with a warm smile. "We've missed your level head these past weeks. I'm glad you're back."

"So am I," the new Marchioness of Kerr said, a feeling of contentment settling over her at being back amongst the inhabitants of Beauchamp House. "It was lovely to be away for a while, of course. But I found I missed you all." She raised a saucy brow. "Even you, Jeremy," she said as she spotted the boy lingering behind the sofa.

"You did?" he asked, looking pleased with himself.

"I did." She confirmed with a nod. "Quill and I even brought you back a present."

The boy's eyes grew wide. "You did?"

"Is there an echo in here?" Quill asked, striding over to the boy and lifting him into his arms. "Let's us gentlemen leave the ladies together so that they can gossip. I have a feeling Maitland will enjoy your gift just as much as you will, Jem."

Leaning down, he gave Ivy a quick kiss and the men left, shutting the doors behind them.

A few minutes later, a tea tray between them, the four bluestockings and Lady Serena were deep in conversation. "He's smitten, I think," Serena said with a grin as she looked to where Ivy and the rest of the bluestockings had gathered at one of the library tables. "And so are you," she continued. "Lady Celeste was quite brilliant to throw the two of you together."

"I hardly think it was that calculated," Ivy said, though in some moments she did wonder if her benefactress had anticipated Quill's strong objection to the way she left her estate. "Surely not?"

"She asked you to find her killer," Serena reminded her. "And you did. She chose correctly. And she knew Quill better than anyone. She always lamented that he was so remote. So alone. I think she must have hoped one of you would catch his interest."

"I suppose we'll never know," Ivy said with regret. She had so much to thank Lady Celeste for. If only they'd been able to meet. Even if only for a moment.

"No. Thanks to her daughter, we won't," Serena said sadly. Then, brightening, she smiled. "I'll just go have a word with the cook about dinner, since there will need to be two more places at the table. I'm so glad you've returned, Ivy."

And without waiting for an argument, she slipped out of the room.

Now, surrounded by the other ladies whom she'd come to love as well as her own sisters, Ivy continued relating the story of how Quill met her father.

"I don't know that Papa was surprised I'd married so much, but that I'd married the son of his childhood crony," she said with a grin. "Neither Quill nor I knew it, but apparently Papa, as the younger son of the Duke of Ware, had visited Kerr Castle any number of times and even played at soldiers with Quill's father. He remembered the late marquess as a bit of a tyrant, which Quill found not at all surprising. But Papa was quite pleased to note that Quill seemed to have taken more of his temperament from his mother than his father."

"How romantic," Sophia said with a happy sigh. "It's almost as if you and Quill have righted some old quarrel between the two families. Like Romeo and Juliet, only without all the dying."

"I'd call it inevitable," Lady Daphne said with a frown for Sophia's sentiment. "There are only so many aristocratic families in the kingdom. That the grandchildren of dukes fell in love and married is hardly a great surprise. If anything, it's to be expected. If Ivy had been the daughter of the late marquess's valet? Now, *that* would have been romantic."

"Oh, Daphne," Ivy said, giving her a quick hug, which Daphne clearly did not enjoy, "I've missed you."

"Thank you, Ivy," Daphne said, pulling away from the embrace as quickly as possible. "I admit that I have missed you and the marquess in your absence. Especially when Sophia and Gemma are teasing me about the duke."

At the mention of Maitland, Ivy exchanged a wide-eyed look with the Hastings sisters. "And how goes your friendship with the duke, Daphne?" she asked carefully. When she and Quill had left, the duke was still avoiding Lady Daphne as if she were wearing a noxious perfume.

"There is nothing of note," Daphne said with dignity. "I have given up my quest to make love to him. He is not the carefree gentleman I thought when we first met. He is instead just as hemmed in by the ridiculous rules of society as any other man. Though as a duke he could quite likely ride his horse naked through Hyde Park without risking social ostracism, he cannot bend his moral code enough to engage in a simple, straightforward affair with me. I am disappointed, naturally. But resigned."

It was a long speech for Daphne, who tended to speak in short sentences. And Ivy felt a pang of sympathy for her. It cannot have been easy to accept Maitland's rejection. She was a lovely woman, and had likely not suffered such a fate much in her life.

"I have turned my attention to other matters," Daphne continued, with a spark of enthusiasm that soothed some of Ivy's worry for her friend. "There are far more intriguing mathematics books here in the library than I'd formerly thought. So I have immersed myself in reading the journals of Sir Isaac Newton and have been reacquainting myself with the *Philosophiae Naturalis Principia Mathematica*. It is quite a brilliant achievement not only for mathematics

but also for England. No matter what that plagiarist Leib-
niz had to say about it."

"We shall have to take your word for it, dearest," said
Sophia patting the other lady's hand. "For I must admit, I
don't even know who those men are."

Daphne looked as if she would tell them, so Ivy spoke
up again. "I presume Mrs. Vance has been taken to the
gaol in Brighton by now?"

"Yes," Gemma said with a nod. "I must confess that it
was a great relief to know she was taken away from here.
I know she was unable to do any more harm from where
she was being kept in Squire Northman's cellar, but just
knowing such an evil person was nearby made me feel a
little ill."

"The duke has determined that she likely killed her
parents—her adoptive parents, that is—as well as Lady
Celeste and Elsie," Sophia said with a shiver. "I know it
must have been upsetting to learn that but for the interven-
tion of the old Duke of Maitland she'd have been born
into a much higher social class, but I cannot understand
how it would turn her mind so."

Ivy thought back to that day in the vicarage. "I don't
think she is mad," she said thoughtfully. "Or rather, not
mad as we understand it to be. She wasn't ill, or unable to
care for herself. She is, rather, prosaically efficient. I daresay if Lady Celeste hadn't left her letter telling me what
she suspected, Mrs. Marianne Vance would have kept on
killing."

"What of the vicar?" Ivy asked. When she and Quill
left for London, the Reverend Devereaux had still been
unconscious. She would visit him at the first opportunity,
if only so that she could tell him how sorry she was that
he'd lost Lady Celeste. It had been difficult to forget his
silent, stricken gaze at her as they both listened to Marianne rant.

"He has recovered," Sophia said sadly, "but I think he will not be able to forget what happened for a long, long while."

"To know that his own daughter killed the love of his life," Gemma said aghast. "If only the old Duke of Maitland hadn't been so determined to keep Lady Celeste and the reverend apart all of this might have been avoided."

"He has gone to live with his sister in Scotland," Sophia said. "I can't say I blame him, really. It would be painful to be so close to where Marianne's crimes occurred."

"Did he and Lady Celeste ever meet after he came back to this area?" Ivy asked. "Surely they must have. Serena said that she attended the little church regularly."

"We'll never know," Daphne said. "Unless there was some mention of it in Lady Celeste's journals."

But none of them could recall reading anything relating to the vicar in their benefactress's diaries.

"So much heartbreak," Ivy said with a shudder. So easily, she and Quill could have ended up dead along with Marianne Vance's other victims.

Which reminded her. "What of Dr. Vance?"

"He was quite overwrought when he came to speak to the duke," Daphne said with an air of disdain. She hadn't quite been able to forgive the doctor for not realizing he was married to a killer it would seem.

"I suppose he was here to discuss his wife's prosecution?" Ivy asked, curious about the doctor's condition. Now that she was married herself, she understood just what a betrayal it had been for the physician's wife to lie to him about her every motive.

"Yes." Sophia set her empty brandy glass on the table. "He looked as if he hadn't slept in days. I must confess that I think the crime against him is as horrible as any Marianne committed against her murder victims. At least they do not have to live with the consequences."

"To spend your whole life helping people only to realize that you're harboring a disease in your own house," Gemma said grimly. "It has to have him going over his marriage with a fine-tooth comb to see if his wife left any more victims in her wake."

"At least she's finally caught," Ivy said. The other ladies echoed the sentiment.

Epilogue

Sometime later, after the ladies had taken tea and caught up on all the other news Ivy had missed while she and Quill were away, the subject turned to living arrangements.

"Where will you and Quill make your home, Ivy?" Sophia asked, stretching a little. "At Kerr Castle or the London townhouse?"

Ah, Ivy thought with a bit of trepidation, *the moment of truth.* She had a proposal for the other ladies, but there was no guarantee that they'd agree to it. After all, the house belonged to all of them equally so long as they remained here for a year. She didn't want to risk her stake in it.

Especially since Quill had such fond memories of his childhood here.

"Would you all mind terribly if we made our home here for the rest of the year?" she asked, tentatively, hoping against hope that they'd agree to the idea. If they didn't, she and Quill could, of course, go to any of his numerous homes. But she'd only scratched the surface of the collection of ancient Greek and Latin texts in the library. And she wished more than anything to use Lady Celeste's bequest to her to the fullest. It was the sincerest way she could give thanks to the woman who had given her more happiness than she'd ever imagined. "I understand if you object, of course. We were supposed to be a sort of bluestocking refuge, and there was never any plan for gentlemen to reside here too. In fact, I know what you'll say. Just give me a short time to let the marquess know, and we'll be on our way back—"

"Will you please be quiet, you ninnyhammer?" Daphne said in a loud voice after each of the ladies had attempted and failed to put a stop to Ivy's monologue.

Her eyes wide, Ivy hushed.

"Why would you think we would wish you gone?" Daphne continued, her puzzlement clear in her eyes. "Lady Celeste left Beauchamp House to the four of us. There is no rule that says you must leave if you marry. Or that one is no longer a bluestocking upon marriage—I have a feeling Madame D'Arblay, the former Frances Burney, would have some strong words at that notion."

"She's right, Ivy," Sophia said with a warm smile. "Besides, I thought we'd agreed when we first arrived that since Maitland, Lady Serena, and the marquess had all but grown up here, it would be cruel to bar them entry now. We can hardly eject you while allowing your husband to remain. It would be a breach of the bluestocking code!"

"Besides all that," Gemma said wryly, "Maitland has all but set up housekeeping here. Why would we toss your husband out on his ear? Lord Kerr can hardly be any more disruptive than the duke, who puts Daphne to the blush at every opportunity and in general makes her impossible to live with."

At a speaking look from her sister, Gemma gave a rueful laugh. "More impossible than usual, then."

"I am not impossible," Daphne protested. "And it is not my fault that the duke will not forget about my indecent proposal to him at the beginning of our acquaintance. It's almost as if he thinks I set my cap at him. When, in fact, it couldn't be farther from the truth. I didn't want to marry the man, I just wanted to f—"

"We understand you perfectly, dear," Ivy interrupted before Daphne could finish her thought.

"If only Maitland did," Daphne sighed.

"So you see, Ivy," Sophia said, returning the discussion to its original subject, "we need you both here—you to give Gemma and me someone besides each other to gossip about Daphne with, and Lord Kerr to give the duke a sobering influence. "

Ivy felt a wave of relief wash over her. She had hoped the others would not object to her living here with Quill, but since they'd begun their tenure here with his vocal objection to their presence in his aunt's home, it would have only been fair if they chose to banish him.

"I promise we will not be one of those annoying pairs of newlyweds who makes everyone feel ill with our constant billing and cooing," she assured them. "You'll hardly know we're here."

"Speak for yourself, wife," said Quill stepping into the room followed by a sheepish-looking Maitland and Lady Serena with Jeremy in tow. "I will bill and coo from sunrise to sunset. And there's nothing you can do to stop me."

Unable to resist him, Ivy turned up her face to his to accept his kiss, which was a bit more heated than strictly proper.

"Oh dear," she heard Serena say. "I am a very poor sort of chaperone, am I not?"

"Thank God for that," Quill whispered into Ivy's ear. "It took a scandal to make me realize I loved you." But Ivy knew deep in her bones, that even if Serena had been a dragon, she and Quill would have found a way to come together.

Scandal or not, they were meant to be together.

And Lady Celeste, who had herself been denied a happy ending, had all but ensured Ivy and Quill had theirs.

The only question now, she thought as her speculative gaze fell on Daphne—who was pretending to ignore Maitland—was which bluestocking would fall next. She knew which of the three she'd place *her* bet on.

And from the looks of the duke, he would not wait long before he set that adventure in motion.

Amid the chattering of the others, she felt a calm wash over her.

Thank you, she said silently, sending up a little prayer to her benefactress.

"What is it?" Quill asked her in a low voice from where he'd taken a seat beside her. "Is something wrong?"

"Nothing." She kissed him softly, her heart full of love. "Everything is just as it should be."

And Ivy knew, from wherever she watched them, that the redoubtable Lady Celeste approved.

THE END

Don't miss the next Studies in Scandal novel
from Manda Collins

Duke with Benefits

Coming soon from St. Martin's Paperbacks